The Accidental Encore

Christy Hayes

DEDICATION

To Jennifer Groover who helped inspire this story.

ACKNOWLEDGMENTS

To Cassie Cox, for her help with this book. To my writing posse, you ladies rock!

CHAPTER 1

Allie Graves pried her lids open slowly as tears began leaking around the edges of her eyes. She lifted her hand when she felt something dripping down her face and was relieved to discover the liquid in question was the diet coke she'd just bought, not blood. The beat from the song on the radio had her reaching for the volume button to dim the sound. The airbag lay like a limp balloon in her lap.

"Hey, lady?" a voice called from outside her closed window. She looked over as if in a dream and, with the press of a button, rolled the window down. "You okay?" the stranger asked.

Was she okay? She wiggled her toes, lifted her knees, and made the mistake of nodding. Her head felt like it was going to explode. The burning in her eyes lessened as the cool autumn air floated into her car. "How bad is it?" she asked.

"Your car?" The guy walked around to the front bumper and scrunched up his face before returning to her window and leaning down so they were eye to eye. "It's gonna need some work."

Great.

"But not as much as the guy you hit."

"What?" She tried to undo her seat belt and exit the car. She'd hit someone. Oh, God. What if he didn't survive? What if she'd critically injured another driver? The man held her door in place when she attempted to get out.

"You'd better stay put." He pointed with his head toward a black pickup truck with a dent in the driver side door. A man

1

with blood running down the side of his face kicked the tire and scowled in her direction. "He's out, and he's mad as hell."

"But he hit me," Allie whimpered. "My light was green." She shoved her door open, ready to explain, when her world began to tip.

"Whoa, lady," was the last thing she heard before everything went black.

***

Craig Archer limped toward the bimbo who'd t-boned his car and noted with disgust that she'd collapsed into the arms of the guy who'd helped him out of his truck. Figured. Damn woman driver didn't know a red light from green. And he'd just had his truck washed.

The man eased her onto the street and hovered over her, blocking Craig's view. It was just as well she passed out. He would have made her cry. Everything about the scene brought back memories, too fast and too painful to acknowledge. So instead of concern for her well being, Craig loathed the woman for bringing his worst nightmare to life in living color.

Had Julie or Becca understood their fate before they hit the pole? Did they have time to feel scared? Or had it happened as the police explained to him and Mark, quick and deadly, without warning, without a chance to evade? He shook away the memories as the uniformed cop approached, eyeing the cut on Craig's temple.

"You okay?"

"Yeah, I'm fine."

"That's a nasty cut you've got there." He pointed to Craig's forehead with a ballpoint pen. "Why don't you have a seat on the curb? Ambulance will be here in just a minute."

"I'm fine," Craig repeated. No way was he going to the hospital for some stupid scratch.

"Can you tell me what happened?" the officer asked as he clicked his pen and opened a palm-sized folder.

"She hit me. Ran the damn red light and plowed right into my truck."

"So your light was green?"

"Green as your partner over there hyperventilating by the lady."

The officer glanced over his shoulder and noted the rookie wiping sweaty hands on his pants as he interviewed the bystander. "She told that guy her light was green."

"Then you might want to do a Breathalyzer or a vision test when she comes to."

The officer looked back at Craig. "Can anyone here corroborate your story?"

"During Atlanta rush hour?" Craig snorted. "We're lucky no one's weaving through the scene."

"What about that guy?" the officer asked, pointing to the man who'd helped him after the crash.

"I don't know where he came from."

The officer let out a sigh and pointed with his pen to the curb. "Have a seat, Mr.?"

"Archer."

"Have a seat, Mr. Archer. I'll be right back."

Craig watched him saunter toward the other party, speak to the man who'd helped both him and the lady, and then listen to the rookie. He kneaded the back of his neck and hoped like hell the man saw the light because the last thing he wanted was a drawn out legal battle on top of the annoyance of having to have his truck repaired.

The lady came to just as the ambulance arrived. She tried to stand up, but the EMTs brought out the stretcher and forced her to lie down. He wondered if she'd passed out for show or if she was really injured. She didn't look any worse for wear. Her shoulder length blonde hair and face were covered in white powder from the airbag and her clothes seemed splashed with some kind of liquid. She'd have to replace her bumper, maybe a side panel or two, nothing like the damage to his truck. Stupid woman.

The officer walked back after they'd loaded her into the ambulance. "She's going to the hospital to get checked out. We'll run some tests while she's there, but she insists her light was green."

"Figures."

"The guy works at the drycleaner. He didn't see a thing."

"So it's my word against hers?"

The officer tapped his pen against his leg. "Appears that way. I'll need to see your license and registration."

Craig stood up. "Yeah, yeah, yeah."

"And you're going to get your head looked at."

"It's fine," Craig muttered.

"Fine or not, we'll just have a look. There's another EMT on the—just pulling up now. We can do it here or at the hospital."

Too bad Craig hadn't gotten the rookie. "Here. I'm not going to the hospital."

"And I'll need to do some tests on you as well, Mr. Archer." At Craig's pointed stare, the officer grinned. "As much for your sake as mine."

"You won't find anything."

"Good. I don't want to have to bring you in. This report is going to be headache enough."

Craig handed the officer his license and the truck's registration. "How are you going to write this up?"

The officer scribbled on a pad. "Depends on what we find. Since you're both saying the light was green, we'll have to do an investigation."

"So I won't be able to file a claim until after the investigation?"

"You can file, Mr. Archer, but the police report won't be ready until the investigation is complete."

Great. Just what he didn't need.

Stupid woman.

CHAPTER 2

Leah Archer opened her front door and scowled at the man limping up the walk. "What happened to you?" she asked. He growled something she couldn't understand and pushed past her into the house. "And where's your truck?" She shut the door and turned to face her uncle.

"Where's your dad?" he asked.

Leah pointed to the ceiling. "Packing." She folded her arms across her chest. "Are you going to answer my questions?"

"You going to quit unless I do?"

"Nope," she said. She loved annoying her Uncle Craig, mostly because it didn't take much work at all. She followed him into the den and watched him ease onto the couch.

"I got in a wreck, which is why I have a Band-Aid on my forehead and why I'm limping. The truck's in the shop."

"Does dad know you were in a wreck?"

They both turned when her dad appeared at the base of the stairs. "You were in a wreck?" Mark asked.

Uncle Craig looked at Leah and lifted one brow. She loved it when he did that. "He does now."

Mark rushed into the room and stood peering down at Craig. "Are you hurt?"

Uncle Craig snorted. "I got a scratch on my head and banged my knee pretty good, but other than that, I'm fine. Wish I could say the same for my truck."

"Is it totaled?"

"No, but the whole damn side has to be replaced."

"What happened?" Leah asked as she took a seat next to her uncle. Her dad stared at his brother, his face pinched with worry. Leah couldn't stand to see her dad upset. Craig must have noticed her dad's reaction because he shrugged his shoulders as if the whole thing were no big deal.

"Woman driver ran a red light and speared me." He looked at Leah and smiled. "Your gender has serious issues behind the wheel."

"My gender takes great offense to your attitude."

"Take offense all you want, sweetheart, it doesn't change the facts."

"Are you sure you're okay?" her dad asked. His hands were clenched into fists and his face looked pale.

Craig smiled so big even his dimples showed. He hardly ever showed his dimples. "I'm fine, Mark. So when are you heading out?"

Leah hopped up and grabbed her dad's hand. "Their flight leaves in four hours," she said. She'd been counting down since she'd woken up that morning. Two weeks with her uncle sounded like paradise after the last few days. "You'd better light a fire under Carolyn, Dad. You know how you hate to be late to the airport."

Her dad stared at Craig for another minute before twisting to face his daughter. "The fire's been lit. She's almost ready."

"You've had this trip planned for almost a year. I don't know why she's running behind."

Dad pulled on her ponytail and ruffled her bangs like he'd done since forever. "Because that's what women do, honey. They primp."

"She's got to be tired of primping after all that fuss last weekend at the wedding." Her dad and Carolyn's wedding had been one long torturous day from beginning to end. Carolyn had even insisted Leah wear makeup.

"Apparently it doesn't wear off," her dad explained. "At least it never did with your mother."

Leah felt the ache, right in the center of her chest, as she always did when her dad mentioned her mother. The ache had gotten stronger since the wedding and all the changes that day brought to their lives. She hated feeling betrayed by her dad, especially when he was so happy, but she couldn't help the way she felt.

"So," her dad said to Craig. "You sure you're up for two weeks with this one?"

Uncle Craig narrowed his eyes at Leah and winked. "How much trouble can she get into while she's making me dinner and doing my laundry?"

Her dad looked at her and gave his usual crooked-smile. "You'd be surprised how much trouble a twelve-year old girl can cause."

Uncle Craig stood up. "You're just too soft, Mark. I've got duct tape and handcuffs and I'm not afraid to use them." He poked Leah in the stomach and tickled her under her armpits.

"Where are your bags?" Mark asked.

"In the tin can rental out in the drive," Craig said. "Come on, squirt. You can bring my bags in and show me to my room."

Leah grabbed his hand and dragged him toward the door. "This is going to be so much fun, Uncle Craig!" She stopped suddenly and looked up into his deep blue eyes. "Where's Blackjack?"

"He's back at my place. We'll pick him up later."

Leah stood on her tiptoes to whisper in Craig's ear. "Did you leave him at home because of Carolyn?"

Uncle Craig shrugged. "She'll have plenty of time to get to know Blackjack when they're back from Hawaii."

***

"You sure you're up for this?" Mark asked Craig. Mark had the same frazzled look he'd had on his wedding day.

"Why do you keep asking me that?"

Mark shoved his hands in the pockets of his khakis. "When I asked you to watch Leah, you weren't hurt."

"I'm not hurt."

"You're limping." Mark lifted his eyes to Craig's forehead. "And I'd bet that scratch came with one hell of a headache."

"Lighten up, Mom, I'm fine." But he could tell Mark was far from convinced. Because Craig understood Mark's fear, he took the time to explain. "It was a fender bender, nothing more. Besides, I might actually get Leah to wait on me if she thinks I'm injured."

Mark laughed. "Whatever works. These days, she's all over the map. One minute she's my little girl, the next it's like an alien has possessed her body. I'm hoping Carolyn can help decipher these mood swings once we're back from our honeymoon."

"Alien possessions? Now you tell me."

Mark lifted his hands in the air. "Hey, you told me not to call Mom."

"I can handle your daughter. Besides, Mom's up to her eyeballs helping Aunt Ginny after her foot surgery."

Carolyn came into the kitchen and wrapped her hand possessively around Mark's arm. "I think I'm ready," she said.

Craig surveyed his new sister-in-law. She was so different from carefree, down-to-earth Becca. But then, Craig barely knew Carolyn. Though she and Mark had dated for over three years, the long distance relationship hadn't offered much opportunity for them to bond. He knew Mark looked happy, if not a little drained by the honeymoon details.

"I don't know what all your fuss is about. From what I remember of my honeymoon," Craig said, "all you need is a bed and some time alone."

"Then we're both more than ready," Mark said and kissed his blushing bride's cheek.

Craig felt...weird about his brother moving on with his life. He didn't blame him. He'd never blame Mark for moving forward, both for him and for Leah. He only wished he could do the same.

"So," Mark said as he picked up a handwritten piece of paper from the kitchen table. "Here's Leah's schedule. Everything is on here, school, piano, lacrosse, chores, friends, phone numbers, everything. Consider this your Bible."

"I got this, bro. I've been watching her for years and she's still in one piece. Go, have a great time, and don't worry about a thing."

"I'm calling every day, just to check in," Mark said, and Craig pushed him toward the door. Their bags were lined up like soldiers. "If you need immediate backup, call the neighbors listed on the back of the sheet."

"Mark," Craig said through gritted teeth. "Just go. We'll be fine."

Leah, who'd been so eager for them to leave just minutes before, launched herself into her dad's arms. "I love you, Daddy. Please be careful."

Mark lifted her off her toes and hugged her hard, his eyes closed. Craig knew Mark loved Leah more than anything in the world. From the look on Carolyn's face, she knew it, too.

"Listen to Uncle Craig, honey." Mark plopped Leah back on the ground and picked up the largest of Carolyn's bags. "And be good."

"I will, Dad." Leah looked at Carolyn. "Have a nice time."

"Thank you," her woefully unprepared stepmother said before following Mark to the car.

After they pulled out of the driveway and Craig closed the door, he turned to face Leah. "Well, kiddo. It's just you and me for fourteen days. What do you want to do first?"

"Let's go get Blackjack," she suggested. "I've got to practice piano and he loves it when I play.

CHAPTER 3

A llie took a deep breath before answering the knock on her door and steeled herself for the scream.

"Oh my Gosh!" Melissa gasped. "Okay, okay." She nodded her head. "I'm glad you warned me." She pushed past Allie and walked into the den, flipping on the overhead light. "Come stand under the light so I can see."

Allie closed the door and faced her oldest friend. "How bad is it?"

"Well..." Melissa grabbed Allie's chin and swiveled her face back and forth under the recessed spotlights. "You look like you were punched in the face. Hard."

"I *was* punched in the face. By me."

"I didn't think airbags did that kind of damage," Melissa said.

"They don't. I was taking a sip of diet coke when the airbag deployed. I'm lucky I didn't chip a tooth."

Melissa narrowed her eyes. "I thought you gave up soda?"

"God, Mel. Only you would hone in on that detail at a time like this."

"If you'd been that diligent with me about chocolate, I'd look a hell of a lot better in these jeans right now."

Patience, Allie reminded herself. She needed an honest opinion, and no one was more qualified than Melissa. "Can we focus on me for just a second, please? I've got clients to see tomorrow and I need to know what reaction to expect. Remember, I'm talking about children. I don't want to scare them or their parents, whose checks pay my mortgage."

"With a little makeup, they might not notice the bruising, but I'm not sure about the swelling."

"I knew it." Allie sat on the couch and flung her arm over her eyes. "I look like the elephant man."

Melissa laughed. "Allie, please. The elephant man never looked as good as you." Melissa sat next to Allie and patted her leg. "Just tell the kids you were in a car accident. What's the big deal?"

"I look like a freak!"

"Says the girl voted most beautiful in high school," Melissa mumbled loud enough for Allie to hear and feel the sting. "Welcome to my world."

"That's not fair."

"Allie, you're stunningly beautiful, even with a bruised and battered cheek."

"Says the happily married mother of one."

"Touché." Melissa pulled Allie's hands into her own. "Look, are you okay? Did this accident do any real damage?"

"No. I was sore for a few days, but I'm better now. It's faded a lot in the last few days. I was just hoping I'd look normal by Friday."

Melissa cocked her head and blinked once, very slowly. Here comes the lecture, Allie thought. "Oh, I get it now. You've got a date."

"I was feeling sorry for myself and signed up for a new site. Lovefinders.com."

"Oh, Allie," Melissa chided in her mom voice. "I thought you were done with online dating."

"I was. Until I got this." Allie reached for the embossed envelope she'd tucked under a magazine on the coffee table. "Sharon Fowler is getting married."

"So?" Melissa shrugged and tossed the invitation aside. "You've gone to weddings alone."

Allie threw her hands in the air. "Sharon Fowler found a man to marry her, and I can't even get a date? Sharon Fowler?"

"Okay, I understand what you're getting at, but I thought you hated the whole online dating routine."

"I do hate it, but what are my choices? I work alone all day. I work with children at night. And all my friends are married or in serious relationships."

Melissa pursed her lips and stared at the ceiling. "I was just reading this article about how alumni associations are a great way to meet men."

"I don't think any Bowden alumni live in Atlanta or even the state of Georgia." Allie got up to pace around her den. "You know as well as I do that I've tried it all. Social clubs, church singles groups, night school, wine tastings. I'm not alone because I haven't tried. Where are all the single men in this town?" She stopped and faced Melissa. "And I don't mean to sound like a bitch when you're listening to me whine, but seriously, Mel, you have no idea what you're talking about."

"Look, Al, calm down. I'm sorry. You're right. I don't know what it's like out there now. But I hate to see you get all worked up over this. You were doing so great before, enjoying work and really getting comfortable in your own skin. I'm so proud of the progress you've made, and I hate to see you backslide like this."

Allie rubbed her throbbing head. "I know. Between the wreck and this invite, I've hit rock bottom."

"I thought you said you didn't have any injuries from the accident."

"I don't, but my car is in the shop for weeks and the guy who hit me is disputing my account. He insists my light was red and I know it was green. You know what a conscientious driver I am."

"So what does that mean?" Melissa asked.

Allie sat down and let out a frustrated sigh. "It means my life sucks, all the way around."

***

"You're late," Leah said after slamming the door of the rental car. "I told you this morning practice ended at five."

It was like talking to a pint-sized version of Mark. "I know, and I'm sorry. I got hung up on the job."

Blackjack barked from the backseat in welcome. Leah reached back and gave him a quick pat. "Hung up how?"

Craig took a deep breath and turned out of the school parking lot into traffic. He'd gotten too used to living alone and not answering to anyone. "You know I'm working on that house in town? Well, when the windows I ordered were delivered, two of them were the wrong size, and by the time I got the bozos at the store to realize it was their fault, I barely had time to lock the place down."

Leah huffed out a breath and rapped her fingers on her leg. "This is why I need a cell phone. If I had a phone, you could have just texted me that you were running late and I wouldn't have worried."

"Did you really think I wasn't coming?"

"No, but that's not the point."

As she dove into all the reasons why a twelve-year-old girl should have a cell phone, Craig zoned out and snuck glances at his niece. How had she gotten so big? It seemed like just yesterday he and Mark were scrambling to figure out how to raise a four-year-old whose mother and aunt had died in a car crash. And look at her. Those long legs and budding breasts. Jesus— Leah had breasts. When the hell had that happened?

"Are you listening to me, Uncle Craig?"

"Huh? Uh, yeah. You said you'd be safer with a phone."

"Exactly. So will you talk to dad?"

"I'm pretty sure he knows you want a phone." And he felt pretty sure Mark wanted to keep her as far away from becoming a teenager as possible. Unfortunately, from the looks of her, there wasn't a damn thing they could do to stop it. "So, what's on the agenda for tonight?" he asked. "Any homework?"

She sighed. "Math, as usual, and a little bit of Spanish."

"You're taking Spanish?"

She smiled, and for a moment, Craig thought he was talking to Becca. "Si, senior. Esta noche tengo piano."

"Say what?"

"I said, tonight I have piano."

"Oh. Okay." He turned onto Mark's street. "Do we have time for dinner first?"

Leah looked at the clock on the dash of the crappy rental. "Nope. According to Dad's notes, tonight's lasagna, so it's got to cook for an hour."

"I'm starving," Craig said. "How about we do something crazy and veer off the schedule? We can have lasagna tomorrow and tonight I'll whip us up a couple of sandwiches."

"Can't," Leah said. "Dad always makes enough for Ms. Allie."

"Who's Ms. Allie?"

"My piano teacher." She rolled her eyes. "Jeez, did you even read Dad's instructions?"

"Your piano teacher stays for dinner?"

"Not always, but we're her last lesson of the day, so Dad always makes enough in case she wants to stay."

Interesting. Homey dinners with the piano teacher was a side of Mark that Craig hadn't expected. "Okay, I guess we're having lasagna."

CHAPTER 4

When Leah walked into the kitchen, Uncle Craig was looking outside through the window. "Somebody's here," he said, but didn't quit staring.

Leah looked over his shoulder. She rubbed her face against the soft fabric of his worn flannel shirt. "That's Ms. Allie."

He brought his hand to her shoulder and let out a whistle. "You didn't tell me your piano teacher was hot. No wonder Mark invites her to dinner."

Leah sputtered. She knew Ms. Allie was beautiful. She'd always impressed Leah with her stylish clothes and fancy shoes, but hot? Weird. She nudged Craig in the arm. "Dad's married now, remember?"

He dropped the curtain and walked toward the front door with her in the crook of his arm. "He may be married, squirt, but he's not dead."

Leah broke free of his embrace and opened the door just as Allie raised her hand to knock. "Oh," she said and clutched her shirt with her hand. "You scared me."

"Sorry, Ms. Allie." Leah opened the door wide. "Come on in."

Allie took two steps into the dimly lit foyer and then jerked to a stop, her eyes wide on Blackjack, sitting calmly at Uncle Craig's feet.

"That's Blackjack. He belongs to my Uncle Craig."

"Oh." Allie flashed her perfect teeth before holding out her hand. "Hello, Uncle Craig."

15

Leah looked at her uncle. Instead of the flirting smirk she expected, his brows were drawn tightly together and he puckered his mouth like he tasted something bad. "Do I know you?"

"I don't think so," Ms. Allie said. "But you do look familiar."

They shook hands slowly and eyed one another as Leah stood waiting. "Well, he *is* my dad's brother."

They dropped their hands. "It's nice to meet you, Craig," Allie said. She glanced down at the large black and white dog. "And Blackjack." She turned to face Leah. "You ready?"

"Yep." Leah walked into the den and sat down at the piano bench. Allie sat her bag on the floor and draped her pretty wool coat over the chair.

"Would you like something to drink?" Uncle Craig asked Allie from the foyer.

"No, thank you." She smiled at him and then opened Allie's lesson book to the song they'd been working on for her recital. "Let's see how much practice you've done this week."

***

Craig leaned against the door casing of the foyer and watched Ms. Allie as she took a seat next to Leah. The gentle curves of her backside nicely complimented what he'd seen of her front. He never looked twice at beautiful blondes, not after Julie. He certainly didn't seek out blondes who wore tailored slacks and silk blouses, but this one, with her light green eyes and dark brows, she packed a punch. He pushed away and went back into the kitchen to check the timer on the lasagna. Thirty minutes. Well, if the beautiful Ms. Allie wanted to stay for dinner, her timing was perfect.

Craig took a seat at the kitchen table and opened his laptop. Blackjack curled up under the window and went back to sleep. Craig checked his email, fired off a few responses, made notes on his calendar for project quotes, and clicked over to the design for the house that was his current obsession.

The challenge of the historic renovation had captured more of his creative spirit than he'd thought possible. Not since the early years of Archer Construction, now a small division of Bell Buildings International, had he gotten this excited about a project. Of course, this wasn't an Archer Construction job, but an Archer Renovation. Both Archer companies had humble beginnings; one had taken on a life of its own and had cost him everything. The other had saved him when his world came crashing down.

Leah pounded a sour note and brought Craig's attention back to the den and the women in the next room. It was getting harder to think of Leah as a child. How had he not noticed the young woman blooming like a flower in front of his eyes? The farther he ran from the past, the more he seemed to count on some things staying the same: Leah and Mark.

But Mark was on his honeymoon. His marriage would change the way Craig popped in and out of this house on a whim. He wondered how Mark's marriage would change his relationship with the girl he considered his own now slowly mastering a song on her mother's piano. He felt relieved to shake off his mood when the timer buzzed.

He pulled the lasagna from the oven just as Leah and Allie entered the brightly lit kitchen. He nearly dropped the pan before setting it on the counter as that niggling thought that they'd met before tickled his addled brain. He usually didn't forget a pretty face.

"Dinner's ready," he announced. "As you can see, we have more than enough if you're interested in joining us."

She'd folded her coat over her arm and had her bag over her shoulder, pulling the material tight across her chest. He caught the tiniest glimpse of white lace between the buttons of her beige top.

"It smells wonderful," Allie said. "Are you sure I won't be intruding?"

Craig liked the sound of her voice, crisp with a hint of smoke around the edges. "Wouldn't ask if you were. Leah, do your uncle a favor and set the table while I open a bottle of wine." He chose a dusty bottle from Mark's stash in the built in Craig had designed. "Red okay?" he asked Allie.

She raised her brows, and he was momentarily distracted by the multitude of shades in her wavy hair. It wasn't quite blonde and wasn't quite brown, but an interesting mix of both. "Don't open it on my account. I'm driving."

"Half a glass won't hurt." He shoved napkins and forks into Leah's hand and scowled when she rolled her eyes. "Besides, if Mark cooks like he does everything else, we'll need a little something to wash this down."

Her answering smile had his nerves on alert. Damn Mark for not warning him the piano teacher was a looker. He'd at least have caught a quick shower and changed his clothes. As it stood, he smelled like he'd spent the day rolling around the lumberyard.

He tossed the premade salad into a bowl, added the croutons and dressing, and brought it to the table. When she turned to take a seat, he noticed a fading bruise on her right cheek that she'd tried to hide with makeup. An abusive boyfriend would undoubtedly explain Mark's disinterest. "Dinner is served."

CHAPTER 5

Allie fought the nerves that had gripped her since she'd walked into the house and spotted Craig in the foyer. Don't blow this, she reminded herself as she took a sip of wine from the glass he handed her—with his ringless left hand. She glanced at him from under her lashes and quickly looked away. Get a grip, Allie. The man looked like a day laborer. Was she really desperate enough to hit on a guy without health insurance or a 401k?

Leah's Uncle Craig had an interesting face. She wouldn't call him handsome, not with his unshaven jaw and the way his nose listed to the left. The injury to his forehead looked fresh and deep. He worked outside; she recognized the scent of a man who used his large, calloused hands doing something physical. His wavy brown hair had streaks of gold, most likely from the sun. His limp made her wonder if he'd injured himself in some sort of work related accident.

"So, Craig," she began. "Do you live around here?"

He lifted one shoulder as he'd done in the foyer and met her gaze. He didn't resemble his banker brother, except around the eyes. Mark's were an honest sky blue, while Craig's seemed as still and murky as the deep waters of the ocean. "Not far."

"It takes me ten minutes to walk to Uncle Craig's house," Leah explained as she picked the croutons out of her salad. "But only if I cut through yards and stuff."

Allie blotted her lips with the napkin after deeming the lasagna too hot to eat. She angled her head toward Leah. "How was the wedding?"

Allie watched as Leah wrinkled her nose. "It was okay."

"Okay?" Allie couldn't imagine anything more romantic than the handsome widowed father taking a second chance at love. "That's all you have to say?"

Leah shrugged. "The ceremony took forever, but the party after was kinda fun."

Craig laughed and drew her attention back to him. She was surprised to see dimples around the edges of his full lips. He dug into the heap of steaming lasagna he'd piled on his plate. "You should have seen her on the dance floor."

Allie smirked at Leah. "Did you go a little crazy?"

Leah shoved back from the table. Allie noticed her pink cheeks as she pulled Parmesan cheese from the refrigerator and skulked back to her seat. "I was just—Ms. Allie!" she said with a gasp. "What happened to your face?"

Allie instinctively lifted a hand and cupped her cheek. She'd thought her bruise had faded when the perceptive girl hadn't said anything earlier. Of course, the light in the foyer was dim and she sat on the opposite side during the lesson. "It's nothing. I got into a car accident, that's all."

Allie felt more than saw Craig pull back from his plate. "You." He fixed her with a pointed stare as sharp as the tines on the fork he aimed at her face. "You hit me."

"Excuse me?"

"That's how I know you. You ran the red light and plowed your little silver sedan right into my truck."

Allie deliberately closed her mouth after it had fallen open. She lifted her chin in the air and straightened her spine. "*You* ran the red light. Mine was green."

"Green my ass!" He scraped his chair back and stood up slowly, settling into a cocksure stance that had her rising from her seat. The dog, with its boxy head and light eyes, got up and wagged his tail at his master's feet. She swallowed hard when she realized the dog resembled a short-legged pit bull.

"Listen," she began with a weary look at the dog, "I don't know what you were doing instead of paying attention to the road, but you obviously don't know the difference between green and red."

"Right back atcha, sister."

Leah raised her hands in the air. "Whoa. Can we call a truce, please?"

Allie reached for her coat and spied her bag where she'd left it, leaning against the kitchen island where Craig stood. She jerked her arms into her coat and retrieved her bag, holding her ground even as Craig refused to move and forced her to stand within inches of his broad chest. Damn him, he smelled even better up close.

"You don't like the lasagna?" he asked.

"I've lost my appetite."

"Ms. Allie," Leah whined as only a child could do. "Please don't go."

"I'm sorry, Leah. I'll see you Thursday."

She sniffed at Craig and bolted for the door.

***

"I can't believe how rude you were." Leah picked up her plate and scraped her practically uneaten dinner into the trash.

"Me?" Craig asked. "She hit me." He pointed down to his leg. "I'm injured because of her."

"You both said the light was green. What if it was?"

Craig scoffed. "That never happens."

"Doesn't mean it didn't, and it doesn't mean you should have yelled at her. I like Ms. Allie."

"Yeah, well, she needs to learn how to drive."

"And you need to learn how to be nice. What if she doesn't come back?"

Craig took a deep breath. He was the adult in this relationship. He needed to start acting like one. "How long have you been taking lessons from Allie?"

Leah pouted. "Three years."

"Okay," he said. "Do you really think she's going to give up on you after three years simply because I yelled at her?" And for damn good reason.

"No."

"Okay, then. She'll be back." And he sure as hell wouldn't ask her to stay for dinner. He sat down and finished eating with the accompaniment of Leah's piano music from the den. He dragged his computer back to the table and tried to focus on work. He wanted to get the windows in before he started on the plumbing and HVAC. He needed to demo the wall between the living room and den before the electrician got started. He was in the mood for demo work.

When the phone rang, Leah stopped playing. From the excited sound of her voice, Craig knew Mark was making his nightly call. He had just loaded the last dish into the dishwasher when Leah carried the phone to him and announced that Mark wanted to speak to him.

"I'm going to take a shower," she said before taking the stairs two at a time.

"Hey," Craig said. He cradled the receiver between his chin and shoulder and closed his laptop so he could sponge off the table. "How's the honeymoon?"

"Good. Great. How is everything at home?"

"Perfect. Course you know Leah likes me better than you."

"I don't think that's true now that you yelled at Allie."

"Jesus, your kid's got a big mouth."

"The biggest. So she's the car you hit?"

"No, I'm the car *she* hit. She may be easy on the eyes and a competent piano teacher, but she can't drive worth a damn."

Mark chuckled. "I wondered if you'd make a move."

"Thanks for the warning, by the way. As it stands, none was needed. What a tight ass."

"Listen, Craig, Allie may look like your standard male fantasy, but she strikes me as being pretty vulnerable. Lose your edge or I'm going to have to look for a new teacher, and I really don't want to have to do that."

"You may have to when Carolyn gets a load of her."

22

"Carolyn's not the jealous type. And she's got nothing to worry about."

Craig knew that saying women weren't jealous was like saying the sky wasn't blue. But leave it to his baby brother to see the sunny side of life. "Whatever you say."

"You know, since the wedding's over and all the craziness has died down, I've had some time to think. Things are going to be different when I get back."

"What do you mean different?"

"I mean I'm going to be married. I *am* married, and I know you're not going to feel comfortable coming over the way you always do."

The stab of hurt was quick and lethal. "Are you trying to tell me to stay away?"

"No, not at all." He blew out a breath. "I'm screwing this up badly. What I'm trying to say is that we want you around, Carolyn and I. We don't want you to feel left out or replaced."

"Look, Mark, I know what you're trying to do and I appreciate it, but you're right. Things have changed. It's time for me to get my own life."

"Craig…"

"No, I'm okay with this. I'm looking forward to not feeling so chained to you and Leah."

"Is that how we've made you feel?"

"No, hell, now I'm screwing this up badly." It was time to be honest, and leave it to him and Mark to do so over the phone. "You and Leah got me through the worst that could happen. I needed to feel needed after Julie died. I feel like we raised her together."

"We did. No question, Craig, we did."

"But she's half grown already, and she needs a woman in her life. The three of you are going to have an adjustment period when you get back, and I'd already planned on making myself scarce. It's for the best."

"I never could have gotten through any of it without you, Craig. All of it—losing Becca, raising Leah. Carolyn and I wouldn't even have had a chance if you hadn't watched Leah every other weekend so we could get to know one another."

Enough, Craig thought. Listening to this was worse than giving the best man speech at the wedding. "Yeah, yeah, I'm a regular saint."

"When was the last time you went on a date?" Mark asked.

"Don't go trying to fix me up now that you're happily married."

"I'm not going to fix you up; I'm just worried about you."

"No, you're not. You don't want to be the only one yanked around by the ball and chain. I'm perfectly happy on my own." And matrimony held less than zero appeal after his first marriage.

"I never said anything about marriage. I said date."

Craig had to think back. His last date was a fix up, and a terrible one at that. "I let Jimmy talk me into taking his wife's best friend to dinner. I'll never do that again."

"I think it's time for you to let someone in. I know it's hard, especially after what happened to Julie, but I want you to be happy."

Who said he and Julie had been happy? he wanted to ask his brother, but he knew better than to speak ill of the dead. If he hadn't told Mark the truth before, he sure as hell wasn't going to tell him now. "I am happy, so just keep your ideas to yourself."

"Fine. Tell Leah I'll call her tomorrow."

"She won't care," Craig teased.

"Yeah, yeah, yeah."

CHAPTER 6

"**Y**ou should have seen him," Allie huffed, "all smug and self-righteous. I had half a mind to punch him in the face."

Melissa reached over and tugged on Allie's sleeve. "Can we slow down a little? You forget I'm pushing thirty extra pounds."

Allie slowed from a run to a jog. "Sorry. Do you need a water break?"

Melissa pointed ahead to where the jog path forked and a pretty bench sat by the river. "No, not yet. Let's stop by the bench and cool down. If we stop now, I'll probably cramp, and Henry likes to look at the ducks."

Allie glanced at the baby, happily chewing on a multi-colored rattle, his angelic face red from the brisk air. "Do you think he's warm enough?"

"He's in head to toe fleece. He's probably sweating."

"His cheeks are red."

Melissa pulled back the retractable cover of the jog stroller and peered over at her son. "His ears are covered. Trust me, if he were uncomfortable, he'd let us know."

They slowed to a stop by the river and Allie stretched her quads while Melissa sat on the bench and gulped down water. "I know this is good for me, but damn, I hate it."

Allie sat down beside her, her breathing back to normal. "Do you want me to push him back? I don't mind, and I think you need a break."

"Maybe," Melissa said. "Let me rest for a minute and I'll let you know."

"So what am I supposed to do?" Allie asked.

"About the guy? What can you do?"

"I have to see him again this Thursday at the lesson. What am I going to say?"

"Why do you have to say anything?" Melissa glanced at Allie and lifted her brows. "Sounds to me like you're interested."

"What? No." She thought of Craig, looking down his crooked nose at her. "He's arrogant and not all that attractive."

"Not all that attractive?"

"Well, his attitude is a big turn off."

"Speaking of turn offs," Melissa said. "Who's the big date with on Friday?"

Allie blew out a breath. She dreaded her date already and that wasn't the attitude she needed when venturing back into the dating pool. "He's a dentist. Divorced. No kids."

"I thought you didn't go out with divorcees?"

"I'm loosening my standards a little. I'm not budging on the kids, but just because a prior relationship didn't work out, that doesn't mean I should dismiss him altogether. What if his wife cheated on him?"

"Or what if he cheated on his wife?"

Allie tried to shrug away the unease in her gut. "I'll never know if I don't go out with him."

"True." Melissa huffed out a big breath. "But all I've ever heard from you is about the sanctity of marriage. I don't think you could fall for someone who walked away from that commitment, no matter what the circumstances."

Sometimes Allie hated that Melissa knew her so well. "Just because my parents' divorce ripped a hole in our family and, let's be honest, my sense of self doesn't mean I can't respect someone else's individual circumstances."

"Allie." Melissa laid her hand over Allie's. "It's okay for you to go out with total strangers you meet on the Internet, but do me a favor and be honest about your reasons."

"Fine." Allie pushed off the bench and began pacing around Henry's stroller. "My criteria are too stringent to pull up anything other than strange men who look like serial killers. If I want to go out with a professional man in his thirties, I've got to be prepared for some baggage. That's just the cold, hard truth. And let's face it," she added with a point to Melissa's innocent face. "I'm no virginal teenager. My relationship with Nick probably equates to a bad marriage."

"Except he never pulled the trigger."

Allie stopped pacing and stared out at the river. "If he'd proposed, I would have married him. I would have married him and then been left to make really hard choices when he cheated on me." She thought of Nick, so handsome, so perfect for her in every way but the one that really mattered. "Thank God he never proposed."

Melissa eased off the bench and stretched her hands in the air before draping one arm around Allie's shoulders. "I'm glad he's out of your life, Al. He was never good enough for you."

Allie laid her head on Melissa's shoulder, so grateful for her friend's support, even if she was wrong. Nick left because she wasn't good enough for him. "It doesn't matter now anyway." Allie grabbed the stroller handle and turned Henry around. "I read this article in Self-Love magazine that said you can't appreciate a good relationship if you haven't experienced a really bad one first."

"Self-Love Magazine?" Melissa handed Henry the rattle when he began to fuss at leaving the ducks behind.

Allie shrugged and began to jog. "I know it sounds hokey, but I think it's true. Looking back, lots of things about my relationship with Nick were messed up, and it never occurred to me to take a stand or rock the boat. I didn't have any other long term relationship to compare it to."

"No, you didn't have the backbone to confront him." She met Allie's accusing stare with one of her own. "Whenever he did or said something that bothered you, you'd complain to me or one of your girlfriends, but you'd never complain to him."

"I just didn't think any of it was worth a fight."

"He wasn't worth the fight. There's a difference."

Allie snorted. Easy for her to say. "You and Ben never fight."

"Ha!" Melissa clutched her side, but kept up the pace. "We just don't fight in front of you."

"But you never complain about him."

"Allie, I purposely don't complain to you about him because I don't want you to think I'm not grateful for my husband. You know as well as I do that you're a little sensitive in that area."

"So you censor your comments with me?"

"No, I just don't bitch to you about Ben. I have plenty of other girlfriends and fellow moms for that."

Allie stopped jogging and frowned at her friend. "Well, what kind of friendship do we have when you can't be honest with me about your life?"

"We have a very good friendship. And I am honest with you, but I don't think you want to listen to me gripe."

"You listen to me gripe all the time."

"I know," Melissa said and started jogging again, forcing Allie to do the same. "And hearing you gripe about men really helps my marriage."

"How?"

"When Nick cheated on you, Ben and I talked about cheating, in real terms. It was the first time we'd ever drawn that line in the sand without just assuming it was there."

"So when my relationship crashed and burned, your marriage got stronger?"

"Exactly. And remember when you went out with that guy who only took you to sporting events on your dates?"

"Yeah." Allie wasn't sure where Melissa was going.

"Well, it made me think about when Ben and I first started dating. We used to go to clubs and restaurants and we'd take turns choosing. After we got married, we only did things with his friends and went to games and concerts of his choice. I put my foot down, and now our rare evenings out are spent doing things we both want to do."

"And all this happened because of me?"

Melissa cocked her head and smiled at Allie. "Yeah, pretty much."

"Well. Perhaps I should charge you a fee for these marriage sessions I didn't realize we've been having."

"I'd say the therapy works both ways."

Allie would have quickened her pace to outrun Melissa if she didn't have the extra weight of the stroller holding her back. As it stood, they were neck and neck. At least Melissa had stopped talking and let Allie digest what she'd learned. The more she thought about what Melissa confessed, the more everything about their lives bounced around in her head, the more she realized what she'd already known: dating sucked. And that, she knew, did little to help her attitude about her upcoming date.

***

Craig dropped the sledgehammer and pulled a section of sheetrock away from the stud. The annoying pain in his knee didn't stop him from enjoying the destruction of a wall that served no better purpose than to close off a corner of the house. Besides, he needed the exertion, the feel of something powerful in his hands and the sweat that crept down his back.

Mark had zoned in on a sore spot and Craig hadn't been able to shake his mood ever since. So what if he didn't date? What was the point? He wasn't looking for a relationship, and whenever he needed sex, he always had his hand if a willing woman couldn't be found. He'd found quite a few willing women in the last couple of years.

He'd spent too much time with Mark and Leah, thinking of the three of them as a unit, a family. He'd known for a while that Mark and Carolyn were getting serious. At first, when Mark had asked Craig to watch Leah while he went out of town for the weekend, he hadn't mentioned a woman. But Mark, being Mark, couldn't keep a secret for long. He'd met someone. She lived in Chicago. They were seeing each other. Their no strings, no expectations weekends together went beyond serious when Mark proposed.

Craig was envious of his brother, for more reasons than just because he was moving on. Mark had grieved for Becca because he could. He knew what they'd had, what he'd lost. He could mourn for the wife who'd loved him and given him his child. If only Craig could've had that chance.

He shook off his mood when Davis Hollingsworth walked in, his Italian loafers popping like dry wood on the unfinished floor. He stood at the threshold between the kitchen and the newly opened room with his hands on his hips.

"Wow, that really opens things up in here," Davis said. "I'm glad I let you talk me into this." He walked around the studded wall and waved his hand at the electrical wires running between them. "What are you going to do with all this stuff?"

What do you think I'm going to do with it? Craig wanted to say, but he bit his tongue and said, "Reroute it through the ceiling and the adjacent walls."

Davis spun around and took in the bottom floor. "I gotta tell you, man, I hope you can put this bitch back together."

"Rehab work is ugly at first. Trust me, you'll be happy with the finished product."

"I damn well better." The words were said with a cocky smile and Craig didn't take it personally. Davis had taken a chance on him, and if the nervous tapping of his foot didn't give away his second thoughts, the constant hair flipping would have done it. "Jimmy knows I'll kick his ass if you screw this up."

"Jimmy'll kick my ass if I screw this up," Craig said and pulled another hunk of sheetrock out from between the studs. "But he won't have to. My work's as good as my word." Craig tossed the sheetrock into the growing pile in the corner by the window. "Did you come by for a reason or did you just want to see how she's coming?"

"A little of both. Stacy had some ideas for the kitchen she wanted me to run by you."

"Okay." Craig dropped the hammer and clapped some of the dust off as he walked to the kitchen.

"She wants an island, like we talked about, but we went to some friends' lake house last weekend and they have this huge island with stools and a sink. Her eyes bugged out, and then she winked at me. All I've heard about since is the island."

"Okay," Craig said with a nod. He knew Stacy would be a problem from the moment he met the perky brunette. "We've only got so much room to deal with here."

Davis held up his palms. "Trust me, Craig, I explained that to her. She's got her mind set, so we're going to have to figure this out."

"You said you wanted to maintain the original structure in here. If you really want a large island, you're looking at ripping all this out and starting over. It's going to cost you."

"Doesn't it always?" Davis slapped him on the back. "Can you work up some of those computer drawings like you did before? Big island with seating, plus she wants one of those range top stoves with the warming drawer."

All good information to have had before. A redesign of the kitchen would set him back a few weeks. "I'll work something up tonight."

"I appreciate it." Davis looked at his watch, a flashy Tag Heuer, and flipped his hair. "I've got to get going. Keep up the good work."

"I'll send the designs over as soon as possible. We'll need to get this finalized soon so I can get the orders in."

After a handshake and a slap on the shoulder, Davis was gone. Craig put his hands on his hips and looked around the kitchen. He was pleased when Davis and Stacy wanted to keep the integrity of the house in tact while updating to modern conveniences. Stacy's kitchen ideas were blowing that right out of the water. "Not your business," he reminded himself. "Do what the customer wants."

That had been the hardest thing for Craig since getting back in the business, but on a much smaller scale. Smaller, hell, he mused. Compared to the Goliath Archer Construction, his new venture was David. Fortunately, they weren't in competition. They weren't even on the same playing field. Making all the decisions, being the one responsible for the success or failure of a project was something he was happy to concede.

He wanted to get worked up about having to redesign the kitchen, but knew the extra work would keep his mind focused while Leah's sneaky piano teacher was at the house.

CHAPTER 7

Allie sat in the drive of Leah's house and grinned as she ended her conversation with Detective Reynolds. Ha, she thought. She knew the detective hadn't called Craig yet and she wondered if she wanted to break the news to him or let him hear it from the police. He probably wouldn't believe it from anyone but the authorities.

She got out of her rental, retrieved her bag from back seat, and walked up the path to the front door. She heard the dog announcing her approach.

Leah opened the door in a less than enthusiastic way. "Hi, Ms. Allie."

"Hi, Leah." She stepped inside and held out her hand for the dog. He didn't look so dangerous now, with his tail wagging and his ears pinned back against his head. He licked her fingers in greeting. Craig descended the stairs wearing jeans and blue t-shirt that brought out his eyes. Damn him. "Hello."

He peeked around her shoulder before Leah closed the door. "I see you made it here in one piece. Did you kill anyone along the way?"

Oh, she was going to enjoy this. "I don't suppose you've spoken to Detective Reynolds yet, have you?"

"Who?"

"The officer at the scene of the accident."

He narrowed his eyes at her and she smiled when she heard his cell phone ring from the kitchen. "That should be him now. You can apologize after the lesson." She gave Leah a scoot into the den with a smirk she couldn't hide. What an ass! An ass that looked great in a pair of old jeans. Doesn't matter, she reminded herself as she settled beside Leah on the piano bench.

"How's the song coming?" she asked, determined to focus on Leah.

"Good. I've got the first two verses down cold, but I get a little tripped up with the third."

Allie flipped open her lesson book. "Let's see what we can do about that."

***

Craig retrieved a beer from the refrigerator and took a long sip before ambling out to the foyer. He leaned against the doorjamb and watched his niece with her beautiful and devious piano teacher.

"That's good," she said to Leah. "Try it again, but this time take it slower and really think about each note. Don't worry about the speed until you get the sequence down."

Leah started playing the piece she'd worked on all week, something slow and melodic that he should know the name of, but didn't. Allie nodded her head in time with the hand she tapped against her pants.

She was a cool one, he'd give her that much. He doubted he'd have been able to keep her secret under wraps for ten seconds, much less thirty minutes. He took a deep breath, and then returned to his computer in the kitchen to work on the designs for the house.

He'd just figured out how to fit an enormous island into the kitchen space when he realized the music had stopped and he heard someone clearing her throat over his shoulder.

"Ready to apologize?"

He turned around and stared up at her stunning face. Damn shame she was such a smart ass. "I'm ready for mine, also."

She splayed those long fingers across her chest and gave a snarky laugh that only emphasized her perfect teeth. "You think I'm going to apologize? Dream on, mister."

"Why should I be the only one to apologize? You said your light was green. It was. I said my light was green; it was. So, I'd say we're even."

Leah snuck her head around the corner as if hesitant to get in the middle of another argument. "You said the female gender has issues behind the wheel."

Allie looked at him as if to say, "Score one for me."

"I said that when I thought she'd run the red light. Now that I know the city's to blame, I might be willing to retract my statement."

"Might be?" Allie and Leah asked in unison. Women.

"Okay, if I say I'm sorry for accusing you of being a stereotypical bad female driver, does that make you feel better?"

"You call that an apology?" Allie asked.

He stood up and delighted when she was forced to look up at him. "It's the best you're going to get."

"I think you can do better." She slapped her hands on her hips and tapped her foot.

"Are you going to sue?" he asked.

"Pardon me?"

"The city. Are you going to sue? The cop seemed a little nervous we'd sue."

"First of all, there is no 'we.' And second of all, what would be the point? They're already paying for the damages to both of our cars. Besides, suing the city is like suing ourselves. It would be our tax money paying whatever damages we recovered."

She was smarter than he'd given her credit for and certainly a hell of a lot more logical than her looks led one to believe. "Valid points, and conclusions I'd already reached."

"Then why did you ask?"

He didn't think she'd appreciate hearing because he enjoyed watching her get riled, and he certainly couldn't help himself from riling her more. "Because I figured you'd want a few extra dollars to buy a pretty dress or get your hair done."

He watched her features change as she inhaled sharply. "You're a sexist ass." She whipped that mane of blonde/brown hair around and said, "Excuse my language, Leah. Your uncle brings out the worst in me."

"No problem," Leah said.

Allie turned her cat eyes back on Craig. Damn if she wasn't more attractive with the heat of anger in her cheeks. "I don't have any dinner to offer you tonight."

"I wouldn't stay if you did."

"Perfect. Then I guess we'll see you next week."

She put on the coat Leah handed her, some ridiculously frilly black trench, and made her way to the door. He should have been irritated that her floral scent lingered. He shooed her hand away and opened the door himself.

After a huffing out a breath, she asked, "When does your brother return?"

"Not soon enough. You've got one more week to slobber over my handsome face."

"You need to wake up, Craig, and take a good hard look in the mirror."

"I have, sweetheart. That's how I know you'll be back."

She pointed at Leah and stepped sideways when Blackjack attempted to scoot past her to get outside. "She's why I'm coming back." She slung her bag over her shoulder and fixed him with a narrow-eyed stare. "You may as well tell your brother I'm billing him extra for having to deal with you."

Craig barked out a laugh as she retreated down the walk. "Ha! He'll get a kick out of that one."

He stood at the threshold and watched her gun the engine, slam the car into reverse, and maneuver a hairpin turn out of the driveway. If it hadn't been so dark, he would probably have seen her tires smoke.

Leah walked up beside him and wrapped her arm around his waist. "I've never seen Ms. Allie get mad at anyone."

"It's just a matter of finding the right buttons to push." He mussed her hair and shut the door.

"I think you pushed all of hers." She walked over to the piano and began straightening her music sheets. "Dad's going to be mad at you for making her upset."

"Then do something crazy and don't tell him."

"You want me to lie?"

"Of course not," Craig said as the phone began to ring. He knew Mark called after her lesson on purpose. "Just don't mention it."

CHAPTER 8

Allie honked her horn and waved when the driver in the car in front of her finally looked up from her cell phone and noticed the green turn arrow. "Go, already," she muttered, nervously tapping her fingers on the wheel and then gunning the engine. She was late for her scheduled date prep that included a hot bath, complete makeup reapplication, and hair styling. At the rate she was going, she might have to forgo the bath for a shower.

What had ever possessed her to teach twins—five-year-old twins—on a Friday afternoon? It was probably a good thing Peyton and Paris had kept her mind off her upcoming date. Why had she agreed to out with a dentist? She loved sugar and candy and sticky treats. She'd already given up soda in an attempt to get healthy. What else would she have to sacrifice?

She pulled into her garage and rushed inside the house, dropping her bag, keys, and purse along the way. She grabbed a diet coke from her emergency stash in the fridge, screw the guilt, and jogged up the stairs to her bedroom. She glanced at the bed. All she wanted to do was to lie on her fluffy duvet and watch a good movie.

"Which is why you don't have a boyfriend," she muttered and forced herself to bypass the bed and head straight for the closet. Allie stripped out of her wool pants and button down and stared at her clothes. First date, probably a nice restaurant, she should wear a dress. She shoved hanger after hanger down the rack, dismissing options as she went. "I hate this," she said when she got to the end of her choices and nothing seemed appropriate.

She went back through her dresses slowly, looking at each one, trying to think about the message they sent. "Too loud," she murmured as she passed up her favorite multicolored wrap dress. She paused at a belted gray dress. "It's a date, Allie, not an interview." She pursed her lips at her cream, boat neck jersey dress. "Too blah," she decided and moved on. Through the process of elimination, she pulled out her black, sleeveless, V-neck jersey dress and paired it with silver hoops and a long strand necklace. "That will have to do."

After a shower and a new coat of makeup, Allie stood in front of the mirror trying to decide if she should wear her hair up or down. When her cell phone rang, she almost didn't answer, but at the last minute rushed from the bathroom and fished it out of her purse before it went to voicemail.

"Hello?"

"Allie?" said a familiar, yet unrecognizable voice.

"Yes."

"This is Craig Archer." In the space of time she tried to hide her shock, he said, "Leah's uncle."

Interesting. "Let me guess. Your conscience got the best of you and you called to apologize?"

"No." He cleared his throat. "Something's happened. Something way outside my area of expertise."

"You have a question about driving?"

"Funny. Listen, I wouldn't call if it weren't kind of an emergency. As a matter of fact, I wouldn't call if I had anyone else to call, but since I don't, you're it."

"Kind of an emergency?" she asked. "What kind of emergency? Is it Leah? Is she okay?"

"Yeah, it's Leah, but she's not okay. Can you come over?"

"I'm kinda busy, so if this *is* an emergency, you need to explain."

He exhaled loudly. "I can't talk about this over the phone. Can you just come over, please?"

"What's wrong? Is Leah hurt? Is she bleeding?"

He chuckled. "She's not hurt, but there's blood. Listen," he said, as impatient as ever, "she needs you. I don't know what to do."

"Well, I…" Allie looked at the clock. She had to leave in twenty minutes or she'd never make it to the restaurant in time. "I don't have much time. How long will this take?"

"If I knew anything about this at all, including how much time it'll take, I wouldn't be calling."

Allie pictured Leah, her sweet face and unruly brown hair, stuck in the clutches of an obtuse uncle during a semi-emergency. "Fine. But I can't stay long."

"Great. Do me a favor and make it fast."

Allie pulled the phone away from her ear when she realized he'd hung up on her. "Urrrr," she growled. She threw her keys, compact, and wallet into her favorite python clutch and grabbed a wrap as she headed for the door. "This better be worth it."

***

Craig opened the door as soon as he saw Allie's car pull into the drive. He heard the click of heels on concrete before she waltzed into the spotlight from the porch lamps. Craig forgot for a moment why he'd asked her to come over and simply stared, concentrating on not swallowing his tongue. She looked like a Victoria's Secret runway model wearing some floaty black dress that pressed against her as she walked, emphasizing every curve and angle of her incredible body. That blondish/brown hair hung free around her sexy, shimmering lips and eyes that seemed to glow in the night. When she stopped in front of him, slapped her hand on her hip, and cleared her throat, he regained his composure, but not before catching a whiff of something dark and sexy. He ushered her into the house.

"What's the emergency?" she asked as Blackjack rushed in from the den. Craig snapped his fingers and ordered him down. The dog reluctantly crept to the floor.

"It's Leah. She…well, I was down here in the kitchen and she screamed and when I got upstairs…" He rubbed his temple and tried to dislodge the image of what he'd seen and what it all meant.

"Spit it out, already," she said. Craig could tell she was annoyed by the tiny line between her brows. "What happened when you got upstairs?"

Craig swallowed his pride, lowered his voice, and whispered, "She started her period."

Those dark brows lifted for just a moment before her freshly painted mouth puckered into a sympathetic pout. "Oh, poor thing. What did you do?"

"What do you think I did? I panicked. I tried to call Mark, but with the time difference, they were either off on some excursion or too busy to answer the phone. I looked over the list of numbers he left, but yours was the only one I recognized. She needs a woman." He thumped his fist on his chest. "I am *not* a woman."

"No kidding." Allie turned her head toward the staircase. "Where is she?"

"Upstairs in her room. Second door on the right."

"Does she have any supplies?"

"How the hell do I know?"

Allie sighed. "Does she know you called me?"

"I told her I'd get someone to help. I didn't specifically mention you."

"Okay." She turned toward the stairs. "I'll be back."

"I'll be right here," he said.

Her scent lingered even after she'd gone upstairs, swaying her hips and drawing his eyes to her surprisingly muscular calves. "Not interested," he reminded himself and walked to the refrigerator to get a beer. He took a long sip, hoping cold beer would help to calm his anxiety and other unwanted urges.

***

Leah's heart rate doubled when she heard a faint knock on the door. *Please, God, don't let it be Uncle Craig or our next-door neighbor, Mrs. Rosenbloom.*

"Come in," she said. Relief swamped her when she saw Ms. Allie, dressed up and looking like she was going to a party. "Oh, Ms. Allie."

"Hi, Leah. Your uncle called." She came inside, shut the door, and closed the distance between them. Leah was too embarrassed to stand up from her desk. "How are you feeling?"

Leah shrugged her shoulders. "Weird, I guess."

"That sounds about right." She placed her very cool purse on the desk and crouched down in front of Leah. "Do you have any pads?"

"Yeah. Dad bought me some last summer before I went to camp. I've got one on now."

Ms. Allie smiled. "Good. You've got a wonderful dad."

"I wish he was here."

"I know you do, sweetheart." She placed her hand over Leah's and squeezed. "Do you have any questions? Do you have the pad on right?"

"I think so. I just put the sticky side on my underwear and folded the wings under. Is that right?"

"Yep, that's perfect." She stood up. With the added height from her heels, she seemed too big for Leah's small room. "Can I see the box to make sure you won't need anything more absorbent for when you're asleep?"

Leah got up and retrieved the box from the back lid of the toilet. She liked the way Allie's heels sounded on the tile.

"This should be fine for both day and night use," Allie explained. "Usually your first few cycles are pretty light. You might want to get some panty liners for the last couple of days when you won't need this much protection."

"Panty liners?" Leah asked.

Allie handed the box back. "I'll bring some when I come Tuesday. They're just a lot thinner."

"Okay. Thanks."

"So, have any of your friends started their periods?"

"My friend Marcy has, but she doesn't like to talk about it." Leah picked at the fingernail polish on her thumb. "I'm not sure about anyone else."

"You know, I started my period when I was thirteen. When I was twelve, some of my friends had already started and I couldn't wait to start. I used to see their stuff in the bathroom and I thought I would feel grown up when I got my period."

"Did you?" she asked. "Feel grown up?"

Ms. Allie pursed her lips. "A little, I guess. But then I started getting cramps and it wasn't so fun anymore."

Leah felt a little sick. "Cramps?"

"Muscle cramps. Do you know what happens in your body when you get your period?"

"Not really."

"Okay." She put her arm around Leah and led her back into the room. Leah watched as she slipped out of her shoes and sat down on the bed for what looked like girl talk. "We women have a uterus, right?"

Leah nodded. She knew from health class that the uterus was where the baby grew.

"The uterus lining swells with blood in preparation for a baby. When a baby doesn't happen, it breaks down the lining and discharges the blood. That's why you get—Oh, my." Allie glanced down at her watch. "I need to make a quick call." She hopped off the bed and grabbed her purse. "I'll be right back."

She stepped into the hallway and Leah inched close to the door to hear what and who she spoke to, but then felt bad about eavesdropping and took a seat on the bed to wait. She was picking at a loose string on her comforter when Ms. Allie walked back in.

"Now, where were we?" she asked and sat back down on the bed.

"You were telling me about how the lining breaks down."

"Yes, that's how you get your period. Sometimes, for most people, the process causes your uterus, which is a muscle, to cramp."

"Like a leg cramp?"

Allie laughed. "Not that acute, but similar. Menstrual cramps are more subtle."

"By subtle, do you mean not that bad?"

"Menstrual cramps are not as quick or painful as leg cramps. They're more annoying than anything. And you might not even get them."

Leah couldn't imagine getting a cramp in her uterus, but figured Ms. Allie knew what she was talking about. Leah had never known anyone as beautiful or womanly as Allie. "Okay. Thanks for explaining all this to me. My dad went over the basics, but he was pretty quick and he didn't say anything about cramps."

"If you ever have any questions, Leah, you can ask me. I know what it's like not to have someone to talk to."

"You didn't have a mom, either?"

"I did. I do, but we've never been all that close."

"I think if my mom was alive, she'd go through all this stuff with me."

Ms. Allie's eyes darted over to the window where the moon glowed bright over the trees. "My mom was…not really there all the time."

"What do you mean? She didn't live with you?"

"My parents got divorced when I was eleven. I got bounced back and forth between my parents' houses. My mom was upset about the divorce and I didn't feel comfortable burdening her with my problems."

"I thought that's what moms were for. I don't think she would have thought of you as a burden."

Allie gave Leah a smile that also looked like a frown. "She probably didn't, but I was young and it just seemed like she wouldn't have cared. I should have asked her." She reached over and patted Leah's knee. "You'll have a stepmom when Carolyn moves in."

Leah's stomach tightened. She didn't think of Carolyn as a stepmom. She didn't think of Carolyn at all. "I guess."

"Are you excited about having a woman around the house?"

Leah shrugged and looked away. She didn't want to lie to Allie, but she didn't want to admit she was dreading Carolyn living in their house and taking her dad's attention away. "Sort of."

"My dad remarried a few years after my parents split up, so I had a stepmom. Of course, I also had my real mom, so it wasn't quite the same."

"I still have my real mom."

"I know you do, sweetie."

"My dad talks about her all the time. I know I was only four when she died, but I feel like I know her. I feel like she lives here, too."

"She doesn't have to move out just because Carolyn is moving in."

Leah got up to pace when she couldn't sit still. "He already took her picture down from his nightstand." She turned to face Allie. "How could he do that? They didn't get divorced. She died. She didn't want to leave us, but God needed her in heaven."

Ms. Allie pivoted on the bed to face Leah where she stood by her desk. "Do you think your mom would want your dad to be alone for the rest of his life?"

"He's not alone. He has me."

"I know he has you, but you won't live here forever. You'll go off to college and start your own life."

She'd never thought about it that way. "But that's not for a long time."

"It'll happen before you know it, and your mom's been gone for what? Eight years? That's a long time for your dad to live without love."

"But why now? Why can't he wait until I'm almost gone?"

Ms. Allie stood up and put her hands on Leah's shoulders. "Because love happens when you least expect it. It doesn't run on a timeline. You can't snap your fingers and magically be in love. Believe me, I wish it was that easy."

"So much is changing, Ms. Allie. I don't want all this change."

"Change is scary, but that doesn't make it bad. I spent years hating my stepmom and she really is a nice woman. I could have saved myself a whole lot of grief if I'd just accepted the fact that she was there to stay. And your period, well, like it or not, that's here to stay, too."

CHAPTER 9

Allie breathed a sigh of relief as she closed Leah's door. She'd walked a young girl through the most frightening aspect of puberty and, even more distressing, the introduction of a stepmother. She hoped she'd advised the girl properly as she made her way along the hall toward the stairs.

Allie felt pretty good about her period advice. That was pretty cut and dried, but what did she know about welcoming a stepmother into a family? She'd been a bitch to Suzanne when her dad had remarried and their strained relationship still endured. She'd tried to encourage Leah to have an open mind about Carolyn when hers had been so firmly shut that she'd never considered letting Suzanne become a real member of the family.

When Craig appeared at the base of the stairs wearing a soft cotton t-shirt and jeans, Allie brought a hand to her chest. She'd been so deep in thought, she'd forgotten he was waiting downstairs.

"How'd it go?" he asked with a voice edged in tension.

She shrugged, stepped over the dog, and moved past him into the kitchen. "Could I have a glass of water, please? I'm parched."

"You're parched," he grumbled as he retrieved a bottle of water from the refrigerator. "So what happened?"

"She'd taken care of it. Mark bought some supplies and she knew what to do. I answered a couple of questions and that was pretty much that."

"Why the hell did it take so long? You were up there forever."

Allie set the water bottle on the counter after taking a long sip. "This is a big event in a girl's life. I couldn't leave without making sure she felt okay."

"So how does she feel?"

Allie didn't mistake the sarcasm in his voice. "She feels weird and confused and more than a little anxious about Carolyn coming to live here."

"Carolyn?" He brought those big hands to his waist and shot out his hip. "How did starting her period morph into talking about Carolyn?"

"She's conflicted. She loves her mother desperately. Starting her period was a milestone she was supposed to share with her mom or, at the very least, her dad. My being here in their place brought up some questions. I told her about when I started my period and that I had a stepmom and then one thing led to another."

"I didn't ask you to come over to counsel her on dealing with Carolyn. The next time you talk to her, I'd appreciate you sticking to the subject."

"Well, excuse me for not turning my back on a young girl in need. What did you expect me to do? Walk out when she started asking questions? She's very anxious about having a stepmother. I was only trying to help."

"Mark wants to handle things his way. Believe me, I've tried to talk to him, but he seems convinced Carolyn and Leah will hit it off once they're all together. I know you thought you were doing the right thing, but damn it, that's not why I called you over here."

Allie was tempted to pour the water over his head. "You know what? I had plans tonight that I cancelled because your niece needed me—or someone, *anyone* but you—and this is the thanks I get?"

"You cancelled your date?" His voice had changed completely and he dropped his hands from his hips. "You didn't have to do that."

She waved a hand in front of her face. She'd felt more than a little relieved to have an excuse not to go. "I didn't even know the guy."

Craig's head dipped and it took Allie a minute to realize he was giving her the once over. "First date?" he asked.

She straightened her back and stuck her chin in the air. "Yes."

"You're wearing that?"

She looked down at her black sheath dress. "Why?" she asked. "What's wrong with this?"

He shoved his hands in his pockets and shrugged. "Nothing."

"What?" she asked. "Your nothing means something."

"No, it doesn't. Not really." He turned his back and tossed an empty beer bottle into the trash.

"Look, do you have any idea how hard it is to dress for a date when you don't know who you're going out with and where you're going?"

"Why don't you know where you're going? He's not picking you up, is he?"

The shock on his face almost made her smile. Almost. "No, of course he's not picking me up, but I've never heard of the restaurant and they don't have a website."

"What's it called?"

"The Stack House. It's in Decatur."

"Decatur? Why the hell are you going all the way to Decatur?"

How did she let herself get into this conversation? "I don't date men around here."

"Why not?" he asked. From the look on his face, she could tell he was truly baffled.

"For a bevy of reasons." When he simply stared at her with his brows raised, she huffed out a breath and explained. "First of all, I work around here. The last thing I want to do is run into a family I teach when I'm on a date. Second, I also don't want to run into someone all over town after our date doesn't go so well. And lastly, one time, someone recognized me from my online profile when I was out with a friend. He used it as an opportunity to talk to me and it was humiliating and uncomfortable. So if I date where I don't work and live, chances of that happening are pretty slim."

"Interesting. You've done a lot of this? Online dating?"

Allie huffed. "More than I care to admit. But you haven't answered my question. What's wrong with this outfit?"

"You really want me to answer that?"

She took a swallow of water and wondered if she really did want to know his thoughts. What the hell, she thought. It might be an interesting peek into the male mind. "I wouldn't have asked if I didn't."

Craig flashed a cocky smile that only made him more attractive. "He's not going to listen to a word you say."

"Why not?"

He gestured with his hand to her dress. "He's going to spend all of his time and attention trying to look at your face instead of your girls."

"My girls?" she sputtered and slapped a hand to her chest. "You did not just call them my girls."

"Okay. Your rack?" he offered. "Your tits? Your breasts?"

"Chest," she said. "If you must refer to them at all, chest seems slightly more appropriate."

"Whatever. He's going to hone in on your *chest* and hear or see nothing else."

"No, *you* would. Most men, thank the Lord, are not you."

"Fine, don't believe me, but don't say I didn't warn you."

"You're an ass."

"No, I'm just honest. And you can't get pissed off at me for being honest."

"You wanna bet?" She turned and grabbed her wrap and purse from the counter.

"Leaving so soon?" he asked. "Leah and I were going to watch a movie if you're interested in joining us."

She gave him her most annoyed expression. "And risk you staring at my girls all night long? Tempting, but I don't think so."

"Suit yourself." He stepped in front of her to open the door. If only his mouth was as well-mannered as his hands. "I guess I'll see you on Tuesday."

"I'm counting the days." She turned around before stepping off the porch and placed a hand on his chest. Damn if it wasn't rock hard. "Call me if Leah starts to freak out about her cycle. I mean it, Craig. I don't want her going through this alone."

"What am I, chopped liver?"

"If you were anything more, you wouldn't have called me in the first place."

* * *

It was the smell of popcorn that brought Leah out of her room. The girl couldn't resist popcorn. What kid could?

"I ordered that movie you wanted to watch," Craig said. "The one with the teenagers who turn into wolves or something."

Leah smiled and grabbed the bowl of popcorn off his lap before plopping on the couch. Blackjack moved down to sit in front of her. "Thanks, Uncle Craig."

He shrugged as if it was no big deal, but he couldn't stand to see her red-rimmed eyes. He'd have done anything to make her smile. "There wasn't much else on anyway."

"No," she said. "I mean for calling Allie."

He stretched his arm across the back of the couch and pulled her hair. "I was a little out of my league with that one."

"I know. I'm sorry."

"What are you sorry about? It's your dad I'm mad at. He should have warned me."

When she smiled at him, his heart squeezed in his chest. His little Leah was becoming a woman and looking so much like her mother it made him ache. "I think he'll be relieved he wasn't here."

Craig took a deep breath and decided to dive into something he shouldn't get anywhere near. Damn Allie for making him feel responsible for talking to Leah about Carolyn. "I doubt it, but if he were here, you would've had Carolyn to help."

Leah averted her eyes and stuffed a handful of popcorn in her mouth. "I guess," she mumbled.

Craig wiped his sweaty palms on his jeans and told himself to man up. He'd helped to raise the girl; the least he could do was ease Carolyn's entry into her life. "How do you feel about her living here with you and your dad?"

She shrugged and put the popcorn bowl on the coffee table. "I don't know."

She didn't want to talk about it. Of course she didn't want to talk about. Craig didn't want to talk about it either. But ever since Allie told him how conflicted she was about Carolyn, he couldn't sit by and let the train wreck he knew was coming just arrive at her doorstep. "You know, it would be weird for any woman to move in here after you and your dad have been alone for so long."

"Yeah."

"And your dad and Carolyn have been dating for a long time. She makes him happy."

"I know that."

"But you don't know her very well."

Leah sandwiched her hands between her legs and sighed. "She never came here, or when she did, it was only for a night or two. She's like a stranger."

"That was your dad's doing, Leah. He didn't want you to get attached to Carolyn if things between them didn't work out."

"Well, things worked out, and now I'm supposed to live with a woman I barely know."

"Can I remind you of something before you go and get all mad at Carolyn?"

She batted Mark's blue eyes in his direction. Damn the girl was going to slay the boys someday. "She doesn't know you either. If I had to guess, I'd bet she's as nervous as you are about living here with you."

"Why would she be nervous about me? I'm just a kid."

"After what happened tonight, I'd have to say that's not true." Craig watched as her face turned three shades of red. "And there isn't anyone your dad loves more than you."

"Except her."

"No, Leah. He loves you both, but you come first. You always have. So from where I'm sitting, I'd have to say you've got the advantage."

Leah looked at him with a glint in her eye. "You really think so?"

"I didn't tell you that so you'd boss her around."

"I know. You told me so I'd feel better, and I do." She leaned over and kissed his cheek.

He put his hand over her face and pushed her to the other side of the couch. She giggled as she pulled the throw from the back of the couch around her shoulders. "Are we going to watch this movie or what?"

CHAPTER 10

Melissa pinched Ben's toe as she reached for the phone. She'd finally gotten Henry down for a late afternoon nap and she couldn't wait another second to talk to Allie.

"I tried to call you earlier," Melissa said when Allie answered. "But you weren't home. Big plans this weekend?"

"I went for a run this morning before church," Allie explained. "I'm glad I did since the sky opened up during the service. I've been kinda holed up today being lazy."

"It's a good day to hole up. I had to run to the grocery store and I got soaked." She stretched out on the floor in the corpse pose to the relief of her aching back. "So, how was your weekend?"

"You mean my date?" Allie asked. "I know that's why you're calling."

"Well, I waited two days to call. I thought that was plenty of time for you to be objective about the dentist."

"I went out with the dentist last night."

Oh, no. How like Allie to jump in with both feet and leave common sense at the door. She really was desperate for a date to the wedding. "Two dates in one weekend? Did you hit the jackpot out of the gate?"

"One date. One emergency."

"What emergency?" Melissa asked. "Is everything okay?"

"One of the girls I teach started her period."

"Oh. Okay." Wait, Melissa thought, her sleep deprived mommy mind two steps behind as usual. "Why were you involved with this?"

"It was Leah, with the dysfunctional uncle who hit me in the car. The guy is…"

Melissa held her breath. There had to be something about this guy for Allie to obsess about him again.

"He's totally immature," Allie continued. "His niece gets her period and he's so inept, he calls her piano teacher. Thankfully, Leah was more grateful to have a woman around than embarrassed. She's an absolute doll. He, on the other hand, is a Neanderthal. Not only did I have to reschedule my date with Allen the dentist, but he got inside my head about my outfit. I swear he may as well have come along for dinner the next night."

Hummmm. So she was thinking of the immature uncle when on her date with the dentist. "So the date didn't go well?"

"It went. He's sort of attractive, if you overlook the thinning hair and his enormous ego. His practice is thriving. He's just upgraded his Mercedes. His ex-wife is a lying bitch, but he's not bitter. Total nightmare. And I swear the whole night he kept looking at my teeth."

Melissa sat up and attempted to do the fire log pose with the phone tucked between her shoulder and her chin. "You have beautiful teeth."

"And yet it wouldn't take him but one appointment to file down my wolf-like eyeteeth."

Melissa gasped. "He did not call your eyeteeth wolfish."

"Not specifically, but what would you think if a dentist offered to file them down?"

"I'd think I'd never go out with him again."

"Bingo."

"So, what now?" Melissa asked. "Any more dates on the horizon?"

"I've had a couple of email inquiries, but after this last date, I remember why I stopped doing this in the first place. You're so lucky you're married."

Melissa glanced over her shoulder to where Ben dozed on the couch. "Yeah, I felt real lucky last night when Ben went out with his friends and didn't get home until the wee hours this morning."

"At least he came home," Allie whined. "At least you wanted him home."

"Allie, I love my husband and I'm very glad I'm married, but that doesn't mean it's always sunshine and roses. It also doesn't mean I didn't suffer through countless awful dates."

"I know. I'm just feeling sorry for myself on this rainy day."

Melissa unfolded herself from the pose and turned toward her husband. "Ben's due for some quality time with Henry, even if he does have a raging hangover. You want me to come over? We could watch a movie, eat something fattening, drink good wine."

Allie sighed. "How soon can you be here?"

"Give me thirty minutes to shower. Pajamas okay?"

"Pajamas required."

"Perfect." Melissa hung up and crawled over to Ben. She kissed his forehead and ran her finger down his nose. "Wake up, sleeping beauty. You're on duty as soon as Henry wakes up."

Ben stretched and let out an enormous yawn. "Did I hear you make plans with Allie?"

"Yes, you did."

"Did I also hear you tell her I was out half the night and have a hangover?"

"Right again."

He opened his eyes. They were the same chocolate brown she fell in love with, but a little fuzzy around the edges. "Why do you tell your friends I'm a carousing drunk who can't hold his liquor?"

"Because it's the truth and it makes Allie feel better about being without a man."

He scowled at her and tried to sit up, but only managed a semi-reclined position. "I feel so used."

"If you hadn't had so much to drink last night, you'd be getting used right now." She ran her hand up his leg.

"I'm up now."

"Now I have plans."

"I don't get Allie," Ben said. He swiped his hands over his face and yawned. "She could have a man—any man—with the snap of her fingers. Why is she always alone and yet complaining about being alone?"

"Come on, Ben. You know Allie. She's the most insecure woman I've ever met. She's also incredibly picky and shy around men. She's uncomfortable around most men, so she ends up alone."

"That makes no sense whatsoever."

"It does when you know Allie as well as I do." Melissa took pity on her hurting husband and scooted behind him and began to rub his shoulders.

"Ummm. What did I do to deserve this?" he asked.

"You made the very wise decision to marry me and ensure that I'm done with dating forever."

Ben grabbed her hands and pulled her on top of him. "Why don't I help you out of these clothes?"

"Ben…"

"What?" He lifted her sweatshirt and yanked it over her head. "Didn't you say you had to shower and change?"

Melissa struggled with loyalty as Ben drew kisses along her jaw. The devil knew just how to tempt her.

"We could shower together," he suggested.

"What if Henry woke up? We'd never hear him."

Ben made quick work of her jeans. "He's in a crib. Where's he going to go?" He'd stripped her to her bra and panties in less than sixty seconds. "On second thought," he said as he pulled off his t-shirt. "We shouldn't waste time. Let's do it here."

"God, I shouldn't be this easy," she moaned.

"Nope," he said. "That's just the way I like you."

***

"I thought you said practice ends at five," Craig goaded Leah as she put her lacrosse bag into the back of the truck and leaned inside to give Blackjack a pat on the head.

"It does. I was talking."

"So I saw." He'd arrived early so he didn't have to listen to another lecture on how she needed a phone. He couldn't believe how many conversations they had that led back to her needing a phone. "I didn't know you had boys on your team."

"What?"

"I saw you talking to a boy carrying a lacrosse stick. I assumed he was on your team."

"Funny, Uncle Craig. That was Brody. He's Cassidy Mizer's brother. He plays on the eighth grade team."

"An older man?"

"An older brother." She rolled her eyes. "So how was your day?"

Craig thought back. He'd had a good day. Davis had gotten Stacy to sign off on his kitchen design and he'd met with his cabinet guy to work up a quote. He'd sheetrocked the newly created great room after the electrician had rerouted the wiring. "All in all, not bad. I got a good bit done."

"Me too. I got an A on my math test."

"Did you?"

"Yep. That ought to make Dad happy when he calls tonight."

"You'd think," Craig said. He was sick of Mark calling, harassing him about putting himself out there, going out with women. His brother didn't know when enough was enough. Didn't he have better things to think about on his honeymoon?

"So what's for dinner?" Leah asked.

"Some chicken casserole your dad made."

"Are you asking Allie to stay?" Before Craig could answer, she said, "I really want her to stay."

He'd thought about it. Wasn't that why he'd pulled the damn casserole out of the freezer? It was a lot harder to invite a woman to join you and your niece for left over pizza. "I'll ask, but don't be surprised if she says no."

"She hardly ever said no to dad."

"Your dad's a lot nicer than me."

"To her he sure is." Leah looked out the window and tried to put her feet on the dash when Craig tapped her leg and shook his head no. She sat up straight and slapped her hands on her knees. "Why don't you like Ms. Allie? She's so nice."

"I never said I didn't like her."

"You didn't have to say it."

Craig blew out a breath. Weren't twelve-year-old girls supposed to think about boys and their friends and…phones? "I like her fine. She's…" Too damn pretty. And he'd spent too much time feeling bad about the way he'd treated her last week. "Fine."

"Good, because I want her to stay for dinner."

Craig turned the radio down and cleared his throat. "Is this about what happened last week? I mean, have you felt okay since…since it happened?"

"Yes," she said quickly. "No. I mean yes, I feel okay and, no, that's not why I want her to stay. I like her. Besides, if I'm going to have a woman living in the house starting next week, I could use some practice of having one around."

"Practice? You think of Allie as stepmom material?"

"I think she's a woman and if she'd married my dad, she could have been my stepmom."

Why did the thought of Mark and Allie sharing cozy dinners suddenly make his hands fist on the wheel? "I don't know Allie real well, but she doesn't seem much like your new stepmom."

Leah considered his question as she bopped her head to a tune. "Actually, she kind of is. They're both pretty—in different ways—and they're both shy."

"Shy?" Craig choked out the word. "You think Allie's shy?"

"Yeah, sort of."

"I wouldn't call her shy." A beautiful pain in the ass is what he'd call her.

"She's been staying for dinner for a couple years now and I get the feeling she's lonely."

Craig looked over at his niece, but she'd recognized a song on the radio and had turned it up loud. Lonely? He certainly knew what lonely felt like. Staying with Leah, having someone to come home to every night, was a nice treat from his usual, but he knew as soon as Mark and Carolyn got back, he'd have to get used to a whole new kind of lonely. "Then I guess we should ask her to stay."

CHAPTER 11

Allie shoved her sheet music in her bag and gathered her coat. The last thing she wanted was another run in with Craig. He sauntered out of the kitchen at the same time she caught a whiff of something baking in the oven. It smelled like Mark's chicken and rice bake casserole. Her stomach growled audibly.

"Lesson done?" he asked. He wore his usual faded jeans and flannel shirt. She could see the fraying edges of his undershirt at the base of his neck. The day old beard added to his scruffy appearance. Why now, of all times, did she have to find his unkempt look so attractive?

"Yep." She patted the dog on his head and dropped her bag so she could put her arms in her coat. "See you Thursday."

He reached behind her and grabbed the coat collar. "I was kind of hoping you'd join us for dinner."

She looked over her shoulder and up into his eyes. Their color perfectly matched the strand of blue in his shirt. "Are you kidding?"

"No. Leah wants you to stay."

Allie turned around to where Leah sat on the piano bench. She nodded her head up and down as if to verify Craig's claim. Allie let Craig pull the coat from her arms and hang it in the closet. "Well, that's very nice of you, Leah."

"Leah?" he said. "What about me?"

"Did you make the casserole?" she asked.

"No," he said with that irritation line between his eyes. "But I put it in the oven."

"If that constituted cooking, I'd call myself a chef."

"You don't cook?" he asked. He led her into the kitchen where he'd opened a bottle of white wine.

"No. Recipes are like braille to me. Where others see a guide to a completed masterpiece, I see nothing but little raised dots on paper."

"No wonder you like eating over."

"It's better than eating a microwave meal alone." She accepted a glass of wine and tried to discreetly peek at the label. Huh. Very nice. She had a bottle of this at home. Allie heard Leah practicing in the den. "So, how's she doing?"

"Leah?" Craig asked. He opened up a bag of salad and poured it into Mark's wooden salad bowl. "She's fine."

"I mean about her period. Any issues?"

"None. If I hadn't seen the blood myself, I'd think I imagined the whole episode."

Allie wished she'd imagined the whole episode. She was still smarting about his 'girls' comment. "Good. I figured, when you didn't call, that she was doing okay."

"Right as wine. Speaking of wine, how is it?"

"Good. Pinot grigio's my favorite."

Craig chuckled. "My wife used to call it cheap."

Allie almost choked. She didn't know what was more surprising, that Craig had a wife or that she'd called her favorite wine cheap. "Your wife?"

"She was a wine snob."

"Oh." Allie inched around the island and watched Craig pull plates from the cabinet. She shouldn't ask. She really didn't care, except the question was out of her mouth before she could stop it. "I take it you're divorced?"

Leah ran into the kitchen. "Allie, did you hear?"

"Hear what?"

"I got it, that last part of the song." Leah's face fell. "You weren't listening?"

"I'm sorry, Leah. I was talking to your uncle." She grabbed the girl's hand and led her into the den. "Will you do it again? I'll watch this time, too."

When she looked up from the piano, Craig stood in the foyer, leaning against the casement in what had become, in Allie's mind, his spot. No wonder he was so bitter and brittle, she mused. Weren't all divorced men clinging to the only emotion they had left for their ex-wives?

"Dinner's ready," he said. When Leah tried to run past, he stood in her path and mussed her hair. "Wash your hands, squirt."

"Yes, sir." She gave a mock salute and had her hands washed and dried before Allie could do the same at the kitchen sink.

Allie took a seat at the table and felt uncomfortable as the outsider of the trio. Despite his overbearing manner, Leah seemed as relaxed with her uncle as she did with her father. She and Craig must spend quite a bit of time together.

Allie unfolded the paper napkin on her lap. "How's your lacrosse team doing, Leah?"

The girl hurriedly swallowed a bite of chicken and washed it down with a gulp of milk. "We're two and three, but the games we lost were only by one point."

"Leah's probably the fastest one on the team," Craig said. "You should see her motor."

"Girls didn't play lacrosse when I was younger. I don't have a clue what the rules are."

"It's kinda like soccer with sticks," Craig explained.

"You should watch the boys play, Ms. Allie. They beat the crap out of each another."

"Hummm," Allie said. "Entertaining."

"They have to wear all these pads." She wrinkled her nose. "I'd hate to play like the boys."

"When I was your age, I lived across the street from three brothers," Allie said. "They used to beat each other up on a daily basis, so I doubt doing it in pads is that big a deal to boys."

"Where did you grow up?" Craig asked.

Allie wondered what kind of answer to give. Should she explain about the in-town house she lived in when her parents were married, the two apartments she was shuffled between during and right after the divorce, or the in-town condo and suburban house her father and stepmother still lived in, neither of which felt like home? "Here. Atlanta, I mean."

"Really?" Craig asked. "You don't meet many natives, especially out in the suburbs."

"I went away for college, but ended back here, even though I swore I wasn't ever coming back."

"What brought you back?" he asked.

"My college roommate. She wanted to live here and I didn't want to start over in a new town without her."

"Where did you go to college?" Leah asked.

"I went to a small music school in Nashville. Melissa, my roommate, she went to Vanderbilt."

Craig waved his fork in her direction. "So you've always done the music thing?"

"Yes," she chuckled and took a sip of wine. "I've always done the music thing."

"I want to go to Alabama," Leah announced as she finished her last bite of chicken and stared at the broccoli on her plate as if it was radioactive. "Roll Tide!"

"Well, I see your father has gotten his crimson blood in your veins."

"Is there any other?" she asked. "Can I be excused, please, Uncle Craig?"

"You going to do your homework?" he asked.

"I did my math, but I've got to study for social studies."

"Finish your broccoli and you can study."

She slumped her shoulders and looked up at him from under her lashes. "I hate broccoli."

"I had to eat it when I was a kid, so now you do, too," Craig explained with glee in his eyes.

"If I eat this, can I have some ice cream for dessert?"

"Who said anything about dessert?" he asked.

"Well," Leah said, "it's in the freezer and we've got chocolate sauce in the pantry."

Craig blew out a breath. "I suppose, but after your homework."

She stuffed the three stalks in her mouth at one time and chewed while holding her nose. "Dad told me you can't taste it when you hold your nose," she explained after swallowing the broccoli and chasing it with milk. "I can still taste it. Yuck." She stood up and gathered her plate and utensils.

"Just leave those in the sink," Craig instructed. "I've got to empty the dish washer."

Before Leah left the kitchen, she turned at the doorway and looked at Allie. "Are you going to be here for awhile, Ms. Allie?"

Allie felt put on the spot. She typically helped Mark with the dishes and stayed to talk after dinner, but couldn't imagine hanging out with Craig. "Uh...I probably need to hit the road."

"Could you come up before you leave?" Leah asked.

The girl wanted to talk, that was crystal clear. "Sure." Leah smiled and dashed up the stairs, leaving Allie alone with Craig and only half finished with her meal. She cleared her throat and took a sip of wine. He'd finished his first helping and was scooping a second onto his plate. "So, you must be looking forward to getting back to your own life."

He dropped the serving spoon and pursed his lips, considering her question. "Yes and no."

When he said nothing more, she felt obligated to ask, "Okay, how yes and how no?"

"Yes, because I get a lot more work done when I set my own hours. No, because I love Leah and I don't consider taking care of her a burden."

"I didn't mean to imply that you would."

"I know you didn't mean to, but I also know that's what you thought."

She set her fork down and took a breath to get a hold on her temper. What was it about this guy that riled her up every time they spoke more than two sentences to each other? "Craig, I don't know anything about your life or what your burdens may be. I was simply trying to make conversation."

"So was I. I'm really bad at small talk mostly because I stopped worrying a long time ago about hurting someone's feelings when I speak."

"How freeing that must be not to concern yourself with anyone's feelings."

He shook his fork at her again before setting it down and taking a sip of beer. "You know, that right there is exactly why I speak my mind. That sounded like a simple statement of fact, when it was really an insult."

"No, it was a statement of fact. When I insult you, Craig, trust me, you'll feel insulted."

"I wonder," he said. He pushed his plate away and sat back in his chair, cradling the beer between his work roughened hands. "Why do you have to use the Internet to get dates?"

The question was so off-topic, so personal, she merely stared at him with a bite of chicken dangling in front of her face. "What?"

"You've got to know you could snap your fingers and men would come running, so why do you go to the trouble of dating online?"

"I…it's complicated." She set her fork down. "And totally offensive for you to assume I could snap my fingers and men would line up at my door."

"Let me guess," he said and tipped back in his seat like a five year old who couldn't sit still. "You're picky and don't want to date someone without reading over his resume."

"Actually, I hate online dating."

"You do?"

"Think about it, smart guy; I know every possible interest from a guy's profile. I already know what he likes to eat, how much he exercises, if he likes pets, and if so, what kind. I know if he likes to read or watch movies or hang out with friends. I know about the size of his family, where he's from, what his religion is, and where he went to college." She was on a roll and began ticking her list off on her fingers. "I know if he has kids, wants kids, hates kids, and I have a decent idea about his dating history. All I have left to ask is what side of the bed he'd like to sleep on and believe me, most guys are more than willing to show me."

She took a deep breath to continue when she realized he was staring at her with a look of wonder on his face. She felt her cheeks heat, averted her eyes, and shrugged. "It takes all the fun out of discovering those things." He continued to stare at her while casually sipping on his beer. "For example," she continued, "this one guy took me out to dinner and ordered chicken and I already knew it was because he didn't eat red meat. How boring is that?"

"Pretty boring."

"Sorry. Hot button issue with several layers of regressed anger. I'm not usually this hostile."

"You mean honest?"

"Well…"

"Look, Allie, I'm not expecting an apology. I told you I prefer honesty."

"Then you'd hate online dating."

The line between his brows was back and he dropped the front legs of his chair on the tile with a thud. "Well, there goes plan A."

"Plan A?"

"To tell Mark I've signed up for online dating. He's been on my back about getting out there. He's been on my back for years, but ever since the engagement, and specifically the wedding, he's really been on my back."

"What's plan B?"

"Plan B is to avoid him and the topic for as long as possible, which is probably the best course of action considering I'm going to have to make myself scarce after the newlyweds get home."

"What do you mean?"

"They need time, just the three of them, to figure out how this is going to work."

"I've never met Carolyn," Allie said. "But Mark doesn't seem like he'd be with a woman who wouldn't put Leah first. He loves her too much."

"Yes, he does. Leah doesn't really know Carolyn either." He set his beer on the table and looked into her eyes. "Sorry I jumped on you about that. Leah wanted to talk about it and I'm glad you were here for her. For everything."

"Well." The apology came out like everything he said: without preamble and right to the point. He sure knew how to stifle her instinct to hold a grudge. "Thank you for apologizing."

"When I'm wrong, I say so."

"Then I'm waiting for another apology."

"For?" he asked.

"You seriously don't know?" When he continued to smirk at her, she said, "My girls? My outfit? Does any of this ring a bell?"

"You want me to apologize for being honest?"

"No, I want you to apologize for being crude."

"They don't call it the ugly truth for nothing." He stood up and carried his empty plate to the sink. "You seem like the kind of woman who wants to be heard. You could have any man you want, and what you want is for someone to listen. You weren't going to get that—you're never going to get that—dressed like you were." He held up his hands. "It's not because your outfit was offensive or slutty, but because it's the cross you bear for the way you look."

What was she supposed to say to that? It wasn't a compliment and it certainly wasn't an apology, but he'd hit on her biggest weakness with men. She *did* want to be heard.

She stood up and brought her plate to the sink. He turned around and leaned his hip against the counter so they were face to face. "I think you should try online dating, Craig."

"I thought you said I'd hate it."

"You would, but I think you need some interaction with the opposite sex. By not getting back out there, you've forgotten how to communicate with women."

He straightened into a cocksure position. "You think I don't know how to communicate with women?"

"You had a wife at some point, so I'm pretty sure you did. Let's just say you're a little rusty."

"Because you don't like what I have to say?"

She patted his shoulder. "You can't prove me wrong until you get back out there."

***

Leah looked up from her notes on the forms of democracy when she heard a faint knock on the door. "Come in," she said.

Allie poked her head through. "You busy?"

Leah patted a spot on the bed in invitation for Allie to join her. She watched as Allie hiked up her fancy pants and sat Indian style facing Leah. "How's the studying going?"

"Pretty good. I think I've got it down."

"Did you want to talk about something before I go home?"

"Yes. I wanted to ask about your stepmother. Are you close with her now?"

Allie seemed surprised at the question. Her eyes bulged and she made a funny fish like expression with her lips. "Not really, but that's mostly because I didn't make it easy for her. I was upset about the divorce, and she was the best person to blame."

"Did your parents split up because of her?"

"No. My parents split up because they didn't have anything to say to one another when they weren't fighting."

"Oh," was all Leah could think to say. "That doesn't sound like much fun."

"It wasn't." Allie reached over and patted Leah's knee. "My stepmother, Suzanne, she was always nice to me, making cookies and offering to make my favorite meals. I didn't like the fact that instead of listening to my mom and dad argue about my mom working all the time, my mom just stayed at work all the time. I didn't like the fact that my dad could move on and get happy when I was so miserable. And when Suzanne got pregnant, I didn't like the fact that they would have their own family when he still had me. So I was never very nice to her, even though she was always nice to me. My dad couldn't understand my behavior, well...he never really tried, and things just went from bad to worse."

Allie unfolded her legs. "I'm not trying to scare you, Leah, I'm just trying to make you understand that you have a big say in how successful this relationship with Carolyn is. My situation was different because I wasn't always with my dad and Suzanne, so I didn't have to change my behavior. I got to escape for a while until my next visit and my mom, because she hated my dad, always backed me up. Carolyn will be here with you and your dad all the time. The harder you try to make it work, the easier it'll be on all of you."

"Uncle Craig said that Carolyn's probably as scared as I am of her living here."

"He's probably right. Looking back, I can see that Suzanne was scared. She was always trying to make me like her because she loved my dad and he loved me. I'm the one who made it hard."

"It's weird to see him with her," Leah admitted. "Kissing and stuff."

"Yeah, but that's just because you're not used to it yet."

Leah twisted the pencil in her hand and tried to think of how to admit what she felt without it sounding strange. "I sort of feel like I'm being replaced. Like I wasn't enough for him."

"Oh, Leah." Allie put her hand on Leah's shoulder. "Your dad's not replacing you. He's fallen in love again and that's a wonderful thing. He's a young man with a big heart and a lot of love to give. Just because he loves Carolyn doesn't mean he loves you any less."

"But I don't need anyone else."

Allie crossed her arms over her chest and stared down her nose at Leah. "You're not planning to have a boyfriend? Ever?"

"Well, yeah." Leah felt her cheeks heat. "At some point."

"And when you get this boyfriend, do you think you'll stop needing your dad?"

"No, of course not."

"Then why would you think your dad doesn't need you just because he has a wife?"

Leah took a deep breath. She thought of her dad and all the ways they took care of each other. It wasn't going to be the same with Carolyn around to take care of her dad the way Leah was used to doing. "I do a lot of stuff for him. He's always calling me his conscience and his alarm clock."

"Maybe, instead of thinking of all the bad ways things are going to change, you can think of the good ways things will change."

"What good ways?"

"Come on," Allie said. "I've heard you complain about having to make dinner. I know sometimes you've felt left out because other girls complained about their mothers and you couldn't complain."

"So now I'll have someone to complain about?"

"And someone to share girl stuff with."

"Hummm." Leah slid down her bed and stared up at the ceiling. She'd never let her dad paint over the clouds her mom had painted when she was a baby. "You've given me a lot to think about."

"Nobody said this was going to be easy, Leah. But it'll be a whole lot easier if you start off with a positive attitude."

"Okay," she said. "I can do that. For my dad."

"For you, too, okay?"

"Yeah," Leah admitted. "For me, too."

CHAPTER 12

Craig saw the Mercedes pull up to the curb and knew he only had a minute or two more to use the clamp saw before Davis swept in for his weekly review. The kitchen demo was well underway, so if Stacy had changed her mind again, she was out of luck. Craig cut the power and lifted the safety goggles from his eyes as Davis rounded the walkway whistling like a man without a care in the world.

"Hey, man," Davis said as he surveyed the damage. "Wow. This is going to cost me some serious time and money."

Craig wiped his brow with his sleeve. Even with the cooler air outside, he'd worked up a sweat. "When your wife decided she wanted to go from a rehab to a refurb, I told you it wouldn't be cheap."

"Nothing about Stacy's been cheap since the day we met," Davis said. "Isn't it always that way with women?"

Did he really want Craig to answer that or just nod his head in agreement? God knew Julie had loved to spend money. "Don't get all freaked out because it looks like a mess. This is just the initial tear out."

"I'm not. You were right about the wall and this was my idea. How far is this going to set us back time wise?"

Craig did some mental figuring. "Kitchen work is precise and a lot depends on the pace of the subs. Did you look over that list of cabinet companies I gave you?"

"Yeah, but I don't want to waste my time on stuff like that. You pick one and I'll be fine with it."

Craig bit back his sarcastic retort. Davis had been the one to insist he pick the cabinet contractor in the first place. "I'd go with Steen & Sons. They've done work for me in the past. They're good and they don't dick around."

"Fine, fine. Go with them, then."

"I'm going to need to set up a meeting with you and them at least once to pick out countertops and wood finishes."

"That's Stacy's department." He put his hands inside his trench coat and eyed the clamp saw as if it were alive and could eat him at will. "I've got a friend I want you to meet. He's bought an old house along the river that needs a lot of work. I told him about you and he's not the kind to drag his feet and interview a bunch of contractors. If I say you do good work, then you're as good as hired."

Craig nodded. "Appreciate that."

"But," Davis said with a wink, "I expect this job to take priority."

When Craig said nothing, Davis chuckled and swung his head from side to side. "I gotta tell you, man. You're one hard nut to crack. I thought you'd jump at the chance for another job."

"I am," Craig said. "I appreciate your recommendation."

"But..." Davis asked.

"But I don't want to over-commit. I'm not looking to take on workers. I like being a one man shop."

"You can't handle both jobs?"

Craig could handle both jobs and a dozen more with his hands tied behind his back. But getting bigger, working with a crew, and juggling multiple projects held little appeal. "I can handle both. I prefer to do one job at a time."

"You must not have the bills I have to pay."

"I've got plenty of bills. I just don't let work take over my life. Been there, done that."

"The beauty of being a bachelor," Davis decided and slapped Craig on the shoulder. "When you've got a wife and a couple of kids in private school, work takes over whether you want it to or not."

"Bring your friend over anytime," Craig said. "I'll be happy to take a look at his job."

"I'll do that, man. Let me know about the cabinet guy."

Craig watched Davis walk out to his car and pull away from the curb before starting the saw and getting back to work. He'd had a wife and a lot of bills to pay years ago, and working like a dog to keep the wolf at bay had nearly destroyed everything. It probably had destroyed everything. The greatest regret of his life was that he'd never know.

But why shouldn't he take on more and more work? If he wasn't willing to jump back into the dating pool, he may as well spend more time at work. He wasn't going to be able to come up for air at Mark and Leah's anymore.

As he started up the clamp saw and watched the blade move back and forth, he knew that his reaction was knee jerk and not based in reality. He'd buried himself in work years before and ended up with a broken marriage and an assload of uncertainty when the world came crashing down. Damn it, Mark was right. He needed to get back out there. The best way to do that, the easiest way, led him straight to Allie.

Convenient that she was coming over that night for Leah's lesson—her last before Mark and Carolyn returned. He'd suck up his pride and ask her to help him get started. She must know how to navigate her way around the various online dating sites.

He still couldn't understand why a woman like her even bothered with online dating. Did she own a mirror? Yeah, she seemed a little insecure about her looks and she could certainly use a little softening around the edges, but most guys—at least guys with a set of eyes in their head—would overlook her prickly manner.

And there he was thinking about her again. "Not your type," Craig mumbled to himself over the hum of the saw. A beautiful, high-maintenance woman with high-dollar taste and a boatload of baggage was the last thing he needed in his life. The best she could do for Craig was to set him up for online dating so he didn't spend his days thinking about her and wondering what the hell was wrong with the men in her life.

***

"Why are you in such a good mood?" Melissa asked Allie. They had just taken their seats in a crowded deli near Allie's house. Melissa sat back after wrestling Henry into the high chair.

"My last lesson tonight with the crazy uncle. God, I can't wait to be free of him."

Melissa pursed her lips. "You're always talking about this guy. I think you like him."

"What?" Allie tried to hand Henry a Cheerio from Melissa's brightly colored snack bowl. "Are you out of your mind?"

"I just think you spend an awful lot of time talking about him, which means you're spending an awful lot of time thinking about him."

"Because he's so annoying. Do you know what he said to me on Tuesday when I stayed for dinner?"

"You stayed for dinner? When he annoys you so much?"

"Leah wanted me to stay. She's worried about her new stepmom and she's been asking me all sorts of questions. I'm trying really hard not to screw this up."

"You don't have a good relationship with Suzanne," Melissa pointed out.

"I know, which is why I'm trying to help her. Leah's mom is dead. If she and her new stepmom don't figure out how to make this relationship work, her teen years are going to be awful."

"So what did he tell you on Tuesday?" Melissa asked. She didn't want to veer away from the subject of the not-that-attractive uncle that was driving Allie crazy. A man who got a rise out of Allie was a rarity.

"He asked me why I online date when I could snap my fingers and men would come running."

Was Allie really expecting her to do anything other than agree he'd hit the nail on the head with his assessment? "And what did you tell him?"

"Come to think of it, I don't think I actually answered his question, but I started to vent about how terrible online dating is." Allie picked up the bowl when Henry knocked it off the table, scattering Cheerios everywhere. "Anyway, he's just annoying and I won't have to deal with him again after tonight."

Melissa couldn't help but stir the pot. Despite her insistence she wasn't attracted, Melissa knew better. "I think I know what bothers you so much about him."

"That he's breathing?" Allie offered with a chuckle.

"He's immune to you and you don't know how to handle it."

Allie's mouth flew open. "What do you mean?"

"I mean he's not swallowing his tongue whenever you're around. You've never experienced that before."

"Oh yes, I have. Not every man on the planet is attracted to me."

"Yes, they are." Melissa knew she had Allie's attention when her friend didn't notice that Henry was throwing Cheerios in her hair. "At least at first they are."

"You mean before they get to know me?"

"I mean on sheer looks alone, all men are attracted to you. And you know it."

"That's ridiculous!" Allie sputtered. "Look at Ben. We met him at the same time and he went home with your number."

Melissa pulled a toy frog from her bag and suctioned his feet to the table in front of Henry to divert his attention. "Ben started talking to me as a way to get to you. I was the warm up act."

"What? How do you know that?"

"He told me."

"No, he didn't," Allie said as the waiter delivered her sandwich and Melissa's salad. Henry made a dive for the silverware before Melissa quickly snatched it out of his reach. "You're making that up."

"No, I'm not. He figured he'd break the ice with me, I'd introduce him to you, and he'd walk away with the real prize." She speared a cherry tomato. "Lucky for me, he never got to you."

Allie scowled at Melissa over her untouched sandwich. "Ben? He and I would kill each other."

"Yes, I know, which is why I didn't let him get to you."

Allie picked up her sandwich. "But just because Ben," she closed her eyes with her sandwich lifted halfway to her mouth, "sorry, I just need a moment to blot out the visual there. Just because Ben thought I was attractive doesn't mean all men are attracted to me."

Melissa pointed her fork at Allie. "If you throw out Gabe as an example, I'm going to slap you."

"Well, he was never attracted to me."

If their college friend Gabe was her only proof, Allie was grasping at straws. "Yeah, and that's how we knew he was gay. Admit it, Allie. You like this guy because he doesn't treat you like some doll that should be set on a shelf and admired."

"He treats me like someone he'd like to run over with his car. Again."

"Sounds to me like the kid who bullies the girl he likes on the playground."

"He's certainly a kid." Allie wiped her mouth with her napkin. "He did mention a wife, so he must be divorced. He's been staying with Leah for two weeks. If there was a wife, she would have made an appearance by now."

"I thought you didn't care?" Melissa asked.

"I don't, but it's interesting that a Cretan like him could get a woman to marry him. It gives me hope."

Melissa lifted her brows, but didn't say anything. She could tell it made her jealous and more than a little intrigued. "I'd like to meet this guy."

"Just look up the word 'asshole' in the dictionary. His picture's right there."

Um hum, Melissa thought. Definitely attracted. For once, things were looking up.

CHAPTER 13

Blackjack and Leah greeted Allie at the door Thursday night. Craig was nowhere to be found and Allie let go of the breath she'd been holding since she got out of the car. She saw his truck, so she knew he was home. Maybe he would lay low and let her slip out after the lesson without making a big deal. She hadn't imagined he wouldn't be there to make a sarcastic jab or two before they parted ways. She felt disappointed she wouldn't get the chance to tell him how happy she was she wouldn't have to see him again.

Leah dove into her recital song. She'd practiced, as was evident by her progress. "That's really good," Allie said. "Try to slow down the intro part of section A and smooth out the rhythm for section B. Remember slow and even."

"Slow and even," Leah repeated with a nod. "I can do that."

"Keep up the good work and you'll be ready for the recital."

"That's my plan," Leah said.

"I wrote down a couple of pages in your lesson book for you to work on and I've circled the octaves." Allie stood up and gathered her notes. "So, are you ready to see your dad?"

"Yes, really ready."

"I imagine he's ready to see you, too."

"I hope so."

They walked to the door and Allie tried to discreetly glance around for Craig. She pulled open the door, turned around to say goodbye to Leah, and took one last look around. Was he really not going to say goodbye? "I'll see you next week. Tell your dad I said hello."

"I'll do it."

Allie walked out to her car, dumbfounded that Craig hadn't gotten one last jab in before she left. She tossed her bag in the back seat and had just opened the driver's side door when he came jogging toward her. His hair was wet and he was barefoot, wearing jeans and a long sleeved t-shirt. The muscles in her stomach clenched.

"Allie," he called and ran a hand through his hair as he rounded the car. He smelled like soap and pine. "You done already?"

She nodded and eyed him suspiciously. He had an open and friendly expression on his face that had her hackles up.

"Are we square on payment?" he asked.

"Yes. Mark paid in advance before his honeymoon."

"Of course he did. He's very responsible."

She nodded once again and watched as he shoved one hand into his pants pocket and grabbed the door with his other hand, encasing her against the car. "It was sort of nice to meet you, Craig."

He laughed, and Allie considered the way his face changed. Gone were the sharp angles and brooding expression, replaced by long dimples and straight, white teeth. "Right back at ya, Allie. Actually, I have a favor to ask of you."

"You want me to teach you how to play the piano?"

"Funny. I've been looking over those online dating sites and I can't make heads or tails of any of them. I was wondering if you'd be willing to help me choose one and get me set up?"

"You want my help? With online dating?"

He shrugged his shoulders and dared her to make fun. "Yeah. If you don't mind."

"You're serious?"

"Well, of course I'm serious. Do you think I'd ask if I wasn't?"

"Well…"

"Look," he said. "It's no big deal if you don't want to. I just thought it would save me a step or two. I can figure it out on my own."

"No, no, I can help. I'd be happy to help."

"Good. Great. Thanks." He dropped his hand from the door and shoved it in the other pocket.

"So when did you want to do this?" she asked.

He blew out a breath. "Mark gets back tomorrow night. How about Saturday?"

Allie's mind went blank and then she remembered the date she'd made. "I'm meeting someone for coffee on Saturday morning. I could do after. Around lunchtime."

"I was thinking later. I'm meeting a sub at the job and I won't be back up here until around five."

"A sub?"

"Sub-contractor."

"Oh. Well…" She hated to admit she didn't have plans for Saturday night, but obviously neither did he. "Okay. Why don't you call me when you're back?"

"Great." He gave her that smile that made her suspicious again. "Should I come to you or do you want to come to me?"

"Why don't I come to you?" she said. "Your computer, your profile."

"Sure. I'm not far from here. You got a pen and I'll give you the address?"

"Just tell me when you call and I'll plug it into Betty."

"Betty?" he asked.

"My GPS."

"You named your GPS?"

"She's British. Queen Elizabeth. Betty." Allie shrugged. "She's helpful, so I gave her a name."

Allie could tell by the pinched look on his face that he wanted to say something nasty, but common sense prevailed and he only shook his head and said, "Of course you did."

"So, I'll see you Saturday, then?" she asked.

"Yep." He stepped back. "I'll call you."

"I'll be waiting by the phone."

***

Craig jogged down the stairs just as the doorbell rang and Blackjack started barking. He glanced at the clock on the mantle and shook his head. He'd asked for fifteen minutes when he'd called her from the truck and she'd given him fourteen and a half.

"Are you always on time?" he asked as he opened the door. She rolled her eyes and sauntered past him into the foyer and he caught a whiff of yet another perfume. "You always smell good, too?"

She turned around and scowled, but only until his dog started begging for her attention. She kneeled down and rubbed him behind the ears with both hands. "Are you bothered by promptness and good grooming?"

"No. I'm just curious."

"I like to be on time." She stood up. "My business demands it. I also have a thing for perfume. Sorry if it bothers you."

"It doesn't."

"Craig," she said and turned around in a circle. "Your house is amazing. I've driven past this neighborhood, but I've never been in here."

"Thanks." He felt self-conscious about the home site Julie had found and insisted they build on in the executive neighborhood. "It's not finished."

She tiptoed around the foyer, peeking her head inside the empty dining room. Her heels clicking on the marble sounded like gunshots in his head. Now that she was here, in the home he'd built for his wife, the home he could barely stand to be in, he wasn't sure this was such a good idea.

"It could use some furniture, but other than that…"

"Come on in," he said and offered to take her coat. She shimmied out of a bright orange wool jacket that made her hair shine like a flame. Her coat smelled like her, rich and exotic. He slung it over the stair banister and led her into the den. "Can I get you a drink?"

She seemed to consider the question as if he'd asked if she wanted to take her clothes off. "Are you having a drink?"

"I'm going to have a beer, but I can get you some wine if you'd prefer."

"Do you have any open?"

"No, but I know how to use a corkscrew."

"I'm fine," she said and turned to look out the two-story Palladian window. "This is a really great view."

"I'm getting a beer," he said as he walked into the adjoining kitchen. He knew she'd followed when her shoes began clicking against the Mexican tile. Blackjack followed on her heels. "If you want something, tell me now."

"Wow. Look at this kitchen." She ran her hand lovingly over the granite countertop and knocked her knuckles against the butcher-block island. "You must like to cook."

"No," he said without explanation.

"Well, you could do some serious cooking in this kitchen."

"I thought you didn't like to cook?" he asked.

"I don't, but someone could."

She eyed him as he opened his bottle of beer and took a sip. "Sure you don't want something?" he asked.

"I'll have one of those."

"A beer?"

"Yes." She put her hands on her hips. She wore jeans and a multi-colored shirt with ties at the neckline. It was the most casual outfit he'd seen her in to date. "I drink beer."

"I don't have any pussy beer."

She sputtered, as he knew she would, and shook her head. "Thank goodness."

"I mean it. I'd rather open a bottle of wine than have you take two sips, gag it down like medicine, and act like want to shave your tongue."

"What is it, million dollar beer? For goodness sake, let me see the label."

He gripped his bottle with two fingers and held out his hand so she could inspect the microbrew.

She speared him with those cat eyes. "That should be fine."

"Fine?" he asked. "Have you ever heard of this?"

"No, but I like pale ale." She lifted her hand and placed it over her left breast, drawing his eye to her chest. "I swear to drink it all."

"Didn't your mother tell you not to swear?"

"No, but she used plenty of swear words."

Damn it, there she went, intriguing him again. What had he been thinking, inviting her to his home, offering her alcohol? "You want to have a sip before you commit?"

"Sure." She grabbed his beer and lifted it to her lips. He shouldn't have watched her, he shouldn't have wondered how soft her lips would feel against his, he shouldn't have envied the bottle for not having to wonder. He pulled another beer from the fridge after she nodded and handed his back. "It's good."

He tried to shake off the uncomfortable vibe from the kitchen and moved past her through the den and into his office. He picked up an upholstered seat from the corner and brought it behind the desk next to his large leather chair. He pulled the chain on his desk lamp and took a seat in front of his computer. Blackjack maneuvered under his desk and lay down in his usual spot.

"This is a very masculine room." She poked around the bookshelves he'd built into the wall. "Is this you and Mark?"

He nodded, but didn't look up. He knew she held the picture of them as kids posing at the base of the hill behind their childhood home.

"Where was this?"

"North Carolina."

"Is that where you're from?"

"Yep."

"Interesting." She put the frame down and slid into the seat next to Craig. When she leaned over to put her beer on the coaster, her knee brushed his under the desk. "So, where do you want to begin?"

"I've been looking at a couple of sites. Some I've heard of, some I haven't."

"I've probably tried them all."

"Which one should I use?"

"They're basically the same. The bigger the name, the bigger the dating pool."

"Which do you use?"

"Right now, I'm using LoveFinders.com."

"I haven't looked at that one."

"It's a moderately sized regional service. The website is pretty easy to navigate and the price is comparable."

He typed in the site and watched two hearts meet in the middle of the screen and explode into a parade of pictures of happy couples. He felt nauseous and had to force himself to stay seated. "Why do they assault you with these dopey pictures? I'd rather not sign up if I end up looking like that."

"They look happy, Craig. They look like well-adjusted men and women who found love online. We probably wouldn't qualify for well-adjusted."

He watched her take a sip and set the beer down. "What?" she asked.

"You don't think you're well-adjusted?"

"On some levels, yes. In the dating arena, absolutely not."

"Well, Allie. Honesty sounds good on you." And looked good on her, too. She was open and relaxed and sitting a little too close.

"I certainly don't have to worry about hurting your feelings." She pointed at the screen. "The first thing you want to do is set up your profile."

He clicked on the profile link and scowled at the screen. He'd probably have to fork over less information if he were applying for a concealed handgun permit. "Why do they need to know all this?"

"They just do. You get to control what other people see on your profile page."

He began typing in his information. Name, address, profession…

"Frances?" she said. "Your middle name is Frances?"

He lifted his fingers from the keyboard. "You know, I don't think I need your help after all."

"I'm just kidding, Frank."

"Seriously, Allie. I don't want to hurt you."

"Touchy." She clasped her hands between her legs and shivered. "It's freezing in here."

"I like it cold."

"This is beyond cold, Craig. This house is like a meat locker."

"There's a blanket on the couch in the den if you want it."

She got up and returned a moment later with the throw around her shoulders. "Is this the only room in the house with any furniture?"

"I use this room, so there's furniture."

"Why do you live in such a big house if you only use the office and, I'm assuming, a bedroom?"

"The market sucks right now. Besides, it's not finished."

"It looks finished to me," she said. "Other than lacking furniture." When he didn't answer, she said, "Okay, so where are we?"

"What's a tag line?"

"A tag line is just a one or two sentence statement about yourself."

"Like?"

"Like, 'I'm a home renovator who loves dogs and lives in a gorgeous meat locker.'"

"That's stupid."

"It's just an example," she said. "You come up with one that's not stupid."

"The whole idea is stupid."

"It may be stupid, but it's required."

He followed her lead and typed, "I'm a home renovator who likes dogs and beer."

"That's so much better," she said. "Okay, next is your relationship status."

"Obviously I'm single, or I wouldn't be online dating."

"Yes, of course, but you need to put divorced." When he turned his head and stared at her, she shrugged. "You are divorced, aren't you?"

He enjoyed the look of panic on her face and knew he'd also enjoy watching her smug expression disappear when he told her the truth. "No."

She sat up straight and blinked those green eyes at him. "You're still married?"

"Technically, yes."

"Craig…" She stood up and moved around the front of the desk, placed her hands on the edge, and leaned over giving him a bird's eye view of her plum colored bra. "I'm pretty sure they don't allow you to date while you're still married."

He reclined in his chair and steepled his hands in front of his face. "You're probably right. I'd better put widower."

She stood upright so fast he feared she'd lose her balance and fall over. Her mouth hung open as she stared at him with a faint crease between her brows.

"Are you hungry?" he asked.

"What?"

"I'm starving. I'm going to order a pizza. You want in?"

She nodded like a robot as he reached for the phone. "I like the works. That okay with you?"

"Yeah," she said. "Whatever."

CHAPTER 14

Allie stood in the middle of Craig's office and listened as he ordered a large pizza with everything for delivery. She felt as groundless as the leaves from the giant oak tree outside his window aimlessly falling. A widower? Craig?

"It's going to be about thirty minutes."

It might take her that long to get her jaw working again. "That's okay," she managed before stumbling around the desk to take a seat. "You're a widower, too? What are the odds?"

"Not bad, considering it was the same accident."

"You lost your wife in the same accident that killed Mark's wife?"

He nodded. "They were friends. Best friends."

Allie picked up her beer, took a long swallow, and set it down on the coaster again. "Wow. Okay, I'm a little speechless."

"I'm going to savor this moment," he said. She knew he was trying to lighten the mood, jolt her out of the shock he'd put her through, but she couldn't even muster a smile.

"I'm sorry," she said. "I can't imagine how hard that must have been."

"It was a long time ago." He pushed back from the chair and stood up. "I want another beer. You?" he asked.

"No. I'm fine."

She sat there in his office staring at the bookshelves lined with architecture books, manuals on every subject a builder might need: plumbing, electrical, code, woodworking, HVAC, framing, renovation. Some novels sat on a lower shelf: thrillers and war books. The only picture in the room was the one of him and Mark as kids. Several framed portraits of Leah were scattered through the house, but nothing else. Was there a shrine to his dead wife in his bedroom? Why did she care?

She rubbed her hands along her jeans and tried to come to terms with the man she'd chalked up as a bitter divorcee. All of her assumptions, stereotypes, and impressions blurred and began forming into a new picture, this one painted with a much more narrow brush. She hated that she'd so easily categorized him like she did with the men she met online. She was too quick to judge, too quick to assume, and too quick to dismiss people for what she thought they were and not what they really were.

He walked back in carrying a beer and a small bowl of peanuts, Blackjack on his heels.

"I owe you an apology, Craig. I've horribly misjudged you."

He carefully set the bowl down between them on the desk and eased into his seat. "I seriously doubt that. Look," he said with a sigh, "I don't want your pity. It was a long time ago."

"I know, but I assumed you were divorced. I assumed quite a number of things about you, and I'm sorry."

"You don't owe me an apology for something you didn't know." He reached for the keyboard, irritation written all over his face. "Can we just get back to this?"

"Sure." She pointed at the screen and tried to steady her roller coaster emotions. "The rest is pretty self-explanatory. Do you have kids, want kids, your ethnicity…"

"Body type?" he asked after filling in the required information. She noticed he checked the wanted kids button. She wondered if they'd tried to have a baby before her death.

"They give you choices." When he selected average, she cleared her throat. "I'd say you're athletic." He turned to stare at her with a cocky grin on his face. What should have annoyed her helped to steady her ground.

"You've been checking me out?"

"No." She should have known he'd twist her words around. "I don't know if you exercise, but you appear more in shape than some of the average guys I've dated."

"Do you want me to flex for you?"

"Put whatever you want, but if you keep making fun of me, I'm leaving."

"No, you're not. The pizza's not here yet and I can hear your stomach growling."

Allie put a hand to her belly as it rumbled like thunder in the sky. "I didn't have lunch."

"Why not?"

"I was working and I just forgot," she said and directed his attention back to the screen. He filled in the rest of his information: height 5'11", faith Christian, he didn't smoke and drank socially. He stopped typing when he came to the age and location range. "What do you think for the age range? Twenty-one to forty?"

"Twenty-one?" she asked. "Seriously?"

"Why not?"

"Craig, you're thirty-five. You think you'll have anything in common with a twenty-one-year-old?"

"Attraction?" he offered.

She rolled her eyes. He laughed and hit the delete button. "I'm just trying to get your goat." He changed his answer to twenty-five to forty.

"Oh, that's so much better."

"Look, if I want kids—which I might—my age range can't go too high. If I start with thirty, most of those women are only looking for a quick husband so they can get on with the family making."

She hated that he was right, and as a woman approaching thirty, she knew exactly what he was talking about. "Fine, but don't say I didn't warn you."

"Warning heard and ignored."

She was curiously surprised to see him include in his list of interests, along with the usual sports and beer, architecture, fishing, and the guitar. "Do you play?" she asked.

"I can pick a tune or two, but I can't read music."

"Have you tried?"

"Yes, and it's like those braille dots in the recipes for you."

It was the second time he'd mentioned something she'd said in passing. The man, for all his faults, and there were plenty, certainly did listen. "See," she said when he put down time at the gym and running. "I knew you were athletic."

He ignored her and moved on to answer the remaining questions. "Astrological sign? What the hell for?"

"Some people believe in that."

"Believe in what?"

"You know, all the signs have ideal matches. Yes," she said when he geared up to argue. "I know you think that's stupid, but some people use that as a gauge."

He snorted in disbelief, but marked himself as a Leo. Of course, she thought. He certainly was a lion. "You went to Appalachian State?"

"Yeah. Did you think I went to Alabama like Mark?"

"Hummm. I just assumed you had."

"Why?"

She shrugged. "I don't know. You seem like a big school kind of guy, like Alabama or Michigan or something like that."

"App State was close to home. After my dad died, I didn't want to be too far from my mom."

"Oh." So his father died young and his wife died tragically. She could feel herself drowning in sympathy for him, but knew that was the last thing he wanted. "Sorry about your dad."

"Long time ago, Allie. Why do they need to know my income?"

"Again, some people want to know that information. You don't have to tell, but most of the men do." She touched his sleeve. "I'll turn my head if you don't want me to see."

"Why? You could always just look up my profile. I'm not putting that down. I own my house and my business. If that's not enough information for these ladies, then screw them."

"That's one way to look at it. Okay," she said as they entered the challenging section. If he didn't want to put his income, which had to be substantially more than she'd first assumed considering his house, he was going to hate this part. "This is where you need to be creative."

"Great."

"You need to write two to three paragraphs about yourself and what you're looking for in a date."

He winced and looked at her like a middle-schooler forced to take a writing test. "Two to three paragraphs?"

"If you put too little, you look like someone who can't communicate. If you put too much, you sound like a bragger. Best thing to do is describe your job, your life, your dog, and then talk about the kind of woman you're interested in meeting."

He blew out a breath just as the doorbell rang. "Saved by the bell."

***

Craig took a bite of pizza and glanced around his den. He tried to see it as Allie did, from the perspective of a woman. She said there wasn't any furniture, but they weren't sitting on the ground. The couch was ancient, but it served a purpose. They were watching baseball on the big screen, weren't they? Couches and TVs counted as furniture.

"Which team are you rooting for?" Allie asked. She'd plowed through one piece of pizza and was eyeing another, but seemed hesitant to ask. He plucked up a huge slice and tossed it on her plate.

"The Braves, of course. Who'd you think I'd root for?"

She shrugged and took a bite. "I didn't know if you were a Cubs fan."

"I've never even been to Chicago. Why would I root for them?"

He snuck a glance at her profile as she watched the Brave's first baseman come up to bat. She was following the game, not asking a bunch of stupid questions. "Do you have brothers?" he asked.

"No. I'm an only child...well, I've got a half-sister."

He waved his crust at the screen. "You understand the game?"

"Baseball?" She set her slice down and wiped her hands with the paper napkin he'd supplied. "You think I'm too stupid to understand baseball?"

"No. I think you're too female to understand baseball."

"I really can't wait for you to start dating," she mumbled under her breath. "I've been going to baseball games and football games and golf matches for years. Hockey, I don't have a clue except I know the puck goes into the goal."

She'd called it a puck, he mused as he threw his crust to Blackjack. The dog caught it in the air and sunk to the floor to savor it like a bone. Most women wouldn't even know that much about a game they didn't follow. "I take it you date the jocks?"

"Some, but my dad's a big sports guy. It was all that was on at his house."

"Was?"

She lifted a shoulder and took a bite. He could tell by the way her eyes darted around the room that she was trying to figure out what to say. "He's still alive. We're not really close."

Didn't want to talk about her father. Daddy issues could explain her problems with men. He tossed his napkin in the half empty box and sat back, patting his stomach. "I'm stuffed."

"Me too." She capped the water bottle he'd offered when she refused another beer. True to her word, she'd finished her first beer without complaint. "You know, sporting events would be a good first date for you."

"What do you mean?"

"I mean it's a good way to figure out if someone likes sports, and there's no pressure to talk all the time."

"Do you have any idea how expensive Braves tickets are?"

She rolled her eyes. "You don't have to get the best seats in the house," she countered.

"But what if she talks the whole time and I can't watch the game?"

"Then I guess you don't go out with her again."

He scowled at the screen and wondered, for the millionth time, why he was putting himself through this again. "Where do you go on most of your first dates?"

"It depends," she said. "I met a guy for coffee this morning."

"I'm not a morning person."

He wondered if he should offer to make her some coffee when she yawned. "I'd have been better off sleeping in. It didn't go so well."

"Why not?"

"He was an overeducated attorney with a job he felt was beneath him and a taste of wanderlust combined with a Peter Pan complex. He was nearing forty, good looking, and had no interest in settling down. I'm not sure why he's bothering to date."

"You figured all that out over coffee?"

"It wasn't hard when he wouldn't shut up. I should have run for the door when he said he was a lawyer."

"You didn't know he was an attorney from his profile?"

"Attorneys get a bad—and in my opinion, well deserved—rap. He said he was a University professional, which apparently is code for legal department patent attorney."

"So, you don't like lawyers?"

"My...old boyfriend was a lawyer, and a liar, and a cheat. I avoid them at all cost."

So, she'd been burned by an old lover and yet she put herself out there time and time again. She was an interesting piece of work, and she was tired, Craig knew, by the sight of her stifling another yawn. "Do you want some coffee?"

"I'd be up all night if I had coffee now."

"Any other suggestions for first dates?" he asked.

"Bowling?"

"Who am I? Archie Bunker?"

Allie laughed. "Are you a late night TV watcher?"

"I'm a man of many levels."

"Yes, yes, I can see that. What about lunch?" she suggested.

"I work for a living. I don't sit behind a desk. I'm not going to run home and take a shower before lunch."

"Drinks, then? If you don't hit it off over drinks, you can part ways and scratch her name off the list."

He grunted as she yawned again.

"I'm exhausted." She glanced toward his office. "Do you mind if we finish up?"

"You go on home, Allie. I think I can manage the rest."

"But you haven't done the hard part yet."

"And I don't need you critiquing my two to three paragraphs over my shoulder. I'm not a dunce; I can come up with something."

"Just read through some of the other profiles to get an idea of what to put. That's what I did."

She helped him carry their dishes into the kitchen, set aside the bottles for recycling even after he told her he didn't recycle, and headed to the foyer for her coat.

"So I just finish my profile and wait for the women to start calling?" he asked.

She laughed, as he'd hoped she would. "Or you can start looking, too."

"What do I do if I see someone I want to go out with? Call her?"

"No." She gripped her chest with a hand. "I'd be so freaked out if someone called me. Just send her an email, or you can nudge her online."

"Nudge?"

"It's this little button you can push to let someone know you like what you see."

"Why would I do that instead of emailing?"

"I don't know. I've been nudged before and then an email usually follows. I'm not real sure what the purpose is except maybe to warn you someone is interested."

"Stupid."

"Yes," she said and slung her purse over her shoulder. "On this I'd have to agree."

He opened the door and felt oddly disappointed she was leaving. They'd shared a meal, some conversation, and he'd probably never see her again. For the best, he told himself as he caught another whiff of her perfume. "Well, thanks for your help."

"My pleasure." She patted Blackjack on his head. "Thanks for the pizza."

He watched her amble down the sidewalk and get into her car. She gave him a smile and a wave before she drove down the street toward the entrance to the neighborhood. He felt…unsatisfied.

He was full, he'd accomplished his goal for the weekend, and yet something didn't feel settled. It was nine-thirty on a Saturday night, he'd just had dinner with a beautiful woman, and hadn't even considered making a move on her. Well, he'd thought about it when she was relaxing on his couch, her feet tucked under her, her hair inches from his fingers where they rested against the back of the couch. Of course he'd thought about it. He wasn't dead, or married, or otherwise engaged. But something about her made him keep things on the up and up. Her connection to Mark, he wondered? Leah? "Leave it alone," he mumbled before stretching out on the couch. He turned his head into the pillow where her scent lingered.

Yep, definitely unsettled.

CHAPTER 15

L eah tiptoed past her dad's closed bedroom door and tried not to wince when she heard voices from inside. They'd been back for three days and she dreaded every morning when she woke up and Carolyn was still there.

She didn't hate her stepmom, not exactly, but she sure didn't like having to share her dad and her home with another woman. And Carolyn was changing everything. Normally, Leah would come home from school, grab a yummy snack, and do her homework at the kitchen table. Yesterday when she got home, Carolyn had a healthy snack prepared for her and expected her to eat it and talk about her day.

Carolyn didn't know any of Leah's friends. She'd never been to her school or to her lacrosse games. How was Leah supposed to tell her about the things that happened during the day when Carolyn didn't know anything about her? Leah was forced to do her homework in her room because Carolyn always had the television on. She'd asked Leah if she wanted her to turn it off, but Leah knew the silence would be worse than listening to the news, and she sure didn't want Carolyn hovering as she tried to do her homework.

Leah had just poured Frosted Flakes into a bowl when Carolyn came into the kitchen with a fuzzy pink bathrobe wrapped around her tiny waist. "Good morning, Leah," she said and poured herself a cup of coffee from the pot she'd set to brew the night before. "Would you prefer eggs?"

"No. I'm fine with cereal."

"I can make some waffles or pancakes if you'd like."

Leah tried not to roll her eyes. If she wanted pancakes or waffles, she'd have made them herself. She wasn't a baby and she didn't need Carolyn treating her like one. "I'm fine."

Carolyn turned on the news and sat at the table with Leah. "Do you have anything after school today?"

"Lacrosse and piano."

"I've enjoyed listening to you practice. When's the recital?"

"In a couple of weeks. Dad has the schedule."

Her father breezed into the kitchen, so handsome in his suit and tie. "Here are my two favorite girls." He kissed Carolyn on the cheek and ruffled Leah's hair on his way to the coffee pot. "What do you girls have on tap for today?"

"Well, Leah's got school, and I'm going to try and make a dent on moving my stuff in the house from the garage. I won't have much of a chance next week when I start my new job."

"Just leave the heavy boxes and I'll bring them in tonight."

"I'm not a weakling, Mark," Carolyn said with a flirty tone in her voice.

"I know you're not, sweetheart, but it'll make me feel strong and useful."

Leah got up and dumped the rest of her cereal down the sink before she threw up. God, this was even harder than she thought. "You picking me up from lacrosse tonight, Dad?"

He looked at Carolyn with his brows raised in plea. "Honey, would you mind? I'm swamped at the office, and if you pick her up, I could be home in time for dinner."

Carolyn forced a smile at Leah. "I'd be happy to. Where do I pick you up?"

"At the school," Mark answered and winked at Leah. "Five o'clock. She hates it if you're late."

"Then I won't be," Carolyn said.

"Have a good day at school," Mark called to Leah as she bolted up the stairs.

Leah could hear her dad and Carolyn kissing and giggling in the kitchen before she shut her door and flung herself on the bed. She didn't want Carolyn picking her up from lacrosse. She didn't want Carolyn making her breakfast, or leaving her snacks, or preparing dinner. She wanted Carolyn to move out of her house and back to Chicago where she belonged.

Leah crawled over her bed and picked up the picture of her mother from her nightstand. "Why did you have to die?" she asked the smiling Becca. "Why did you have to leave us?" Leah ran a finger over her mother's deep brown hair. "I don't want a new mom," she said to the picture before setting it down and staring up at the ceiling. Truth was, she didn't want anything but her dad back all to herself. Just the way it was before.

***

Allie rushed up the walk to Mark's house and took a deep breath and straightened her scarf before ringing the bell. She wanted to make a good impression on Mark's new wife, and being on time for Leah's lesson was the best way to start off on the right foot. She wasn't late, but Timothy Beven's mom liked to talk, and leaving their sprawling home on the other side of town and maneuvering through traffic had taken a while.

A pretty woman with shiny black hair and honest brown eyes opened the door and greeted Allie with a haggard smile. "Hi. You must be Allison."

"Allie. And you must be Carolyn."

"Must be," she said and stepped back so Allie could enter. After closing the door, Carolyn stuck her hand out for Allie to shake in an oddly formal manner. "I've heard a lot about you, Allie. Leah is very fond of you and Mark can't say enough."

"Well, they're very special, but I don't have to tell you that."

"No," she said on a sigh. "You don't." Carolyn moved to the base of the stairs. "Leah? Ms. Allie's here."

Carolyn turned back around and wiped her hands on her jeans. "I'm sorry about my appearance. I've been moving stuff in all day."

"I imagine you've had lots to keep you busy." Allie looked up the stairwell, surprised that Leah hadn't come down. The girl was usually eager for their lesson to begin.

"I have. Mark told me you usually stay for dinner after Leah's Tuesday lesson, but I haven't had a chance to prepare anything."

"That's okay, Carolyn. I wasn't expecting to stay, and you don't have to feed me every week."

"Well, it sounds like a tradition, and I don't know anyone in Atlanta. If you don't mind staying, I'd love for you to join us next week after things are more settled."

"If it works out for you next week, I'd be delighted," she said as Leah moseyed down the stairs. "Ready?" she asked the girl.

"Yep."

"I'll be in the garage if you need me," Carolyn said before disappearing around the corner.

Allie followed Leah into the den. When they were both settled in their places, Allie asked Leah to start with her recital song. Leah nodded and began the song at a tempo much faster than she'd learned. "Whoa, slow it down, Leah." Allie tapped her leg in rhythm to the beat. "Start over and watch the pace."

Leah started again, but she kept messing up at the chorus of the song she'd had down for weeks. "Arrrrh," she grunted. "I can't do it."

Allie placed her hand on the girl's arm. "Yes, you can. You can do this in your sleep. Start over from the top and relax. You're all tense. Your fingers won't cooperate if you try to push it."

"My fingers won't cooperate anyway." Leah slammed her hands on the keys and bolted from the bench.

Allie sat in stunned silence as Leah ran upstairs and slammed the door. Uh oh. Leah was upset about more than her piano lesson and Allie had a good idea why. She thought about getting Carolyn, but quickly disregarded that idea. If Allie wanted Carolyn, she would have run to the garage and not her room. With a quick look around the corner to the closed garage door, Allie followed Leah up the stairs and quietly knocked on her door. "Leah?"

"I can't do it, Ms. Allie. I can't do anything."

"May I come in, please?"

After a muffled, "Yeah," Allie pushed open the door and frowned at Leah, her face buried in the pillows on her bed.

Allie closed the door and sat down at the foot of the bed on Leah's aqua blue blanket. "Leah, what's wrong?"

"Everything." Leah flipped over and stared at Allie with red-rimmed eyes. "I don't like her at all!"

Just as Allie feared, Leah was upset about her stepmom, not her piano playing. "Sweetie, you have to give it some time."

"Time's not helping. I like her less and less every day."

"More time. It's still too new."

She sat up and rubbed the heel of her hands over her face. "Everything is different. She's changing everything. Her stuff is all over the house. It doesn't even feel like my home anymore."

Allie remembered what it felt like when her dad and Suzanne moved into their new home. They'd combined their belongings and her dad had gotten rid of a lot of his furniture—her furniture—to make room for Suzanne's things. The worst were the pictures of the two of them she scattered all over the house. "I know this is hard, but you need to think about Carolyn for just a minute. She moved half way across the country into your house. You can't expect her to throw all of her stuff away."

"Why can't she leave it in her room?"

"You mean their room?" Allie pointed out.

"Whatever. I didn't marry her, so why should I have to live with her things?" Leah crawled off the bed and grabbed a framed photo from her dresser. "She moved the picture of us—my mom, dad, and me—from the mantle to in here and put a snapshot from the wedding in its place. She's getting rid of my mom already."

Tread lightly, Allie warned herself as she tried to think of a way to pacify Leah without making it seem like she was taking Carolyn's side. "Leah, I don't think she was trying to get rid of your mom. She probably thought she was doing a nice thing by moving the picture in here, but the only way to know for sure is to ask her. You need to talk to Carolyn about this and give her a chance to explain." Allie stood up and faced Leah. "You two are probably experiencing some of the same emotions. I know it's hard, but I really want you to try and talk to her."

"I can't, Ms. Allie." Leah kneaded her elbow with her hand as if it hurt, but Allie knew she was just about to crawl out of her skin with anxiety. "If I tell her what I'm feeling and thinking, I'm going to get in trouble. My dad always said if you don't have anything nice to say, then say nothing at all."

"Usually that's true," Allie countered. "But in this case, the longer you keep your thoughts bottled up, the more likely they'll eventually explode and, trust me, you'll be in bigger trouble then." Allie stepped closer and patted Leah's arm. "Talk to your dad. Ask him to help you talk to Carolyn. The three of you can work this out, I know you can."

"He'll take her side."

The girl was intent on being right. Of course, Allie remembered how being twelve and feeling totally displaced felt. "There aren't sides here, Leah. The three of you have to figure out how to get along, and when you do, I think you'll find you might just be happier than before."

Leah snorted. "That's not going to happen. It didn't happen with you."

"I didn't have to resolve anything because I could always run to my mom." Not that she did anything other than fan Allie's already burning flames. "My parents hated each other, and neither one of them was capable of putting their differences aside for my benefit. Your dad loves you, and Carolyn is feeling like an outsider. Everyone here wants you to be happy."

"I wish I had some place to escape."

Allie wrapped her arm around Leah's shoulder. "You do. You can lose yourself in your music."

"Is that what you did?"

The piano had saved her even before the divorce. She'd play for hours to block out the sound of her parents arguing. Before she knew what had happened, the music, her ability to control the song, fed a hunger where nothing else could. "Yes, that's exactly what I did."

CHAPTER 16

Allie couldn't help but speculate as to Craig's motive for wanting her to come over. She'd been surprised when, after her lesson with Zoe Thomas, she had two missed calls and a text message from Craig. *Come to my house ASAP*, he'd texted. So like him not to ask, but to order.

She'd thought of him since Saturday. She couldn't help but think of him. A widower. A man with a beautiful, empty home and a lonely heart. She'd felt a connection with him over pizza and conversation. He's the one who said she wanted to be heard, and damn him and his listening skills. He was unpredictable and funny and he kept her on her toes. So why did she feel so uncertain about him calling her? Was he interested in seeing her on a personal level, and if so, what would she do?

She liked him, despite his unconventional attitude about women and pretty much everything. She'd never met a man who didn't play games or mask his true feelings. As strange as it seemed, they were friends. Allie had never dated a friend.

He met her at the door with a scowl on his face and his dog at his heels. "You've really done it now, Blondie."

"Excuse me?" she asked.

Instead of inviting her in, he stepped onto the porch with her and shut the door behind him, leaving Blackjack inside. He hadn't changed from work and he smelled like sawdust and sweat. "Leah's here."

She lifted her brows and stared at him, waiting for further explanation.

"I found her here when I got home."

"Is she okay?"

"She was alone and upset." He shoved his hands in his jeans pockets and glared at her. "Apparently someone told her it would help to have a place to escape when she was feeling bad about Carolyn."

Uh oh. Allie hadn't said that. Not really. "I never told her that."

"That's not what she said."

"I told her my situation with my stepmom didn't get better because I didn't have to face it every day like she does. I was trying to make her realize she had to be honest with Carolyn and Mark."

"Well, you misfired. She took off and didn't even leave a note. Not to mention the fact that she walked here alone in the dark."

"Do Carolyn and Mark know she's here?"

"They do now, and I look like the bad guy."

"Can I talk to her?" Allie asked. She knew Craig blamed her for what Leah had done, and while she knew this wasn't what Allie had told Leah to do, she did feel responsible.

He grabbed her arm as she tried to walk past him. "You need to fix this, Allie. She can't run away from her problems."

When Allie turned to face him, they were practically nose-to-nose. Absurdly, she felt a tingling in her belly at being so physically close to him, even though he looked as if he wanted to spit on her. "I'll try. I didn't mean for this to happen."

He opened the door for her and followed her inside. "Where is she?" Allie asked.

Craig pointed up the curving staircase. "First door on the left."

Allie tiptoed up the hardwood stairs, the tapping of her heels echoing off the empty walls. She spun around midway when she heard Leah say, "I'm in here," from somewhere down the stairs. Craig stared at her with a bitter look of accusation on his face before nodding with his head into the den. Great. No matter what she did, no matter what she said, he was going to blame her for Leah's actions.

"I thought I asked you to wait upstairs," Craig said to Leah where she sat huddled in the corner of the couch. Blackjack nestled against her and set his head in her lap.

Leah shrugged. "I didn't want you talking about me."

"Well, what did you think Allie and I were going to talk about? The weather?"

"Look, I'm sorry," Leah said. "Obviously, I shouldn't have come here." She stood up, but made no attempt to leave. "I thought you'd help me."

"You thought wrong." He walked to stand over her and peered down at her tear-streaked face. The man was tough as nails if the trembling of her lip didn't sway him. "You scared your dad and Carolyn half to death. They didn't know where you were or what in the world was wrong to make you leave like you did. I don't know what Allie told you, but I'm pretty sure it wasn't to run away when things got tough."

"He's right," Allie said, figuring she had a better chance of getting out of this unscathed as Craig's wingman. "You have to talk to your dad and stepmom. I never told you to run away."

"I tried to talk to them, I really did," Leah whispered through tears. "But they don't care about me. All they care about is each other."

"That's the biggest load of crap I've ever heard," Craig said, not even trying to hide the disgust in his voice. "Do you have any idea how many times and how many ways your dad has bent over backwards for you? The only reason you don't know Carolyn right now is because your dad was trying to protect you in case their relationship didn't work out. He's always put you first, and it's about time you started to show him the respect he deserves." Craig stared at his niece as a vein in his neck pulsed menacingly. "He's in love, Leah, and he's happy. He found a woman who makes him feel good about life again. After your mom died, I didn't think he'd ever feel good about anything ever again. He loves Carolyn and he loves you and you're breaking his heart by being such a brat."

Allie walked closer when she worried Craig's honesty might make Leah burst into tears. To her credit, Leah stood her ground, although Allie could tell by the flush of her cheeks that he'd hit a sore spot dead center. "You don't know what you're talking about!" she yelled back.

"Oh no?" Craig slapped his hands on his hips. "Who do you think was there after your mom died? Who do you think watched him work his fingers to the bone being both mother and father to you? Who do you think listened to him worry for two years about whether to ask Carolyn to marry him because he didn't want you to think he was rushing into something?"

"I love my dad. I want him to be happy."

"Then you'd better grow up and act like it. Carolyn's here. She's his wife and she's your stepmom. You don't have to love her, Leah, but you damn sure better treat her with respect."

"Craig's right," Allie said. "You won't get anywhere with either one of them if you disregard the rules and are mean to her. Your dad loves you both, and it's not fair of you to make him take sides. You have to be willing to get to know Carolyn and try to forge your own relationship. It's not up to your dad or your uncle to do it for you."

"I don't know how," Leah cried. "I don't know what to say to her."

"Start with 'good morning' when you get up and 'hello' when you get home from school," Allie said, thinking of all the ways she'd screwed up with Suzanne. "You said she's been putting her stuff out. Ask her about it. 'Where'd you get this?' or 'why is this special?' If you don't talk to her, you won't ever find any common ground. And Leah, you've already got one giant piece of common ground—you both love your dad."

Leah sniffled and wiped her nose with the back of her hand. "She keeps asking me about lacrosse and school and stuff."

"Do you answer?" Allie asked.

"No."

"Your dad taught you better than that," Craig said.

"I know that."

Craig reached out a hand and lifted Leah's chin where it had fallen to her chest. "I think you know what to say to her. I think you can start with an apology."

Allie scooted between Craig and the coffee table and crouched down so she and Leah were eye-to-eye. "Leah, I'm twenty-eight years old and I have a terrible relationship with both my dad and my stepmom. I never tried with either of them, and I'm telling you it doesn't get any better or any easier by just ignoring the problem or trying to wish your stepmom away. I'm not going to sugar coat this for you. I'm going to tell you straight out. My mom is a cold woman who never wanted kids. The best chance I had for a normal mom was Suzanne, and I blew it because I was too jealous and too selfish to let her in. Don't make the same mistake I did. Give Carolyn a chance. You have so much to gain and everything to lose if you don't."

Leah grabbed onto Allie and hugged her with so much strength she almost pushed Allie over. Craig righted her with a hand on her shoulder and kept it there as Leah sobbed into Allie's coat. Allie shushed her and ran her hand down Leah's soft, dark hair. "Let it out, sweet girl," she cooed as memories of her own tortured childhood surged through her pounding head.

She wouldn't have noticed the doorbell if it weren't for Blackjack's barking and the feel of Craig's hand leaving her shoulder. Allie stood up and wiped the tears from Leah's cheeks.

"Leah?" Mark said from behind them.

Allie's throat tightened when Leah leapt into his arms and buried her head against his chest. The look of relief on his face at having his daughter back made Allie turn away. She'd never had anyone, not anyone, look at her with so much love in his eyes.

"I'm sorry, daddy," Leah sobbed. "I'm so sorry I worried you."

"Leah, you can't ever leave the house without telling us first. Promise me you won't ever do that again."

Leah nodded and looked over Mark's shoulder to where Carolyn stood at the entrance to the den. Her arms were wrapped tightly under her chest, her fingers making indents into her sweater. "I'm sorry, Carolyn, for being disrespectful."

"Oh, honey. We were just so worried."

"I know, and I'm sorry. I won't do it again."

Carolyn timidly crept to where Mark held Leah and enfolded both of them in her arms, settling her head against Leah's back. Allie walked around the couch and into the foyer where Craig stood by the door. "May I use your restroom?" she whispered.

He pointed with his head to a door off the adjacent hallway and she quickly disappeared inside before the dam of her tears broke and she made a fool of herself. She could only stare at her pale reflection in the mirror and watch the tears silently pool around the corners of her mouth. She closed the toilet, sat down on the lid, and buried her face in a wad of toilet paper, hoping to muffle her sobs. Like everything else in the house, the bare walls only magnified her sniffles.

***

Craig didn't wait for Allie to emerge from the bathroom, but dragged his weary butt into the kitchen and fished a bottle of red from the rack he'd built into the island. He uncorked the bottle and reached for the largest glass he could find.

"Craig?" he heard her call a moment later.

"In the kitchen."

She'd done the best she could to mask the tears he'd heard her shed. Her eyes were swollen and she'd chewed off her lipstick, but she gave him a dazzling smile and accepted the glass of wine as though she hadn't just cried her eyes out in his bathroom.

"It hasn't had time to breathe," he said.

He tried not to flinch when he saw her hands tremble as she lifted the glass to her lips. "So," she said after taking a large sip. "That went well."

He chuckled. "You think that went well?"

Allie tossed a shoulder in the air after easing out of her coat. She wore a silky button down blouse that tied at her waist. The mustard color made her appear pale as a ghost, but seemed to illuminate the golden color of her eyes. "It could have been worse," she said. "Did they go home?"

"Yep."

"Are you still mad at me?"

He poured himself a glass and contemplated his answer while taking a sip. He really wanted a beer, but this wasn't half bad. "It's hard to stay mad at you when you look like I could knock you over with a weak poke."

She snorted and sank onto a stool. "Sorry," she said. "That was hard."

He worried she was going to start crying again and needed to lighten the mood. He said the first thing that popped into his mind. "So, what's a music transposer, anyway?"

"What?" She laughed at him, but her smile didn't reach her eyes.

"Music transposer. That's what your profile says."

"You read my profile?"

He shrugged and wished something else had popped into his head. "You're in my age range. Did you read mine?"

"Yes."

He wiggled his brows and leaned against the butcher block.

"But only to see how you did on your paragraphs," she said.

"And what do you think?"

She took a sip. To his great relief, her hands were steady. "I think you did okay."

"Okay?" he asked. "I sweated over those two paragraphs for hours. Days. And all you can say is that I did okay?"

"What do you want me to say, Craig? That it was the best, most descriptive string of words I've ever read?"

"I wouldn't want you to lie."

"Then okay is the best you're going to get." She splayed her hands on the counter and tracked him with her eyes as he pulled bread and sandwich meat from the refrigerator. "I transpose music."

"I'm familiar with the -er suffix. What I want to know is what it is."

She huffed out an impatient breath. "I change musical scores for different instruments."

"I thought all instruments used the same music."

"Most do, but some instruments' pitch is transposed. The saxophone, the French horn, the clarinet, and a couple others."

"So how do you figure out how to transpose their music? Do you play all of those?"

"No. Notes are vibrations of air. Their frequency is measured in hertz."

"So, it's math?" He slapped ham and roast beef on bread. He didn't ask, but put mustard and mayonnaise on both sandwiches.

"Yes. There are computer programs that transpose music, but they're not always accurate. For complicated pieces, musicians pay me to do it for them." She shrugged. "It helps pay the mortgage."

"Sounds complicated."

"Not really. I've got a math mind."

He slid the plated sandwich in front of her and retrieved a jar of pickles from the fridge. He slapped one on her plate without asking.

She sat up. "You don't have to feed me."

"Sure I do." He tapped her almost empty glass with his finger. "You won't be able to drive home without food in your stomach."

"You're right about that," she said and put a hand on her forehead. "Do you mind if I grab some water?"

"Water's free." He poured what was left of her wine from her glass into his and took a bite of his sandwich. "So, how old were you when your parents divorced?"

She twisted the cap off the bottle she'd retrieved from the fridge and took a dainty sip. "Eleven."

"Ahhh."

"Yeah," she said. "It's hitting a little too close for comfort."

"Eat up," he said when she sat staring out the window.

"Sorry." She picked up the sandwich. "You probably have plans for tonight."

"Not tonight, other than a shower. I've got my first online date on Friday."

"Do you?" She smiled at him with a smudge of mustard at the corner of her mouth.

She licked it off and he looked away. Allie eating and drinking wine in his kitchen, swollen eyes and an unpainted mouth aside, also fell under the category of a little too close for comfort. He'd been so pissed off at her before, when he thought she'd planted a seed in Leah's mind. She had, but unlike his initial assumption, it wasn't intentional and it certainly wasn't malicious. "I'm going the traditional route. Drinks with an option for dinner."

"What's her name?"

"Jealous?" he asked.

She gave him a haughty stare. "No, just curious."

"Emily," he said. "Emily Brand."

"Huh." She wiped her mouth with a napkin and took another sip of water. Food was bringing all the color back to her face. "I've got a date on Friday, too. We're going to see the Gladiators play."

He set his wine down without taking a sip. "I thought you didn't like hockey."

"I didn't say I didn't like it; I said I don't know the game."

"Why hockey?"

"I don't know. He's from up north, so I figure he's a fan. Like I said before, it's a good way to spend an evening together without having to fill up every second with chatter."

He'd never had any lapses in chatter with Allie and he hardly got along with anyone, but he wasn't going to point out the obvious. He wasn't dating her. "So what's his name?"

"Steve Kellman. He's an architect."

Craig thought back to the bevy of architects he used to work with through Archer Construction. "Never heard of him."

"I don't think he does residential," she said and gave her pickle a sniff.

"It's kosher." It shouldn't have bothered him, her assuming he was nothing more than a handyman. He'd lost everything because of Archer Construction, but he'd busted his butt building that company up from a one-man shop to a three million dollar operation. "I used to work with commercial architects. I'm pretty familiar with most of them."

"Oh." She sat her sandwich down and pushed her plate away.

"You're not going to eat the crust?" he asked.

"No."

"You ate your pizza crust. Why wouldn't you eat your sandwich crust?"

"Why are you so observant with trivial things?" she asked. "I like pizza crust. It's basically a breadstick. I don't like sandwich crust."

"But it's just bread."

"I don't like it," she insisted. "You didn't eat your pizza crust and you ate your sandwich crust. What's the difference?"

"I save the pizza crust for Blackjack." The dog sat up at the mention of his name. "The sandwich crust is part of the sandwich."

"Technically, so is the pizza crust." She took both of their plates to the sink and rinsed them with water.

"No," he said. "It's more like a handle for the pizza."

"You're an odd man, Craig."

He carried their glasses to the sink and snuck a sniff of her hair. She smelled like pumpkin tonight.

She turned off the water and pivoted so they were face-to-face. Their gazes locked and stayed locked as his pulse beat in his head. She looked relaxed and vulnerable and way too tempting. He deliberately took a step back when every instinct in his body pushed him to do the opposite. "Are we becoming friends, Craig?"

It was an interesting question considering he felt light headed from being in such close contact. He was pretty sure a friend had never made him feel like he'd been punched in the gut with just a look. "I've never had a female friend."

"I've never had a male friend, at least one that was straight." She placed her palm on his chest and he felt anything but friendly at the intimate contact. "I guess there's a first time for everything." She pulled her hand away and retrieved her coat from the chair. "Thank you for dinner."

"Don't mention it. Thanks for…helping out with Leah."

"I'm glad you called. If she pulls another stunt, will you let me know?"

"I don't think she will after tonight, but yes, you'll be the first to know."

He walked her to the door. "Go grab your shower, Craig, you don't have to see me out."

"I wasn't born in a barn, Allie. I think I can manage."

"Good luck on your date," she said as she turned to face him on the porch. Her breath came out as tiny puffs of smoke in the chilly night.

"You too."

Halfway down the walk, she turned around. "Do me a favor, would you? Call me and let me know how it goes."

"Why?"

"I'm curious. I'd like to know what it feels like from the other side."

Right now, watching her saunter toward her car, it felt damn uncomfortable having thoughts of her swirling around his head. "Yeah," he said. "I'll let you know."

CHAPTER 17

Craig wasn't surprised when he saw his brother's number on his cell phone. Mark was either going to thank him or give him a hard time about Leah.

"Hey," Craig said to break the ice. Mark couldn't be mad at a man who sounded like he didn't have a care in the world. "How's it going?"

Mark huffed out a breath. "That's a loaded question. Look, I'm sorry about last night."

"What are you sorry for?"

"Leah. I'm just not sure what to do with her lately."

"Talking to her would be my suggestion." Craig measured the stain grade trim and marked his spot while cradling the phone between his ear and his shoulder.

"I have. We have. We talked for a long time last night. She's feeling displaced by Carolyn and Carolyn's feeling in the way. I should have listened to you when you tried to tell me to have them spend time together sooner."

"Too late to worry about that now. How'd you all leave things?"

"We're all going to try and understand how the other feels. Respect is the number one priority in the house, and that should eliminate a lot of our troubles."

"Good. I don't like the idea of Leah walking to my house at night."

"Me neither," Mark said. "I don't think she'll pull another stunt like that again."

"I hope not."

"So," Mark said with a distinctive change to his voice. "What's going on with you and Allie?"

Here we go, Craig thought. He should have known Mark would hone in on her like a drone missile. "Nothing."

"Nothing? The last person I expected to see at your house—at night—was Allie."

"She and Leah have a bond. I told you I called her when Leah got her period."

"Yeah, but...what was she doing there? And more importantly, how long did she stay after we left?"

"I called her because Leah mentioned something Allie said to her. I thought Allie had given her the idea to run away and I was pissed. I was wrong, believe it or not, but I called Allie so she could clean up the mess I thought she made."

"And that's it?"

He thought of Allie last night, the feel of her hand on his chest. He only wished it was the first time he'd thought of her that day. "Of course that's it. What are you getting at?"

"She's a beautiful woman," Mark prodded.

"I've got eyes, Mark."

"So what are you waiting for?"

"Why are *you* asking me that question? She's been at your house twice a week for years, befriending you daughter, having intimate dinners." It wasn't until he'd said it out loud that he realized he was jealous.

"I was dating Carolyn."

"She was 700 miles away and you weren't exactly committed."

"I've never been one to juggle women, Craig. Besides, she's Leah's piano teacher."

"Exactly. And she's not my type."

"Ha!" Mark barked into the phone. "She's exactly your type. I thought..."

"What?" Craig asked quickly, a little too quick to hide his interest.

"I thought it might freak you out how much she looks like Julie."

Craig sagged against the counter. Allie looking like Julie? "How so?"

"Come on, Craig. She's blonde, beautiful, a little bit mysterious."

"Allie's nothing like Julie. I didn't even put that together until you mentioned it."

"And now?" Mark asked.

"And now I have to get back to work. Some of us do that, Mark. Work for a living."

"Yeah, some of us do," Mark said with a snicker. "You're not one of them."

"You'll be happy to know I've got a date tomorrow night."

"Really? With who?"

"Her name's Emily Brand. She's a paralegal who likes dogs and sports."

"Why does it sound like you answered a personal ad?"

"Get with the times, Mark. I met her online."

"You?" Mark sputtered. "You're online dating?"

"Yep. Allie helped me get set up with that, too."

"So all roads lead back to Allie."

"I'm hanging up now, Mark. I've got work to do."

"You coming to Leah's game on Saturday?"

"I'll be there," Craig said before pocketing the phone and zoning back in on the trim.

Or trying to zone back in on the trim. He couldn't get thoughts of Allie out of his head. He'd gone straight to the computer when she'd left and looked up Steve Kellman, the architect. He looked like a prick and sure sounded like one in his snappy two paragraphs about his white picket fence upbringing and the type of woman who would make him complete. Craig wanted to twist the trim in half just thinking about him making a move on Allie.

He'd just talked himself out of doing anything harmful to the trim when Tommy Steen, cabinetmaker extraordinaire, walked in, his tool belt swinging in rhythm to his gait. "Archer. What's up, man?"

He offered his knuckles for a bump. Craig tucked the pencil behind his ear and obliged. "Just a whole lot of kitchen to work on."

"So I see." Tommy stood in the center of the room, hands on his hips, and turned in a circle. Craig could see the wheels in motion in Tommy's head. "Nice space."

"It is now. You should have seen it before I took that wall out and got all the original stuff out."

Tommy crouched to examine the flooring Craig had discovered under two layers of linoleum. "They just don't build houses like they used to, do they?"

"That's for sure. Did you get my plans?"

Tommy slung his head toward the front of the house. "They're in the truck. I wanted to get a look at the space first."

"Look all you want. They want to be in the house by Thanksgiving, so we've got plenty of time to do this right."

"I do everything right," Tommy said with a goading smile. "Did I hear you say you're online dating?"

Hell. Just what he didn't want to talk to his contractors about. "Maybe."

"You know, since the divorce, I've been dating online." Tommy shook his head. "I'm more confused about women than ever."

"What do you mean?" Craig asked.

"I mean I don't get it, man. Melody and I didn't have sex for almost two years before the divorce. I couldn't get my damn wife to have sex with me, and yet the only thing these ladies want is to have sex. I want to call Melody up and tell her that I may not be attractive to her, but these other women out here can't get enough of me." He took his hammer out of his belt and absently twirled it around his finger like a gunslinger. "And the hell of it is, I don't want to have sex with any of these women. I still want to have sex with my wife."

"Really? All of them want to have sex?"

"Well, maybe it's just me." He smiled and shot the hammer back into his belt. "I'm not looking to have any more kids. I've already got three of them. I seriously think the women who are beyond the kid stage just use it like an escort service. I know I shouldn't complain, especially after my dry spell, but it makes me feel kinda used."

Interesting. If a five-foot-eight, overweight, balding carpenter had women throwing themselves at his feet, Craig was more than a little afraid of what he'd find. After all, he did have a full set of hair. But as Tommy went out to his truck to get the plans, Craig decided a quick romp in the sack with Emily might be just what he needed to get Allie out of his head.

***

Leah was more than polite and profuse in her apology for her behavior the previous night at Craig's house. Allie felt as though she were stepping into a television drama when she entered the Archer house on Thursday night. They all greeted her at the door, Mark, Carolyn, and Leah. The only ones missing were Craig and Blackjack. She wished they were around to deflect attention.

After the lesson, Leah thanked her and went upstairs to her room before Allie even had her bags packed. Mark and Carolyn walked her to the door.

"I can't thank you enough, Allie, for everything you've done for Leah," Mark said. "Craig explained how helpful you've been with her while we were on our honeymoon. And last night..."

Allie felt uncomfortable. Mark seemed genuine—he didn't have a disingenuous bone in his body, but Carolyn was eyeing her nervously and offered to walk Allie to her car after grabbing a sweater from the coat rack in the foyer.

Carolyn seemed more formidable tonight with her wool pants and tidy makeup. Although Allie was taller than the petite brunette, she felt as if she were about to receive a scolding. She was pretty sure she deserved it.

"I'm not trying to overkill the thanks, Allie," Carolyn began. "But I know what you said to Leah the other night. She told me you were trying to make her understand how I felt moving in here with her and Mark."

Allie stopped walking and turned to face the woman she'd thought of quite regularly that day. "I feel like I'm butting my nose in where it doesn't belong. I am, I know I am, but Leah opened up to me while you were gone about her concerns about all of you living together. I spoke to her about my experience with my stepmom and tried to advise her to make more of an effort than I did at her age."

"I appreciate that."

Allie shrugged. "I have a terrible relationship with my dad and stepmom and my behavior growing up is the main reason why. It probably wasn't all my fault, but since I'll never know for sure, it seems the most likely excuse." Allie passed her bag to her other arm and cinched her coat tighter. The temperatures had dropped and she knew Carolyn had to be freezing in her thin sweater. "Leah and her dad are so close. They have such a special relationship."

"Yes, they do. I'm having trouble…I mean, I'm not sure…" She ducked her head, tucked her hair behind her ears, and looked up at Allie with doleful eyes. "I'm floundering, as I'm sure you can tell. We talked about what happened, about how she can't run to Craig every time she feels upset. She agreed to be respectful and I'm doing the same. We're all walking on egg shells."

Allie remembered the polite silence that reigned in her father's house on the rare occasions they weren't fighting. She much preferred the fighting. "You probably will, for awhile."

"I start my new job next week. I know I'll be slammed for a couple of weeks, but I'd like to meet for lunch one day if you've got the time. I could use some pointers with Leah and you know her better than I do."

"I'm not sure how much better I know her," Allie said. "She's only just opened up to me."

"That's more than she's done for me. Please," Carolyn begged. "I don't know who else to turn to."

Oh boy. Getting more involved with the Archer family didn't feel like such a good idea. "Okay, sure. Go on in. You're freezing. Call me anytime for lunch. I'll see you Tuesday."

Allie watched Carolyn go inside as she started the engine. She turned up the heat and backed out of the driveway wondering how she'd gotten so drawn into the lives of her client. She'd befriended the father, counseled the girl, and now agreed to help the stepmom. Not to mention her burgeoning friendship with Craig. How would he feel about her meeting Carolyn for lunch? She wondered if she'd tell him.

CHAPTER 18

"Wow, you're as pretty as your profile picture." Allie thought the same could have been said for Steve Kellman. "That almost never happens."

She knew Steve wasn't lying. She'd heard it from every man she'd ever met online, but it still annoyed her to hear it. Don't be so hard on him, she told herself as they stood in line for their tickets from will call. "You must be a hockey fan?"

"I used to play." He took a sip of his non-fat latte. She'd ordered her usual from the coffee shop where they'd met: a large cinnamon blend with cream and sugar. Did she really want to date a man who was more concerned with calories than she was? "So you teach music?"

"Piano. My clients are kids, mostly."

"All day with kids?" He visibly shuddered. "You're braver than I am."

"I like kids," she said in defense of her profession and her students. "They're refreshingly honest."

He held up his hand and Allie noticed his large class ring. He already mentioned he went to Stanford and UC Berkeley. "Don't get me wrong," he said. "I like kids. I mean, I want to have some. Someday. But I wouldn't want to be around them all the time."

Allie took a gulp of coffee and hoped the date would improve. It was going to be a very long night. He got their tickets and led her to their seats behind the Gladiators' bench. "So how long have you been in Atlanta?" she asked.

"Couple of years. I moved out after college."

"Quite a change from California."

"I grew up in Maryland, so I was ready to head back east." He flashed a perfect smile to show off his over bright teeth. He'd either had them whitened recently or this was his first coffee ever. "Never did quite fit into the California scene."

The music blared and their conversation stopped while the teams were introduced and, after much fanfare, the game began. "I've been to San Francisco," she said once play had been underway for a minute or two. "It's beautiful, but I don't think I could live there."

"The people are different. The lifestyle's different. It was fun for a while, but I'm glad to be back."

"Do you think you'll stay in Atlanta?" she asked.

He shrugged and kept his gaze on the ice. "Depends. I like my job and I like the city, but I'm not opposed to moving. I'm young, I've got no real ties here, so if the right opportunity came up, yeah, I'd consider moving again."

They lapsed into silence and Allie took another sip, wondering if perhaps he'd like to know anything about her. This wasn't an interview, and she'd learned pretty much everything she cared to know so far. He was a west coast educated architect with a job he liked, but didn't love. He was good looking, better looking than most of the guys she went out with, and from his comments about having kids way in the future, he had no interest in settling down. Why, she wondered, did he choose to go out with a woman who spent her time with kids and desperately wanted to find her soul mate? She made a mental note to revisit her profile and reread her 'About Me' paragraphs.

"Do you ski?" he asked, pulling her out of her thoughts.

"Pardon me?"

"Ski? Snow ski? I'm going out to Utah in a couple of weeks."

"Oh, no. I've never been."

"I can't wait. The slopes on the east coast don't compare to the fresh powder in the West." He eyed her over the lip of his cup. "We should go some time."

"Ummm," she said and inwardly flinched. Who asked a woman to go away on their first date? More importantly, did he think she'd agree to go? She glanced at her watch. An hour into her date and she was already bored. They had, it appeared, zilch in common.

As she watched the players skate around the ice chasing the puck, she thought of Craig and wondered how his date with Emily was going. She didn't like Emily Brand, the perky paralegal with fake auburn hair and a profile that read like she'd been created for men. Who had time to teach yoga and spin class while hitting the trendy hotspots all over town? They were probably done with drinks by now. Were they having dinner? Why did she care?

He bought her a slice of pizza and a beer at half time and found a small thread of common ground discussing their parents. Steve's divorced when he was little and, strangely enough, he seemed to enjoy playing one off the other. "My dad paid for college after my mom threatened to sue him again. They hate each other."

"Yeah," she said. "Mine do, too. I have a hard time picturing them being in love."

"Mine weren't," he said. "They got married because she got pregnant with me. I don't think they were ever happy."

"Sad, don't you think?"

He took a bite and shrugged. "I've got a friend from college who got his girlfriend pregnant. He tried to do the right thing by getting married, but they're struggling. He's trying to finish his degree, she's nagging him all the time about the baby. I think they'd have saved themselves a huge headache by not getting married at all."

A giant red flag waved in front of Allie's face, blinding her vision before it swooped away and she was watching him chew. Not get married? She couldn't imagine that would be better for any of them.

"You know, my girlfriend Melissa has a new baby. They did it the right way—they fell in love, got married, and then had the baby. She tells me all the time how hard it is to focus on her marriage now that the baby's here. I think new parenthood is just tough at first."

"But marriage throws a whole other layer of complication into an already complicated situation," he countered. "Both parties want to have a baby, fine. Do it. But don't add marriage into the mix unless you both want it in the first place."

"You see, I think we're too cynical based on our situations," Allie said. "That, to me, is the worst part about having divorced parents. We can't even think about marriage without doubts creeping in."

"Fortunately," he said with a charming grin and an irritating wink, "I don't ever think about marriage. You ready to head back to our seats?"

She wanted to say no. She really did, but he hadn't said or done anything wrong. She liked discussing heady topics, she liked digging beyond the 'what do you do for a living' questions that seemed to dominate these tedious first dates. Steve, it seemed, wanted to keep it light. Keeping it light, Allie knew, meant there wouldn't be a second date.

**

Craig accepted his second drink and closed out the tab while Emily was in the bathroom. He wasn't sure he wanted to have dinner with her, but didn't think it wise to keep the tab open, as she'd had no problem sucking down two fifteen dollar glasses of wine and seemed headed for a third.

There hadn't been any lapses in conversation, not with all her talk about yoga and the gym where she taught spin three times a week. Apparently she forgot to update her profile to mention that she'd been laid off as a paralegal, which would explain her gusto for expensive wine on someone else's dime.

He signed his name, left a generous tip, and considered eating at the bar. He was hungry and he didn't feel right ending the date when she'd had two glasses of wine without any food on her stomach. He thought of Allie and how lightheaded she'd been after just one glass of wine. He cursed himself for thinking of Allie. Again.

When Emily returned and hopped onto the barstool like a teenager, she flashed a brilliant smile and Craig told himself he could man up and handle another hour with the annoying little cheerleader.

She downed her last sip of wine and drummed her fingers on the bar. "Boy, it's really getting crowded in here."

He had to lean in to hear her and caught a whiff of her overly sweet perfume. "Yep. I guess it's to be expected on a Friday night."

"I don't ever come here," she confessed. "The crowd is so..." She looked over her shoulder and scanned the room. "Old, I guess."

Old? Where did she normally hang out, a dance bar? "You okay to drive home?" he asked. No way was he paying for dinner when she'd just called him old.

"Yeah, sure." She slid off the bar stool and pulled her mini dress down before sauntering toward the entrance with her fur lined jacket slung over one shoulder. Craig felt as if he'd spent the evening with a hooker.

She gave him an uncomfortable hug in the parking lot that did nothing to peak his interest and left him smelling like her perfume. Perfect. He started up the truck, backed out of the space, and considered going somewhere, anywhere to ease the discontent with his night. It was still early, only eight o'clock, and he could think of nothing more enticing than an evening at home with his dog.

He headed for home with thoughts of Allie at the hockey game stuck in his head. The game was just getting started. Was she hitting it off with Steve Kellman, graduate of the Berkeley school of Architecture? Would she kiss him? Sleep with him? He forced his hands to unclench from the wheel and took a calming breath. He had to stop thinking about Allie, wondering where she was and whom she was with. He wasn't going to ask about her dates. He wasn't going to contact her at all. She spelled trouble with a capital T and he didn't need any more drama in his life.

Two hours later, with his feet propped up on his desk and her profile pulled up on his computer, he cursed himself when the phone rang and her name popped up on caller id. Damn. He shouldn't answer. He should let her think he was still with Emily.

"Hello?" he said on the third ring.

"Hey, I saw you online."

He dropped his feet and sat upright with a jolt. How did she know he was looking at her profile? "How?"

"I'm on LoveFinders.com. You have a smiley face next to your name, which means you're online."

Great. Nothing like being caught in the act. "Oh. What are you doing online? I thought you had a date?"

"I did. It was kind of a bust. I'm looking at my profile to see why I keep attracting the same kind of guys."

"What kind of guys?" he asked as he felt himself relax for the first time all night.

"A little immature."

"Immature?" Craig chuckled. "He couldn't have been more immature than Emily."

"I could have told you she was immature," Allie said.

"How? And why didn't you?"

"I looked at her profile. I wasn't checking up on you," she immediately amended, "I was just curious. Anyway, I'd guess she was a club-hopping adolescent."

He wouldn't admit she'd nailed Emily, not when he couldn't keep the admiration out of his voice. "You'd be close. I could have told you Kellman was a prick."

"I didn't say he was…that word. I said he was immature."

"Whatever."

"So how did you know?"

"Every architect from a fancy school thinks his shit doesn't stink. Let me guess, whatever job he has now it just a stepping stone to bigger and better?"

"Probably. He's not tied to anything, or looking to be." She sighed and he wished he could see her face. "I mistakenly assume these guys are looking for someone special to share their lives, when really, they're all just looking to have a good time. I like to have a good time, but I feel like the only person on the planet who's looking to find one person to spend the rest of my life having a good time with." She laughed. "And now you know I'm a typical female nearing thirty."

Now he knew Steve Kellman was the stupidest prick on the planet. "Yeah, but I already knew that."

"Maybe we should pick each other's dates?" she suggested.

"You want me to blame you when my dates don't work out?"

"Good point," she said. "I'm never going to find a date to this wedding."

"What wedding?"

"Oh, this girl I've known since high school is getting married in a couple of weeks. I need a date and I'd rather it not be a first date."

He felt tempted to offer to take her. He wanted to know what it felt like to have her all to himself for one night. "You'd take a first date to a wedding?"

"I wouldn't want to, but so far I've got no one and I'm not going alone."

"What's so bad about going alone?"

"I don't like the bride, and I won't give her the satisfaction of knowing I couldn't get a date to her wedding."

Craig moved to the couch and relaxed into the cushions. He scratched Blackjack behind the ear. "If you don't like the bride, why are you going?"

"Because if I don't, she'll think it's because I don't have a date."

"You don't have a date."

"Not yet, and by the looks of these guys, I won't have one."

He didn't want her to have a date for the wedding. He didn't want her dating at all. Jesus, being around her, being friends, was the worst idea in the history of bad ideas. He needed to deflect and fast. "How did your lesson with Leah go yesterday?"

"Fine," she said. "Have you talked to her?"

"No. I'm trying to stay out of the way so she doesn't get any more brilliant ideas about running to me when things get tough."

After a long pause, she said, "I agreed to have lunch with Carolyn."

"Why?"

"She asked. She thinks I can give her some insight into Leah, but I don't know what to tell her. I think she's struggling, Craig. I think they all are."

"Yeah, I know it, but I'm not sure how to help."

"I'm getting too involved. I don't want to be in the middle of their situation. It makes me feel responsible."

He was just about to comment about her butting her nose in when she groaned. "What's wrong?" he asked.

"I just got nudged."

He felt the muscles tense in his neck. "Who by?"

"Jeremy Feckler. Let's have a look."

Craig jogged back to his computer, typed Jeremy's name into the search bar, and pulled up his profile. "Jeez, do you think he's posted enough pictures?" The dizzying array of poses made Craig want to vomit. "Look at him, Allie. What kind of guy posts a picture of himself flexing?"

"He's a teacher," she said in a voice that told him she was reading his 'About Me' description with more interest than he could stomach. "He likes animals, is close to his family, and has lived in Atlanta for the last ten years."

"He's a cheeseball," Craig countered. "He's flexing for the camera."

"You're right. Those pictures are gross."

"Speaking of pictures," he said, "you only have one of you and it's not a close up."

"So? I'd rather men judge me by my words instead of my picture."

"What do men say when they meet you? They're pleased, I'm sure."

"Did Emily look like her picture?"

The bubbly redhead looked exactly as she'd been: a pubescent party girl. "Yes, and it should have been my first clue."

"We're hopeless, Craig," Allie sighed.

He was hopeless, all right. Hopelessly distracted by the wistful sound of her voice, the lonely tone she couldn't hide, and his ever increasing need to soothe her. Damn it, he didn't want to care about a beautiful blonde who had the power to crush him. "Yeah," he admitted. "But at least we're trying."

CHAPTER 19

Allie had a difficult transposition and more students than she should have had on her calendar each afternoon and evening. She was hopping all around town, working on her music, and making plans for the upcoming recital. She was too busy to date, she told herself each time she passed on an invitation or ignored an email. She still scanned the site most nights and every time ended up on Craig's profile.

So typical of him to put only one picture, a shot he'd cropped of him smiling. She recognized Mark's arm around his shoulder and Leah's hand on the other. She hadn't heard from him in over a week and she missed him. Was he dating? Did he meet someone? Was that why he hadn't called?

His lack of contact shouldn't have bothered her. After their last conversation, she'd ached to go to him, lay her head on his shoulder, and be held. He'd never offered comfort, and certainly never touched her in a way to suggest he would, but it was there. She couldn't control her desires any more than she could control her heart. But was it her heart that hurt because of the lack of communication or was it her pride?

A brisk run with Melissa would cure her mood, she thought as she laced up her sneakers and pulled on her gloves. Ben had taken Henry on some errands and the girls had the morning free to run and grab some coffee. She'd missed spending time with Melissa, too.

"What's new on the dating scene?" Melissa asked before they rounded the first curve.

"Ho hum," Allie said. "I haven't had time to do much at all."

"What about tonight?"

"No plans." She'd received more than a handful of emails, not to mention the endless nudges. Craig was right; they were stupid.

"On a Saturday? Why not?"

Allie stopped running and began to walk. Talk of her non-existent dating life drained every ounce of her energy. Melissa sensed her frustration and wrapped her arm around Allie's shoulder. "You okay?"

"I'm just sick of going out with guys I have nothing in common with searching for a relationship that's never going to happen."

"Isn't that why you quit the last time?"

"Yes, but now I've got a wedding to go to and no date."

Melissa let the issue stand for a moment as their shoes crunched on the gravel path. "Why don't you ask Craig?"

Allie pulled a tissue from her pocket and wiped her nose. "I've thought about it," she admitted as she upped her pace to a jog. "I mentioned the wedding the last time we talked, but I couldn't pull the trigger."

"Why not?"

"He could say no. He probably will say no."

"Why?" she asked. "If you're friends."

"Because he doesn't put himself out for anyone. Asking him makes me needy and he hates needy women. I think losing his wife years ago really scarred him, much more so than Mark."

"Uh oh," Melissa said.

"What do you mean, 'uh oh'?"

"You love a wounded puppy, Allie."

"Ha! He's no puppy, trust me. He's more like a ferocious lion who's been king of his own jungle for too long."

"What's the latest with the kid?"

"Leah? She seems fine. Back to normal except maybe a little more guarded. I haven't been called back in for advisement, so I guess all is well."

"Any more word from the new wife?"

"Nope. She said she'd call me for lunch and I haven't heard from her. I stayed for dinner last Tuesday and I get the feeling they're all on their best behavior, which is good. I certainly never even tried with Suzanne, and if she tried with me, I was too pissed off to notice."

"I hope I never get divorced," Melissa huffed as they ascended the only hill along the trail.

"Mark didn't get divorced," Allie reminded her friend. "And neither did Craig."

"Thanks. That's a much more cheerful scenario."

"I'm just pointing out the difference. There's no ping-pong effect for Leah like I had, bouncing back and forth between two angry parents, each of them filling my head with nonsense that had nothing to do with me. It's a wonder I even want to be in a relationship considering what I grew up with."

"Everyone wants someone to love, Allie."

True, Allie thought as she settled into a nice, steady pace. But what Allie wanted most of all was for someone to love her.

***

Craig nearly spilled the cup of coffee he'd just bought at the gas station when he saw Allie's name pop up on his cell phone. He quickly placed the cup in the holder and took a contemplative breath before answering. He'd avoided calling her. He hadn't needed to avoid her when she hadn't called him. He'd like to think he hadn't missed her, but he knew better than to lie to himself.

"Hello?"

"Hi, Craig." She sounded overly perky on the phone, as if she were trying too hard to sound casual. This new friendship they were building on top of his veiled attraction felt like quicksand.

"Hey," he gave his best attempt at spontaneous. "What's up?"

"Nothing, well…I've got a favor to ask. I was hoping to ease into it after a little small talk."

"I don't do small talk."

"Yes," she chuckled. "How could I forget?"

"What's the favor?"

"You know that wedding I told you about?"

Oh no. Not the wedding. Anything but the wedding. "Yeahhhhh."

"I need a date."

He kneaded his forehead and tried to come up with an excuse not to go. "Are you really that desperate?"

She let out one long breathy sigh that had him fidgeting in the seat. "Yes. I'm sorry," she said. "I know you don't want to go. I know I'm asking too much, but I *am* that desperate."

"When is it?"

"This Saturday. I know it's short notice, but I've tried to find someone else. I've had three bad dates this week, and I just can't do it anymore."

He wanted to say no. He wanted to feel nothing but pity for her ridiculous efforts to impress some girl she didn't even like. But damning all common sense, he felt drawn to the idea of her needing him. "Okay, okay, okay. I'll go. But I'm not wearing a tux."

"Really?" she said, her voice finally sounding normal. "You'll go even though it's the last thing you want to do?"

"I said I would."

"Oh, Craig," she said as he started the truck and slammed it into reverse. "Thank you. I owe you big time for this."

"Where's the wedding?"

"Some funky warehouse on Ponce."

"Will there be food?" he asked.

"Yes, a buffet dinner."

"I suppose that helps to ease the sting."

"I can't thank you enough, Craig. I've spent the last two weeks interviewing my dates for the job of wedding guest and none of them were suitable."

"Your standards aren't very high if you think I am. I still don't understand why you have to go to this stupid wedding."

"You don't have to understand, you just have to put on a suit and take me."

He'd take her, all right. That was the problem. Spending an evening with her, pretending they were an item, or at least interested in becoming one, meant dancing and alcohol and too damn much temptation. He was screwed. "Text me the details including your address and I'll pick you up."

"You're my hero!" she belted.

"Yeah, yeah, yeah." He'd better be a hero because it would take super-human strength to keep his hands to himself.

CHAPTER 20

Allie shouldn't have felt nervous. She'd had four dates in the last seven days, and yet she quaked like a schoolgirl at the thought of going out with Craig. Only they weren't really going out. He was doing her a favor. A big one.

She stood in front of the mirror as second and third thoughts whirled around her head. She told herself she'd dressed for Sharon, the bride she disliked, the bride she wanted to snub. She told herself she dressed for her, to feel good about the body she'd worked hard to sculpt.

She told herself lies.

She'd dressed for Craig, to dare him, to tease him, to taunt him into wanting her. That, she knew, was the reason her stomach fluttered with butterflies and her hands weren't quite steady as she dotted her neckline with perfume. She'd never had to work hard at making men want her. Ever.

The question she couldn't answer was why she wanted to tempt him. Because she was tempted? She didn't want to find him attractive, but from the very beginning, something about him had taken root and wouldn't let go. She didn't want to find his gruff and unsophisticated manners so appealing, but he'd somehow managed to make those qualities seem honest and refreshing. She didn't want to compare every man she went out with to him and wonder what it would feel like to be chosen by him.

So tonight was an experiment. After tonight, she'd know what it was like to be with him on a date, even though she'd orchestrated the evening and wheedled him into going. The results were the same: they would be a couple for one night and she'd know how it felt to be his. She slipped her feet into her coral, peep toe platform pumps. They weren't red—that would be tacky. They were a subtle variation on the flashy color that added a nice punch to her navy dress. She descended the stairs, needing to shake her nerves, and turned to the one thing that had always helped clam her down.

***

Craig pulled into the drive of the small cottage in the oldest part of town. He thought the butter yellow siding and rust colored shutters suited Allie to a T. She'd planted pansies and ivy in concrete planters flanking the front door and had a miniature hedge leading along the path.

He heard the music before he hit the porch steps, something dramatic and sad. His first reaction was to feel nostalgic for Leah's nightly practices before the rushing crescendo made him realize this was unlike anything Leah could play. A touch to the front door had the music vibrating through his fingertips. He could feel the power and the passion of the song and marveled again at how he'd been so wrong to peg her as a depthless beauty. When he used the doorknocker, the music stopped with a jolt.

It was like getting slammed in the stomach by a fist or whacked upside the head with a board. Holy mother of God, the woman had nerves of steel and curves that made a man want to weep.

"Well, well, well," Allie said with a provocative hand on her hip. If Craig didn't know any better, he'd think she'd posed for him, cocking her sleeveless shoulder in the air while her other arm, the one with a full sleeve to the wrist, lightly grasped the doorknob. "You certainly clean up well."

He had the pleasure of returning the favor and giving her the once over from her perilously high heels to her dangerously painted mouth. "So do you, Blondie, but I think you already know that."

She dropped her hands as her cocky smile morphed into a sexy pout. "If you make me feel like a slut, I'm going to deck you."

"You should feel like a beautiful woman, which you are."

He must have hit the mark, because she stepped back and waved him inside. "Come on in. I've got to get my bag."

"Nice house," he said. Every inch of the place felt homey, from the creamy sofa to the bold red and yellow pillows that adorned the well-worn piece. The soft tan walls and seagrass rug served as a neutral background for her upright piano and old leather chair with patterned pillows. He ran his fingers over the keys of her well-used piano. "I heard you playing. It was beautiful."

"Thanks," she called from the kitchen where she took items from her large carry bag and plopped them into a tiny orange purse.

"I assumed you'd have a grand."

"No room," she said. "Ready?"

When she turned around and flashed him a smile, he knew he wasn't anywhere near ready to spend the evening with her on his arm. "Do you have a coat?"

"My wrap. It's by the door." He draped the flimsy material around her shoulders and tortured himself on her scent. Tonight she smelled like sin, straight up.

She locked the door behind her as he tested the wood of her porch stairs. "You need to replace this step."

"I know," she said. "I just haven't gotten around to it yet."

He gripped the porch rail and wiggled it back and forth. "This banister is loose."

She stopped dead when she saw his car and he wondered, not for the first time, if he should have brought his truck. "Whose car is that?" she asked.

"Mine." He held open the passenger door to the German import he'd bought on a whim when he'd felt restless last year. He had a past full of expensive whims that had never satisfied for more than a day or two.

"Why did you drive around in that rental car if you had this gorgeous sedan?"

"I don't take this to work," he explained. "It sends the wrong message."

"So where do you drive this?"

"Dates, long trips." He shrugged and wished he'd hung his suit coat up before getting behind the wheel. "It mostly stays in the garage."

"Speaking of dates," she said. "Have you had any in a while?"

"One or two."

"Which is it?" she asked. "One or two?"

He consciously relaxed his hands on the wheel instead of gripping them as if they were around her nosy throat. "One."

"And?" she prodded.

"And it went fine. We had dinner."

"Oh." She tapped her long, manicured fingers on her leg, drawing his attention to the hem that rose to mid-thigh. Her legs went on forever. "Are you going to see her again?"

He struggled to put the woman out of his mind. His head was too full of Allie to think of Kathryn, the twenty-eight year old dietician he'd taken to bed and had yet to contact. She'd seemed okay with him leaving in the middle of the night without a promise for more. He'd never felt as though encounters like theirs were anything more than what they were: mutual gratification without any strings. He doubted Allie felt the same. "Maybe."

"Oh. That's progress. I haven't contemplated a second date in longer than I can remember."

"Why is that, Allie? What's wrong with all these men you go out with?"

"Nothing. Or, nothing specific. Jared, my Monday date, he seemed a little too unfocused about his career. He has a degree in finance, but didn't want to be a banker or a stock broker, so he worked in a pawn shop before starting his own nursery."

"Plants or kids?"

The sound of her laugh had him stifling the urge to roll the windows down and press on the gas pedal for the sheer pleasure of doing something wicked.

"Plants. I think he's using that finance degree to try and keep himself out of bankruptcy. I know this sounds petty, but I don't want to date a guy who's floundering in his career."

"Makes you wonder if he'd get bored with women the way he does with his job."

She grazed his leg with her hand and had him gritting his teeth. "Exactly."

He could have mentioned he felt the same about the women he dated, but didn't want to encourage her after the way her eyes lit up after his last statement. "You said you had three dates."

"Ah, yes. Bradley was a chiropractor, so his job wasn't the problem."

"Chiropractors are quacks," Craig said.

"Ummm, I used to think so, but I saw one after I hurt my back running and he really helped."

"It was all in your head."

"You've obviously never been to a chiropractor."

"So what was Bradley's problem, other than his occupation and pretentious name?"

"He kept staring at my chest, and before you say anything, I covered my girls up, thank you very much."

He lifted a brow at her. "Your girls?"

"I'm just trying to speak your language."

"Do you ever call these guys out when you catch them staring at your rack?"

"What? No. Good grief, what in the world would I say? *Please stop staring at my chest? My eyes are up here?*" She gave a self-conscious chuckle. "I just take off major points."

"Oh, you keep a tally?"

"Well..." She swiveled in the seat to face him. The shifting of positions brought her perfume fluttering to his side of the car. "Don't you?"

He considered her question. "I guess, yeah. I suppose I do."

"So what was it about this woman you went out with that makes you maybe want to go out again?"

Nothing, if he were honest. Nothing but the fact that she didn't mind him using her for sex and attempting to purge his mind of Allie. "I'd say because she was nice and didn't seem to have too many character flaws."

"Such as?"

"Such as whining about her job or former boyfriend or life in general."

"So what did you talk about?"

"Her job. She's a caterer. Our backgrounds." He shrugged. They hadn't covered much ground before she'd placed her hand over his on the table and suggested they skip dessert and go to her place. Who was he to refuse and why had he felt guilty the moment it was over? "The usual. What about the third date?"

"Carlton."

"I'm sorry for calling Bradley pretentious, but go on."

"He's a doctor—doing his fellowship, actually. Good looking, obviously smart."

"So what was his problem?"

"He kept getting beeped during dinner. I'm not sure we discussed more than our names and occupations."

"That does sound petty, Allie. He is a doctor."

"Exactly. So if I'm bothered by it now, do you think it'll get better or worse in the future? Besides, there were no tingles or bolts of electricity."

Craig pulled into the parking area for the address she'd given him. "This is it?" he asked as the valet came around to his window. The twinkling lights around the arbored entrance only added to the not-very-wedding-like feel of the location.

Allie ducked her head and leaned closer to his shoulder. He could feel her breath on his cheek as she said, "Apparently so. Ready?"

He worried about the tingle she brought to every orifice of his body and wondered how long he could resist the giant bolt of electricity that would strike at a moment's notice. "Ready or not."

CHAPTER 21

Mark brought the pizza in from the kitchen and set it on the coffee table next to the plates and napkins Leah had placed beside the salad Carolyn had made. Both of his women sat on the couch with a space in the middle reserved just for him.

"So what movie did you ladies decide on?" he asked.

Leah crossed her arms over her chest and Carolyn took a deep breath he now recognized as a calming mechanism when dealing with her stepdaughter.

"I suggested we watch The Lorax," Carolyn said.

"That's a baby movie, Dad. I want to see One for the Money."

"I've never heard of either one," Mark admitted. "What's the money one rated?"

"It's PG-13," Leah said. She leaned forward, jutting her head around him to look at Carolyn. "I've seen lots of PG-13 movies."

"I looked it up online, Mark." Carolyn put her hand on his leg and gave him a glare with her eyes that said he'd be a fool to let his innocent daughter watch the film. "It's got violence, sexual references, drugs, and partial nudity. I don't think that's appropriate for a twelve-year old."

Be careful, he told himself. Carolyn's by-the-book parenting style was the cause of much of the tension in the house. "Well, why don't we watch the trailer, and then we'll see?"

Leah pressed the preview button on the remote and Katherine Heigl's face appeared on the screen. He wouldn't mind spending the evening with Katherine Heigl. Carolyn pressed her elbow into his side as a grandma said bastard, squeezed his leg when an older man covered his privates with a newspaper, and threw her hands in the air when the clip ended on a couple of hookers.

"Hookers?" she said. "Need I say more?"

"I know what a hooker is, Carolyn," Leah spouted. "I'm not five."

"I know you're not five, but twelve-year olds don't need to watch a movie with guns, hookers, and naked, old men."

"How about The Vow?" Mark offered. He'd heard both of them, on separate occasions, express an interest in seeing the chick flick. He could stomach a sappy love story if it meant keeping the peace.

Leah tried not to act excited, but raised her chin in the air. "That would be okay."

"Well, at least they're married," Carolyn said. "I guess that would be fine, but you don't want to watch The Vow, do you, Mark?"

"I do now." He leaned over and kissed his wife's cheek. "Leah, order her up while I dish us up this homemade, special order pizza."

An hour and a half later, with a full belly and both of his girls crying, Mark flicked off the television. "Well, that was predictable."

"It was awesome, Dad. How could you not like it?"

"I just said it was predictable, not that I didn't like it." Although he hadn't, but he knew better than to fight her on the merits of a chick flick.

"You slept through half of it." Carolyn gathered their plates and shuffled into the kitchen with Mark on her heels with the salad bowl.

She put the left over pizza in a storage bag while he covered the salad and hoped to get another day out of the lettuce. He placed both containers in the refrigerator before backing his wife against the counter out of view of the den.

"How about I cash in on all that romance? After my power nap, I'm feeling recharged."

She snaked her hands up the back of his shirt as the corners of her lips lifted into a smile. He loved the way her dark eyes grew even darker at his touch. He nipped at her lip and had just angled his head and taken their playful kisses deeper when Leah walked into the kitchen and slammed her glass on the counter.

"Gross."

Mark straightened as Carolyn shoved at his chest.

"What's so gross, Leah?" he asked. "We are married."

"You're also my dad."

"You don't think it's normal for husbands and wives to kiss?" he asked. "Didn't we just watch an entire movie where that's pretty much all they did?"

"That was a movie. I'll bet they wouldn't be all over each other if they had a kid in the house."

"Honey," Mark said and grasped her arm as she tried to sprint out of kitchen after sending a withering stare in Carolyn's direction. "I love Carolyn. People in love kiss and hug and touch. I know you're not used to seeing me kiss a woman, but you need to get used to it and know that it's normal."

"Whatever, Dad. I'm going to bed." She stormed out of the room, up the stairs, and slammed her door.

"That went well," Carolyn said. "I just can't win with her, Mark."

"We can't win. I have a feeling we aren't the only parents dealing with hormonal angst at her age."

"This isn't hormonal angst. This is 'I hate my stepmom' angst." She rubbed her temples with her fingers and leaned back against the counter.

Not only had Leah upset his wife, but she'd pretty much ruined the mood he was hoping to segue into the bedroom. "She doesn't hate you, sweetheart. She's just adjusting. We've been pretty careful to shield her from the physical side of our relationship. Maybe it's time we started acting like the newlyweds we are."

"You want to have sex on the counter?"

"I'd suggest the table first. The height seems like it would work better."

She slapped him on the chest. "Nice to know you've given this some thought."

"Sweetheart, there isn't a surface in this house that I haven't imagined making love to you on, but that's not what I mean. If I want to give you more than a friendly peck on the lips before I go to work in the morning—which most days I do—I think I should."

"Don't you think that'll be a little too in-your-face for Leah?"

"No. I think it would be normal activity that she needs to see and get used to. We don't need to smother the physical part of being in love. She doesn't know what normal looks like. Becca died when Leah was four. She doesn't remember much about her mother, and I'm certain memories of us touching and kissing aren't what she remembers."

Carolyn sighed. "She's just going to hate me more if you attack me before going to work."

"No, she'll learn how husbands and wives treat each other when they're madly in love."

"I don't think I'll be able to relax and let you attack me."

He glided over to stand in front of her and put his hands on her shoulders. "Then maybe we should practice." He felt her muscles tense and then relax against him as he nibbled along her neck and gave her jaw a friendly bite. He swallowed her moan as she melted against him and ran her fingers through his hair in the way that never ceased to excite him.

"Maybe next weekend we can get Craig to watch her and try out the table."

"Just the table?" he asked.

"For starters."

***

"Is that a bathtub?" Craig asked as they approached the entrance. "And what is that metal thing? A bug? A warrior?"

Allie rolled her eyes and wrapped her hand around Craig's arm. She wouldn't let herself worry if she invaded his space. He'd agreed to be her date and that required a certain amount of touching. "It's different and fun. I've never been here before, have you?"

"No," he said with a scowl. "Why would I have been?"

"Oh!" she said as they entered the space. The thrum of jazz greeted their entrance along with the subtle scent of gardenia. There were tea candles on every shelf and ledge in the enormous space. "It's an antique mart."

"We're supposed to buy something?"

"No." She slapped him playfully on the arm. "But look at all this great stuff."

Craig lifted the tail to a fox stole wrapped around the neck of a dressmaker's dummy. "What the hell is this?"

"It's a stole." When he looked at her as if she'd spoken Russian, she said, "A wrap."

"People pay money to wrap a dead animal around their neck?"

"It's vintage. I remember my grandmother used to have one. I'd play with it like a pet before she'd shoo me away." She plucked a glass of champagne from a bow tie wearing server and looked down at the cement floor with a red painted trail. "I think we should follow the path."

They wound their way around the store, through booths featuring retro light fixtures, scrap metal art, and hundreds of other unique items. "Look at this," she said when she spotted a denim colored glass bud vase. "It's so pretty."

"It's tiny. What would you do with it?" He looked at the price tag and lifted his brows.

"Put a small spray of wildflowers in it or a single stem."

"Seems kinda silly to me."

"Says the man with an empty home."

She held it up to the light and, on impulse, brought it next to his cheek. "I'm too big to fit inside."

"It's the color of your eyes." She set it down when he looked like she'd kneed him in the balls. "Why don't we find the bar and get you a drink?"

"Sounds like a plan."

They wandered along the path, but could have found the bar by simply following the buzz of people. She spotted Melissa and Ben nestled against a red velvet chaise with a life-sized mannequin peering over their shoulder. "I see some friends." She had to raise her voice in the thick crowd.

"Why don't you go say hi and I'll bring you a drink?" he said. "Wine?"

"Perfect." She watched him make a beeline to the bar and threaded her way toward Melissa.

Her friend squealed and hopped up to give Allie a hug. "Isn't this place fabulous?" Melissa asked. She looked stunning in her chiffon shift dress.

"It's an unusual setting for a wedding and a whole lot of fun—pretty much the last thing I expected from Sharon."

"So where is he?" Melissa asked, her eyes darting around the room.

"At the bar getting us a drink."

Melissa craned her neck. "Which one? There are so many people here."

"He's up by the front. Gray suit, blue tie." Allie's stomach fluttered with nerves at the prospect of Craig meeting Melissa and Ben. She wondered if he'd feel ambushed.

"Very nice," Melissa purred. "I knew you were lying when you said he wasn't that attractive."

Allie tried to look indifferent. "Every guy looks good in a suit. Even you, Ben," she said when he stood up after tucking the phone in his pocket.

"Hey, Al," he said. "Looking good."

"Thanks. You too."

Ben looked at his wife. "Your mom said Henry's asleep and she's got the Law & Order marathon to keep her company. I think we're good to go."

They clinked their glasses as Craig arrived and handed Allie her wine. "Just in time for the toast," he said.

"Melissa and Ben Carter," Allie began the introductions. "Meet Craig Archer."

Ben and Craig exchanged handshakes while he and Melissa nodded in greeting. "Melissa was my college roommate."

"Vandy?" Craig asked.

Melissa grinned and nodded, shooting a smug look at Allie.

"They look pretty good this year for basketball," Craig said.

"It's usually our only shot at the bigs," Melissa said. "Ben went to Duke, so Vandy gets second billing in our house."

Craig and Ben began the male ritual of discovering their professions while Melissa and Allie peered around the room. "Where's the wedding going to be held?" Allie asked.

"From what I gather, behind that door is a stage set up for the wedding."

"A stage? Is this for real or a theater production?"

"You know her fiancé is in the music business," Melissa said.

"I thought he worked for a TV station."

"Maybe that's it. I can't remember." She squeezed Allie's arm when the door to the main room opened and the guests began descending the ramp. "The show is about to start."

Allie and Craig filed into the room where four-top tables draped in black linens and topped with red votive candles surrounded a red carpet leading to the stage. They snagged a table in the middle and looked around as guests took seats at tables and lined up against the back wall bar.

"This keeps getting weirder and weirder," Craig whispered into her ear. She could feel his arm braced against the back of her chair.

"I'm not sure what to expect. This isn't exactly Sharon's style." Or at least not that Allie knew.

When the groom and his attendants began lining up on stage and a song Allie recognized began playing over the speakers, she shot her brows up and smirked at Melissa.

"Is this "Here, There and Everywhere" by the Beatles?" Melissa asked with an astonished look on her face.

"I do believe you're right." Allie stifled a giggle. Despite the unusual song, when the bridesmaids started down the aisle wearing knee length dresses right out of the 1950s, Allie felt her pulse quicken. "I don't recall Sharon being cool enough to pull this off." But when her long time acquaintance stepped onto the red carpet wearing a form fitting mermaid dress and a vintage hat with birdcage veil, Allie gasped.

"I'd say she's pulling this off," Melissa whispered. "She looks beautiful."

Allie tore her eyes from Sharon to stare at the groom. From half way across the room, Allie could see the sheen of tears in his eyes and the adoring look on his ruddy face. Allie didn't envy Sharon her groom, but would have cut off her left hand for a man to look at her with that much love in his eyes. She sniffled as her throat closed.

Craig leaned in again, his breath tickling her neck. "Tell me you're not crying."

"I can't help it. They look so happy."

"Jeez, Blondie." He rolled his eyes when she looked back at him, but he pulled a tissue out of her purse and handed it to her. She dabbed at her eyes as Sharon and her groom held hands and chuckled their way through the short, but emotion filled ceremony. They marched out of the room to Frank Sinatra's "Fly Me To The Moon."

"Well," Craig said as the crowd began mingling around the room. "At least it was quick."

"That was very heartfelt," Allie said to Melissa. "Unusual, but lovely."

"Where's the chow?" Craig asked. She could tell he was trying to lighten her mood. "You promised me food."

Ben pointed up the ramp to the room where they'd started. "I see a buffet line forming now."

"I'm going to hit the restroom first," Craig said. "I'll meet you in line."

She nodded and watched him walk away.

"How'd you meet Craig Archer?" Ben asked.

"He's the uncle of one of my clients. Plus I ran into his car, or he ran into mine. We had an accident."

"What was he driving?" Ben asked. "A Maserati?"

"Why would you ask me that?"

"Allie, that guy's worth a few million."

Allie dropped her wine glass away from her mouth before she could take a sip. "What are you talking about, Ben? He's a home renovator."

"I'm sure he can dabble in whatever he wants since he sold Archer Construction a few years ago."

"How do you know this?"

"I'm an engineer, remember? His company built some of the biggest buildings in Atlanta and the southeast. He sold out to Bell Buildings what…" He looked up at the ceiling where a fan lazily spun the fragrant air. "Five, six years ago, before the market went to crap. He's loaded."

Craig? Loaded? "Are you sure?"

"Positive," Ben said. "You reeled in a big fish this time."

CHAPTER 22

Melissa returned to the table from the buffet line before Craig and Allie. They had gone to the carving station together. They made an incredible couple, so easy on the eyes and easy with each other.

Ben sat down next to her before frowning at his empty glass. "You need another drink?" he asked. "I'm going to the bar."

"No, I'm good for now."

"I'm getting you another."

"Are you trying to get me drunk?" she asked.

"Not a bad idea." He rubbed her shoulder and then leaned down to nip at her skin. "But the bar's packed and I don't want to have to fight the crowd ten minutes after I get back."

God it felt good to get out of the house, get out of their suburban bubble, and be with her husband again. She loved her son more than anything in the world, but it felt exquisite to be something other than a mommy for a night. She popped an olive into her mouth and sat back to wait for someone to return to the table before she dug into her plate. She glanced up in time to see Craig leading Allie back into the room with his hand at the small of her back.

"Would you please quit talking to me as if I've always had men at my beck and call?" Allie said to Craig. "I didn't even go to prom, and not because I didn't want to. Nobody even asked."

They set their plates down and Craig helped her into her seat. He had great manners.

148

"That's because you were beautiful, smart, and quiet," Craig countered. "Not many teenagers can work up the courage to ask a girl like you out."

"You would," Allie said, snapping her napkin onto her lap. "So, what unattractive, stupid chatterbox did you take to prom?"

Craig's smile brought out an adorable set of dimples Melissa hadn't expected to find on such a rugged face. "Annabeth Collins."

"So you admit she wasn't pretty, smart, or quiet?"

"She was easy, which was my only qualification back then."

"Of course it was." Allie picked up her fork and moved food around her plate. "Why do I even bother trying to have a conversation with you?"

Melissa had never seen Allie so relaxed with a man and felt her enjoyment of the night kick into high gear.

"Where's Ben?" Allie asked.

"At the bar. He needed a refill."

Craig glanced at his and Allie's glasses. "Not a bad idea." He stood up and pointed at Allie's wine. "You want another?"

"Sure," she said and smiled as he walked off.

"He likes you, Allie, and you like him. I don't know why you refuse to admit it."

"We're friends. Why can't you accept that for the first time in my life, I have a male friend?"

"Because friends don't look at one another the way the two of you look at each other."

Allie peered down her nose at Melissa. "Would you please stop putting ideas into my head? Yes, I like him. I like having him as a friend. He's helping me understand the men I date and I'm trying to do the same for him. Why do you have to ruin it with all this talk?"

"I'm not trying to ruin your friendship, but you have to admit he's good for you. I've never seen you like this around a guy, so comfortable and so…you. You act like yourself around him, and I think that's great."

"That's because there's no pressure. He's not interested in me, so I don't have to worry about what I say and how I look and what I do. I can be myself and I'm enjoying it. So, yes, I'm enjoying him. If there's an undertone of attraction, believe me, it's one sided."

"For him to be so uninterested, he sure is careful to watch where you are and who you're talking to."

"He's probably afraid I'm going to ditch him."

"He doesn't look afraid, Allie, he looks interested."

"He's not. And neither am I."

"Really?" Melissa asked. "So you don't mind that he's talking to one of the bridesmaids?"

Allie whipped her head around to where Craig stood talking to Ben. She'd turned too quickly to pretend not to be jealous. "Ha. Very funny."

"You didn't seem too uninterested."

"Look, quit stirring the pot. He's made it abundantly clear that I'm not his type."

"We've covered this, Allie. If he's not gay—and if he is, my gaydar is broken beyond repair—then he's interested. And I say that for more than just the obvious. He's at a wedding where he doesn't know the bride or groom. He's just met Ben and me, so we're not the appeal. He's having a good time. He's having a good time with you."

"Which is why we're friends." Allie speared a lobster filled ravioli with her fork and glanced up, only to blanch before Melissa's eyes. "Oh, God."

"What's wrong?" Melissa asked.

Allie nodded with her head behind Melissa's shoulder. "Nick's here."

***

Craig returned to the table with his beer and a wine for Allie just as she bolted from her chair and made her way through the crowd. "Everything okay?" Craig asked.

"Allie's going to the restroom." Melissa dropped her napkin on the table and stood up. "I think I'll join her. Excuse me, please."

Ben shrugged at Craig and, after depositing the drinks on the table, sat down and started eating.

Craig tried to listen as Ben asked him question after question about Archer Construction and the sale and his renovation work. He answered, ate, and all the while couldn't help but worry about the look he saw on Allie's face before she barreled past him. He couldn't imagine what could have upset her in so little time, leaving her pale and anxious. When Melissa returned to the table without Allie, his sense of dread felt justified.

"Did you lose someone?" he asked.

"Allie needed some air. She said to tell you she'd be back in a minute."

Needed some air? In this neighborhood? Craig stood up and grabbed Allie's wine. "Which way'd she go?"

Melissa pointed to the corner of the room to a set of double doors. "Up those stairs and out back to the deck."

He nodded and navigated through the crowd, past funky couches and an elevated seating area set for the bride and groom whenever they made their grand reentry. He pushed open the doors and felt the cold air hit him as the scent of cigarette and cigar smoke lingered in the air. Allie stood in the corner of the deck next to an enormous metal replica of the Eiffel tower with a gorilla climbing its side, staring out at the skyline.

When he tapped her on the shoulder, she let out a startled gasp and then gave him a brilliant smile that didn't reach her eyes. He handed her the glass of wine. "You okay?" he asked.

She nodded and took a sip. He slipped his suit coat off and draped it over her shoulders. "No," she said. "I'm okay."

"You're shivering, Allie." He walked behind her and ran his hands up and down her arms. He didn't know what had happened to upset her, but he would do anything to see the sparkle back in her eyes. "So what happened?"

"Nothing. I just..." She lifted her shoulders, let them drop. "I just needed some air."

"Allie." He gently turned her to face him. "What's wrong?"

She sighed and took another sip of wine. "My ex-boyfriend is here. I didn't think...it was...unexpected. I don't know why I'm upset."

"Do you still love him?"

She let out a startled laugh. "Love him? No, I don't think I ever did. I thought I did when we were together, but it wasn't love. I'm not quite sure what it was."

"Then why do you care that he's here?"

She looked over his shoulder. "It's painful to see him, to remember how vulnerable I was. He made me feel so small, so absolutely pointless."

For that and for putting the sad look in her eyes, Craig wanted to punch him. "You don't need me to tell you you're not pointless."

"No. I don't, but I appreciate you saying it." She grabbed his hand and squeezed. "I'm feeling sorry for myself, and I'm just about done."

"Is he still here?" Craig asked.

"I'm sure. It wouldn't faze him to see me. As a matter of fact, I'm sure he'd waltz his date up to my face just to make me squirm."

"He sounds like an ass."

"He was. He probably still is." She turned around and leaned against the deck rail. "I don't want him, Craig. I'm so glad to be rid of him, but…it hurts my pride that he didn't want me. That he tossed me away as if I didn't mean a damn. And I should be ashamed of myself saying this to a man who lost his wife. I'm sorry."

Craig didn't think. If he had, even for a second, he wouldn't have let compassion and an odd need to soothe overrule his common sense. "My wife cheated, Allie, and I didn't have a clue until after she was dead."

Her gasp of surprise nearly did him in, but the pitiful look in her eyes and the trembling fingers that grazed his face had something inside of him cracking. He could almost feel the fissures in the wall he'd built straining for release. "Oh, Craig."

"Three months after I buried her, I found some emails on her computer. I didn't know who he was. It didn't matter. It still doesn't matter, but knowing she'd turned to someone else made everything we had feel like less."

"Yes," she said. "That's exactly it."

He felt fate connecting them, like a spider making a web around the two of them on the deck under the watchful eye of the gorilla. Standing under the starry sky with Allie's hand on his chest and her heart in her eyes, he didn't know why he'd told her what he'd never told anyone else, but he knew the rest had to stay with him.

"Only I don't have to run into her at parties and put on a happy face."

"Oh, Craig." She kissed his cheek and rested her forehead against his. The web became tighter and much more dangerous. "I wish you could see her at parties. I don't like Nick very much, but I don't wish him dead."

"In a way, I'm glad that choice was taken out of my hands." He wrapped her shoulders in his arm and plucked the empty wine glass from her hands. He didn't know what was making her get to him, but he needed to break free of the web for some distance. "You're freezing. Come on," he said and pulled her toward the building. "You hardly ate and you've sucked down that glass of wine. If I don't want to have to carry you out of here—and I don't—you'd better put some food in that belly."

**

Melissa watched them reenter the room, Craig's arm draped over Allie's shoulders, their faces red from the cold. Allie didn't look so unnerved, and she didn't even look around the room for Nick like Melissa expected her to do.

"Boy, it must be freezing out there," Melissa said as Allie slipped out of Craig's coat and handed it back before taking a seat at the table.

"It was. Thank goodness it's not in here."

"Not with all the dancing going on." Melissa nodded with her head to the dance floor where couples were dancing to the eclectic mix of tunes from the DJ that had her toe tapping under the table. "Your food's got to be cold. Why don't you get another plate?"

Allie shrugged and glanced back toward the buffet. There were only a handful of people in line. "I guess I should." She looked at Craig's empty plate. "Do you want seconds?"

"No, I'm fine." He stood up when she did. "I'll get you a drink."

Allie settled a hand on her stomach. "Just water for me, thanks."

When they both left the table in different directions, Ben leaned over and pulled on a lock of her hair. "What're you thinking?"

"Huh?"

He patted her temple with his finger. "The wheels are turning in there, Mel. I can see them. What are you planning?"

"Nothing. I don't think I have to plan anything." She pushed her plate away and picked up her wine glass, turned to face her husband. "They're more than friends, don't you think? I think they really care about one another."

"So?"

"So I think Allie is falling for this guy in a normal, healthy way."

"Then why do you look like you're going to stick your nose in where it doesn't belong?"

"Because that's what friends do."

"Melissa…"

"You know Allie, Ben. You know how she's her own worst enemy with guys."

"Craig doesn't seem like the kind of guy who spooks easily," Ben said.

"He doesn't seem like the kind of guy who sticks his neck out at all. From what Allie's told me, he's pretty closed off with women. He likes her. A blind man could tell he likes her."

"So why don't you let them figure it out themselves? If you stick your nose in, you're going to be the one they blame if it falls apart."

"I'm not going to stick my nose in," Melissa said as she saw Craig returning to the table with a glass of water for Allie. "I'm just going to give him a gentle prod."

Ben stood up. "I'm not going to be an accessory. I'm getting another drink, and when I get back, you're going to dance with me."

Craig set the water down and took a seat, but not before glancing over his shoulder to where Allie stood talking to a college friend. "So which one of the guys in here is the prick who broke Allie's heart?" he asked without preamble.

Good, Melissa thought. He was making this easier than she could have hoped. She twisted in her seat and studied the crowd. She spotted Nick near the edge of the dance floor with a brunette beauty wrapped around his arm. She turned back to Craig. "Behind me," she said. "Ten o'clock. Dark suit, pink tie, with a Megan Foxx lookalike on his arm."

Craig's eyes narrowed as he locked on the target. She only hoped Nick saw him and squirmed under his stare.

"He sure likes the pretty ones, doesn't he?"

"He likes himself, mostly." Craig's glare shot to hers. "I didn't care for him. At all. And he didn't break Allie's heart, but he sure gave it a nice big bruise."

"How long did they date?"

"Over a year. Allie expected a proposal after she'd molded herself into what she thought he wanted her to be. Instead he told her—without remorse—that she wasn't enough for him and that he'd met someone else. The guy's dirt."

"No argument here." He sat back after finishing off the last sip of his beer.

"They made a stunning couple and, on paper, they seemed destined for a Cinderella wedding. He was all wrong for her and she wanted so desperately to be in love that she couldn't see what an ass he was."

"I think she sees it now."

"Yeah. She's better now. Happy in her own skin. Most people can't understand how someone so physically beautiful could be unhappy. Allie doesn't feel beautiful, she just feels unloved." Melissa scooted her chair closer to Craig and leaned in so she wouldn't be overheard. "Do you know what she told me once?"

Craig lifted his brows and tried his best to look uninterested, but Melissa could tell by the way he shifted toward her that he was more than curious. "She asked me if the guys I dated—back when I was dating—ever closed their eyes when they kissed me because the guys she dated never closed their eyes. She said she couldn't relax because they always watched her, and she couldn't stop thinking about what she looked like and how they expected her to act."

Craig gave her a look that said, "So?"

"No one has ever kissed her and made her stop thinking." Melissa took a sip from her wine and tipped the glass in his direction. "I think you're the man for the job."

He lifted his hands from the table in a gesture of surrender. "We're just friends."

"You're friends, but I don't believe the just."

"Believe it or not," he said as if he could have cared less. "Trust me, I'm the last person Allie needs in her life."

"If I believed that, Craig, you wouldn't be sitting here right now."

CHAPTER 23

As soon as Allie sat down, Ben came back from the bar and whisked Melissa into his arms for a turn around the dance floor. Allie smiled as she watched them until she saw Nick and his date talking with another couple by the dance floor.

What a creep. His date must be his girlfriend as her dress perfectly matched his tie. She remembered how important it used to be for Nick that their outfits coordinate. What had she ever found appealing about him in the first place?

She shook thoughts of him away and let the bombshell Craig had dropped try to settle in her head. How had he done it? How had he survived after discovering the worst thing about the person who'd sworn before God to love, honor, and cherish him when she wasn't around to defend herself or explain?

"You keep scowling into your food and people are going to think the stuff is bad."

Allie grinned up at Craig. "Sorry."

He lifted a shoulder and flashed her a dimple. "I'm not the caterer."

"It's actually very good. Of course, I was starving, so that might factor in."

"Did you skip lunch again?"

He paid too much attention. "Yes."

"Why do you do that? If you tell me you're dieting, I'm going to punch you."

"I'm not dieting, I just forget to eat. By the time I realize I'm hungry, it's too late to have a meal, so I wait for dinner."

"You need to take better care of yourself."

She pushed her plate away and rested a hand on her full stomach. "I could stand to lose a few pounds."

Craig punched her lightly in the arm. "Allie, you've got to be kidding me."

"I am. Sort of." She glanced at Nick as his hand sneaked around his size two date's waist. "Nick used to encourage me to lose weight."

"If you believed him, I'm losing respect for you by the minute."

"It's hard not to believe the person who sees you naked."

Allie watched as Craig shifted in his seat, scanning the room with his jaw clenched. She felt uncomfortable for revealing too much of herself to him, especially about Nick.

"Since I haven't seen you naked, I can't really comment, but I'm more certain than ever the guy needs glasses. For you to spend a moment of your time second-guessing your looks is absurd. You're the most beautiful woman in the room and that includes the pixie stick your ex is draped over."

She felt her cheeks heat. "I wasn't fishing for compliments, Craig. I know my weight is fine. He just gets to me; he gets inside my head." She rested her elbows on the table and set her chin in her palm. "How did you get through discovering your wife cheated? How were you able to move on and have normal relationships?"

"Who said I have relationships?"

"Well, you want a relationship, don't you? Isn't that why you signed up at LoveFinders?"

"I signed up at LoveFinders to get Mark off my back. He's happy now, married and looking toward the future. He wants the same for me."

"Don't you want that for yourself?"

"I had that, and look where it got me." He sat up and looked around the room. "I'm better off on my own."

"Craig, you don't really mean that, do you? You don't really want to be alone forever?"

"Allie. I don't want to talk about this." He flipped a napkin over and over on the table while staring at it as if he'd find the answer he was seeking underneath. "No one knows Julie cheated."

"You didn't tell anyone?"

He shook his head from side to side, daring her to question him.

"Not even Mark?"

"Julie and Becca were best friends. Becca had to have known and if she knew, chances are Mark knew too."

"But you don't know for sure?"

"Knowing won't change anything."

"You might be able to figure out why."

"Do you know why Nick cheated on you?" he asked. "Does it help?"

Allie felt the sting of his question like a slap, but she'd started this conversation and she owed it to him to be honest. "He said I was boring, and whether or not it's true, it's how I think of myself now. So I guess there might be some solace in not knowing."

"First of all, you're not boring." He sat back and linked his fingers in his lap. "And second of all, I'm pretty sure why she cheated."

"Okay," she said, anxious for him to go on. He'd already told her more than he'd told anyone. Would it hurt to finish the story? "Why?"

"I worked all the time. I told myself it was for her, for all the stuff she wanted—the house, the cars, the lifestyle, but my business was growing and I couldn't let go of the reins. The bigger and faster it grew, the longer and harder I worked. I knew it was affecting her and our marriage, but I couldn't give up the control."

"I wouldn't call you a workaholic, Craig. You spend plenty of time with Leah."

"Some lessons are learned a little too late."

"Ben said you sold your company."

"Couple years ago. It was easy to let it go when it didn't mean very much anymore."

"Much harder to let your wife go."

"It about killed me—the grief and regret. Until I found those emails and it didn't mean very much anymore."

He was kidding himself about that, but she wasn't going to argue with a man so obviously haunted by his demons. "Thank you for telling me, Craig. It puts this whole situation with Nick into perspective."

"I don't want you thinking you're boring, Allie. I've never been bored around you."

"Give me time," she said to lighten the mood. "I'm not the most exciting person in the world, but I know he was wrong. It's kind of like the dates I've gone on. Mostly I feel nothing towards the men I meet online. No interest, no spark, nothing. I would have settled for nothing before. I did with Nick."

Craig reached over and ran his hand down her back. "Life's too short to feel nothing."

He may as well have scraped a match along her spine. She struggled not to shiver. Amazing how a simple touch could ignite her skin and send prickles of excitement through her body. He hadn't meant to set her insides on fire, and she felt sure he'd be shocked if he knew what he'd done.

"I know." She reached over and rested her hand on his leg. "Look at you. I've never felt nothing around you."

She recognized the panic that crossed his face, the way he gaped at her in stunned silence. Because she had no intention of making a move on a man who clearly had zero interest in her, she threw her head back and laughed. "Don't freak out, Craig. I was going to say that my irritation with you was worlds better than the nothing I usually feel for men." She wished the only emotion she felt toward Craig were irritation. "Besides, look at the lovely friendship that blossomed out of irritation."

***

Craig wasn't sure what possessed him to do it. It could have been the way she looked at him when he thought she'd meant more than irritation. It could have been the way she continued to touch him, a squeeze here, a tender graze there. It could have been the idea of waltzing her across the dance floor in front of her ex and watching him seethe in anger for what he'd given up. No matter what her ex had told her, no matter what she thought, any man who'd had a taste of Allie and walked away didn't walk away unscathed.

"Come on," he said after hopping to his feet. "Let's work off some of that food."

"You want to dance?" she asked.

He pulled her to her feet. "Why not? Isn't that what you do at weddings?"

He'd forgotten how powerfully her scent could entice him with all the other smells that littered the air. When he had her in his arms, her sinful fragrance kicked him in the gut. He forgot they weren't dating, he forgot he was doing her a favor, he forgot he didn't want the woman in his arms to match him step for step, sway for sway. If they were this in tune on the dance floor, how good would it be if he took her to bed?

"You're full of surprises, Craig Archer."

"My mom teaches dance at the Y back home. Her boys know how to dance."

"I'll say."

He expertly swung her around and back into his arms. He closed his eyes as her laughter filled his ears. "Ben told me you're loaded."

"What?" He pulled back and recognized the smirk on her face.

"He said you sold your company for several million."

"So?" he said when she continued to stare at him. "Does it matter?"

"No, I just didn't have a clue. I should have figured it out when I saw your house and that fantastic car we arrived in."

"Does it change the way you think of me?" he asked before he could stop himself. Now who was fishing for compliments? He'd lost his mind and was wading into dangerous territory.

"Ummm," she purred as his hand inched lower on her waist. "You're more complex, which I suppose makes you more attractive."

They were too close; the music, some seductive song that had images of New Orleans and sweaty sex mingling through his head, was too intoxicating. That stupid challenge Melissa had wagered kept running through his head. He was the man for the job, all right, but the job just might kill him.

Their gazes locked, and in Allie's eyes, he saw fear and desire. He wasn't so far out of the game that he couldn't recognize a woman begging to be kissed. His gaze drifted to her mouth where the tip of her tongue wet her bottom lip.

"Ouch," Allie said as the couple behind them slammed into Craig's back, causing him to slap his forehead against Allie's.

It was the douse of cold water he needed. Fate had stepped in and saved him from making a colossal mistake. A mistake that could have cost him a friendship and the very carefully erected walls he'd build around his heart. "Sorry." He gave his head a rub to ease the sting.

Did he really think he possessed enough self-control to stop with just a taste of Allie? He'd have gobbled her whole in a room full of her friends, embarrassing them both. It was better to never start something he had no intention of finishing. "I think that's our cue to end the dance."

"Oh, look," Allie said and pointed to the corner of the room. "They're cutting the cake."

"Are you going to cry again?"

"No, but I think I'd like another glass of wine."

He didn't need her drunk and willing, that was for sure. "How about some cake to wash it down?" he suggested.

"I'll get the cake," she said. "You get the wine."

"Deal."

They met back at the table and ate, drank, and watched as the happy couple danced and mingled around the room. When the bride approached their table, Craig marveled at how the women hugged and preened as if the best of friends. If Allie hadn't told him she didn't like the bride, he would never have guessed.

When the bride shifted to an adjacent table, Craig leaned over and asked, "So what is it you don't like about her again?"

"I'm not sure anymore." She played with the stem of her wineglass and pursed her lips in thought. "She was petty and jealous and sometimes mean." She looked over her shoulder to where the bride hugged an older woman. "I think falling in love and being happy has changed her for the better."

"For a little while, at least."

"Come on, Craig," she said. "I know you've been hurt in the worst possible way, but even you can't look at her, at them together, and think anything but the best for them."

"I wish them luck," he said. "They're going to need it."

"My parents had a terrible marriage. To this day, my mother is bitter and angry. My father moved on and he's been married now for almost twenty years." She looked him square in the eye. "Don't be like my mother, Craig. Don't choose to be unhappy."

"I'm not unhappy, Allie. Being alone doesn't mean I'm unhappy."

"Choosing to be alone forever may feel like the safe option, but being safe and being happy are two completely different things."

"Yeah, yeah, yeah. Is that free advice, or do I owe you something for your analysis?"

"Just keep your eyes open for the possibility of love. It's out there, Craig, for both of us. I, for one, am going to be ready when it arrives."

She would, Craig knew. She'd fall head over heels into the arms of some lucky bastard who could never appreciate all the fascinating aspects of Allie. He knew it would happen sooner rather than later and would bring an abrupt end to their friendship. Damn shame, he thought, because he'd never had a friend quite like Allie.

CHAPTER 24

C raig used one hand to balance on the ladder and used his other to retrieve his ringing cell phone. He was going to turn it off and continue spackling the drywall when he saw Mark's name on the display.

"Hey," he said, dropping the trowel and carefully descending the rungs. "What's up?"

"You're a hard man to get in touch with," Mark said. "I called you on Saturday and you didn't answer. Big date?"

He knew he should lie, tell Mark he'd gone out with some woman he'd met online, but he'd never felt comfortable lying to his little brother. They'd been through too much, shared too many things for him to be so callous. "I had a wedding."

"A wedding? Whose?"

Mark had always been nosey. "No one you know."

"*You* put on a suit and went to a wedding and all for someone I don't know? Now I'm not just curious, but intrigued. What gives?"

Damn it, did the man have any responsibilities at work? "Fine, I'll tell you, but I don't want you giving me any grief." He sighed and gritted his teeth before saying, "I went to a wedding with Allie. She needed a date. End of story."

"End of story? Sounds like the beginning of the story to me."

"Look, you were friends with Allie for years, so I'm not sure why you have such a hard time believing the two of us are just friends."

"I was friends with Allie because I was in love with Carolyn. Which is actually why I'm calling, but you don't have an excuse to be just friends with Allie."

"Sure I do. She's a woman in the classic sense of the word. She's bossy and nosey and full of opinions." And beautiful and vulnerable and so damn multilayered that she kept him on his toes every time they were together. When he'd dropped her off at her house, she'd kissed him on the cheek and he'd almost— almost—turned his head and discovered her exact flavor. His last thread of sanity and the offhand remark she'd made on the ride home about going to church the next morning were the only things that had kept him from giving in.

"And beautiful, and available, and probably hoping for a little Archer love. I don't know what happened to you, man, but you never used to try so hard to hide your conquests."

"Allie's not a conquest, you ass, she's a friend. Why is that so hard to believe?"

"Because I've known you all my life and I'm not stupid. The more you deny it, Craig, the more I know there's something going on. Just admit it. Do you think I'd have a problem with it?"

"There's nothing to admit other than the fact that you're wrong. Why are you calling me?"

Mark huffed out an impatient breath. "Carolyn and I could use a night alone. Any chance Leah can hang out with you on Saturday night, maybe have a sleepover?"

"Yeah," he said. "Of course. I'm meeting a potential client Saturday afternoon in Buckhead at three. I could pick her up on my way back, say five or so?"

"Perfect. She'll be excited. She wants to see that Katherine Heigl movie and Carolyn doesn't think it's appropriate."

"Are you warning me or telling me to let her watch it?"

"It's your call."

"But I'll catch hell from Carolyn if I let her watch it?"

"Not if she doesn't find out."

"You think Leah will keep her mouth shut? Not a chance."

"That's why it's your call," Mark said. "Listen, I've got a meeting. I'll have her ready on Saturday."

***

Allie reluctantly answered an email from LoveFinders when half the week had gone by and Craig hadn't called. She needed to get over her fascination with him and move on with her life. Greg Wallace, a six-foot-three, brown hair, brown-eyed environmental engineer seemed as a good a way as any to stop obsessing about Craig.

Why wouldn't he call? The better question, the one she knew she didn't want to answer, was why she wanted him to call. He'd been so compassionate with her at the wedding, admitting his most tortured secret to ease her embarrassment and pain. He was alone by choice and, if the circumstances were reversed, she might very well have chosen the same. Their circumstances weren't the same, and she wasn't about to turn her back on the possibility of love. Suffering through bad and mediocre dates was a small price to pay for finding love at the end of her rainbow. Her date with Greg, so far, hovered somewhere around the vicinity of mediocre.

"So what does an environmental engineer do, exactly?" she asked over a late afternoon coffee.

"I'm basically a consultant. I mainly work with the oil and gas industry and help them navigate the myriad of governmental regulations." He took a sip of his black coffee and chuckled as he set the cup on the table. "I don't know how you lean politically, but the current administration has been a boon to our business."

Allie cringed. A disagreement about politics could end the afternoon fast. "I try not to discuss politics on first dates."

"That's probably smart. I'm all about saving the environment—obviously—but some of these regulations are down right crazy. The oil industry in particular is getting hammered. If I didn't have family in Louisiana who worked off shore and know first hand how the oil and gas industry supports entire towns and regions of the country, it'd be easy to shake my fist at the big corporations. As it stands, I just keep my head down and try to do my job the best I can. I figure, hey, I'm not the one writing the regulations, I'm just trying to help companies operate within their boundaries. I wish my family felt the same."

"That's got to be tough, Greg. Do they give you a hard time?"

"Yeah, but then I come home in my new Mercedes and suddenly saving the planet is cool again."

Oh, goodness. That was the second time he'd mentioned his car. Not another one of those guys. "So you're from Louisiana?"

He nodded. "Went to LSU. Geaux Tigers!" He raised his fist in the air.

Allie wouldn't have been surprised if he'd had Les Miles' head tattooed on his forearm. She hoped never to find out. "How'd you end up in Atlanta?"

"I did my graduate work at Georgia Tech and interned for the company I'm with now."

"Do you think you'll stay in this area?"

"I kinda have to," he shrugged and lowered his eyes to the container of sugar packets on the table between them. "With the kid and all."

Allie's stomach dropped to her knees. "Kid?"

"Oh," he said and gave that jug head chuckle once more. "I haven't updated my profile yet. Just found out an ex-girlfriend named me in a paternity suit. I can't even think about leaving town until I get that squared away."

"What are you going to do if the child is yours?" she asked, although she couldn't have cared less. Greg, with the warm brown eyes and barrel chest, had just eradicated any prospect of a second date.

He shrugged. "Get a lawyer."

Get a lawyer! How about get a life. Allie slammed her silverware drawer shut and measured honey into a spoon. She knew she was overdoing it on the caffeine, but she couldn't shake the chill that had stayed with her since fighting the biting wind back to her car after her date. She brought her mug of tea to the table where her latest project for hire sat scattered along the surface. She needed to get this latest piece finished and off to the composer before her next project showed up on Monday as expected.

Her indignation about Greg's situation wouldn't let her go, and she needed to vent. She thought about calling Craig, but didn't want to sound desperate and alone on a Saturday night when he was probably out enjoying himself. She called Melissa instead.

"Hey, what are you doing?" she asked.

"Just walking out the door. I'm coming," Melissa said before apologizing. "Ben's heading for the car, threatening to leave me."

"Go on then. I'll call you tomorrow."

"What's up?" she asked. "You sound weird."

"I'm fine. Where are you headed?"

"Date night," Melissa squealed. "My mom said that since Henry is on a regular sleeping schedule, she wanted Ben and me to spend some regular time together. He's honking. I've got to run."

"Have fun," Allie said before hanging up the phone. Her married friend was having date night and she was all alone. Better than being with Greg, she told herself and got back to work.

An hour later, with the project done and tucked neatly in the mailing envelope for her to send on Monday, she looked around her den. She could practice the music she was playing at church the next morning, but she'd played it a hundred times over and knew each keystroke by heart. She could call her friend Beth. They'd reconnected at Sharon's wedding and she'd said she'd call so they could go out. Beth, with her steady boyfriend, held little appeal. She eyed the phone and walked around the den, straightening magazines and folding the throw she'd left tossed in a heap on the couch. Her house could certainly use a good cleaning, but even wallowing seemed a better use of her time on a Saturday night.

"What the heck," she said and dialed Craig's number. She sat on the edge of the couch with her free hand sandwiched between her knees. When a voice on the other end of the line said, "Hello," a voice Allie didn't recognize, a decidedly female voice, Allie blurted, "Wrong number," and tossed the phone away as if it were toxic. Oh crap, she thought and pulled the neatly folded throw over her head.

***

Craig watched the popcorn swirl around and around his microwave, listening for the pops to stop before the buzzer went off and burned the bag. Leah had already started in on him about the movie and he hadn't made up his mind about whether he'd let her watch it. They'd seen that stupid vampire movie, for God's sake, so how much worse could this one be? At least the characters were human. Of course, he hadn't had to worry about Carolyn's wrath back then.

He'd let Leah sweat it out a little longer.

He shook the popcorn into a bowl, poured two sodas, and called Leah to the kitchen for a hand.

"Allie called you," Leah said as soon as she walked into the kitchen.

"I didn't hear the phone ring," he said. Craig threw a piece of popcorn to Blackjack, who'd waited patiently for it to pop.

"I answered when I saw her name on the screen, but she said, 'wrong number,' and hung up. Why would she do that?"

Uh oh. "She probably thought you were a woman and she didn't want to interrupt."

"Like a date?" Leah giggled.

"Yes, squirt." He ruffled her hair and gave her armpits a poke with his fingers. "A date. I do that every now and again."

"Why don't you date Ms. Allie?" she asked as she carried the sodas to the den.

"Are you and your dad tag teaming me now or what?"

"Huh?"

"Never mind." He took a fist full of popcorn and tossed a piece into his mouth.

"Are you going to call her back?" Leah crossed her feet on the coffee table, mimicking Craig's posture.

He shrugged and began flipping through the list of movies they could order on the screen. He wasn't sure which topic would cause him more grief—the movie selection or discussing Allie. "I don't know."

"She called you for a reason," Leah pointed out. "Aren't you curious what it was?"

Unfortunately, his thoughts of Allie had moved well beyond curiosity, but he wasn't going to admit that to a twelve-year old. "Not really."

Leah held the phone in his face, blocking the screen. "Call her back, Uncle Craig. Tell her it was me and invite her over to watch the movie."

"You want me to invite her over? I thought you were looking forward to some special time with your uncle?"

"It won't be any less special with Allie here." She shook phone before his eyes. "Call her."

Craig sighed dramatically and took the phone from her hand. He went through his call history, saw her name, and hit talk. The phone rang three times before she answered.

"Hello?"

"Hey, Blondie. Did you call?"

He thought he heard her swallow. "Yeah, but it wasn't important. You can get back to your date."

He snuck a glance at Leah and lifted his brows suggestively. "My date's the one who insisted I call you back. She's pushy that way."

"I'm so sorry for interrupting, Craig. It was nothing, just another miserable date I thought you'd get a kick out of."

"What happened?" he asked.

"Go back to your date, Craig. This can wait."

"She's in the bathroom." He held his finger up to his lips to keep his giggling niece quiet. He may as well have a little fun with both of them. He tossed some more popcorn to Blackjack. "I've got some time."

"Craig, really. I'll call you later."

"Allie, really. Tell me what happened."

When she huffed into the phone, he knew he wouldn't have to ask her again.

"I've gone out with some idiots before, Craig, but this one takes the cake. He's just been named in a paternity suit with an ex-girlfriend and he doesn't even have a lawyer. He's got multiple graduate degrees, but not a lick of sense. Of course, he hasn't updated his profile to mention any of this, so us unsuspecting women wade into the mess he's made of his life. I mean, really, in this day and age, if he didn't wear a condom or ask if his girlfriend was on the pill, then he deserves the mess. I mean, I'm on the pill and I can't even remember the last time I had sex. The one I feel sorry for is the kid."

He didn't hear a thing but the word sex in her righteous tone. "Would you like to come over?" he asked to stop her tirade. "My date insists."

"What? Are you kidding? No."

"It's Leah, Allie. We're just trying to pick a movie. We could use a tie breaking vote."

"What are the choices?" she asked.

"One for the Money and Joyful Noise."

"I'm sure Joyful Noise is more appropriate—"

"I didn't ask which was more appropriate. Which one do you want to see?"

"Katherine Heigl or Dolly Parton? Do you really have to ask?"

"So which is it?" he had to ask.

"Katherine Heigl," she said. "So who's my new best friend?"

"We both are." He flashed a thumbs up to Leah. "But we may have to use you as cover for Carolyn."

"Understood. Popcorn?"

"Already popped."

"Twizzlers?" she asked.

"Uhhh..."

"I'll make a quick stop. Any requests?"

"Only you," he said and hung up the phone.

"Is she coming?" Leah asked.

"What can I say, squirt? I'm irresistible to women."

CHAPTER 25

Allie pulled the sheet music from her bag and rested it on the stand in front of Leah.

"What's this?" the girl asked.

"A little something I thought you could work on. It's challenging, but I think you can handle it. I'd like you to try and work on this for the recital."

"The recital? I already have my recital song down."

"Exactly. You won't continue to progress if you don't keep pushing yourself. I know you can do this, Leah, and you're ready to perform more than one piece at the recital."

"Urggh," Leah groaned. "Can you play it first?"

"I'd be happy to." They swapped places on the bench and Allie opened the sheet music. She'd chosen this song, a song she'd mastered as a girl, especially for Leah. Like it or not, she and Leah had formed a special bond thanks to Craig.

Mark walked in the door as Allie finished playing the tune. He stood in the foyer in the exact spot Craig used to stand and clapped his hands. "Wow. That was beautiful."

Carolyn came out from the kitchen. Her white blouse had a splash of sauce on the front. "I didn't expect you home," she said and popped up on her tippy toes to kiss him.

"Speaking of beautiful." Mark wrapped his arm around her waist and held her there while he deepened the kiss.

Allie felt her cheeks heat and whipped her head around to face the piano. Leah made a gagging noise while Allie hopped up and took her seat in the chair. "Now you give it a try."

Leah puffed out her cheeks, placed her fingers on the keyboard, and slowly began sight reading the piece. Allie kept time with a pat on her leg while her mind drifted back to the scene she'd just witnessed in the foyer. They were so in love. Mark, with his bright blonde hair and sunny personality, seemed to shine all of his light on dark and unsure Carolyn. The woman seemed to glow under his adoration. How could Craig not want what his brother had for himself?

She wasn't going to think about Craig. Not tonight.

By the end of the lesson, Allie knew Leah could easily perform the song in the Christmas recital. "Very good. I think you'll have this mastered in plenty of time."

Allie put her coat on.

"You're not staying for dinner?" Leah asked with a plea in her voice.

"Nope. I've got a date."

"With Uncle Craig?"

Allie placed her hand on Leah's shoulder. "Leah, you know we're just friends."

"You don't like my uncle?"

"Of course I like your uncle. That's why we're friends."

"But you're not going to date him?"

"No." Allie stepped into the foyer and peered into the kitchen. She didn't want to leave without saying goodbye, but she also didn't want to interrupt whatever was going on in the kitchen.

"Why not?" Leah asked.

"Why not what?"

"Why aren't you going to date my uncle?"

Allie sighed and gathered her patience. "For one thing, he hasn't asked."

"What if he did?"

"Leah, go tell your parents I'm leaving."

"*She's* not my parent."

"Fine." Allie glanced at her watch. "Go tell your dad and stepmom that I'm leaving."

Carolyn came into the foyer wiping her hands on a dishtowel. The splash of sauce had disappeared and was replaced by a water stain. "I thought I heard you stop playing. Will you stay for dinner?"

"I'd like to, Carolyn, but I can't tonight."

"She's got a date," Leah offered. "And it's not with Uncle Craig."

"Oh, well," Carolyn said, clearly unsure of how to answer. "Have a good time."

"Thanks. Leah did great. I gave her a new song and if she practices," Allie narrowed her eyes at Leah, "she should be able to perform two songs at the recital."

"We'll make sure she does."

***

Leah grabbed the portable phone from the den and bolted up the stairs after dinner. She closed herself in her room and dialed the number she knew by heart.

"Allie's on a date," she said as soon as her uncle answered.

"Hello to you, too."

"Did you hear what I said? Allie's on a date."

"So? She's a beautiful, single woman who's looking for love. That's what they do."

"You don't care?" she asked.

"About what?"

Leah sighed in frustration. She hated it when adults treated her like a kid. "That she's going on a date and it's not with you."

"Leah..."

"I know you like her. I don't understand why you don't ask her out. When she left tonight, she said the only reason she's not going out with you is because you haven't asked."

"She said that?"

"Yes, so why haven't you asked?"

Leah heard him sigh as time stretched out. The second hand of her cat clock went from the five to the eight before he spoke.

"We're friends, Leah. Friends don't date."

"My friend Nicole's older sister dates a guy who used to be her best friend."

"Yes, and if I were in middle school, I might just have to ask Allie out for that very reason."

"Nicole's sister's in high school."

"Drop it, squirt. Don't you have homework to do? Boys to chase? A dad to pester?"

Why couldn't her uncle see how perfect Allie was for him? "I've done my homework," she lied. "I'm not old enough to date according to my dad, and he's too busy playing kissy face with Carolyn to pester me."

"Do you need me to come over and mess with you then?"

"No. I need you to ask Allie out on a date. Please, Uncle Craig. Just one date. For me."

"I'd do just about anything for you, squirt, but not that. When your dad's done playing kissy face, have him call me, will ya?"

"Yeah," she said. "Whatever."

She turned off the phone and fell back on her bed. Nothing was turning out the way she wanted.

***

Craig picked up the phone on the first ring. "Mark?" he asked.

"Hey. Leah said you wanted me to call. What's up?"

"I'll tell you what's up." Craig took a swallow of beer and set the bottle down gently before he did something stupid and threw it against the wall. He wasn't sure why he was so angry, but Mark was going to suffer the brunt of his assault. "You and your daughter need to butt out of my life."

"Excuse me?"

"B-U-T-T O-U-T," he said slowly as if speaking to a toddler. "I don't need either one of you trying to fix me up with Allie. What she does on her own time is none of my business."

Then why did he feel like she'd stabbed him in the back and twisted the knife? "I don't have any idea what you're talking about," Mark said.

"Oh hell yes, you do. Your daughter called, announced Allie had a date, and pleaded for me to ask her out." But wasn't that why he felt so betrayed? Because after the evening the three of them had spent together, he'd spent a restless night dreaming of her? Because every time he logged onto that stupid dating site, he ended up staring at her profile wondering which Bozo would ask her out next? Because he couldn't get the image of her, snuggled up next to Leah on his couch, under his blanket, out of his mind?

"I didn't know she'd done that, Craig. I'm sorry. I'll have a talk with her."

"And tell her what?" Craig demanded. "To stop doing the very thing you do every time we talk?"

"Look—"

"No, you look. I'm sick of you two trying to set us up. I'm sick of having to defend my friendship with her, and I'm sick of you and Leah butting into something that is none of your business."

"Okay," Mark said. Craig could picture him standing somewhere in the house, his hands raised in the air. "Did you and Allie have a fight?"

"Urrrrrrgh!" Craig stomped into the den. "This is why I don't need women friends!" He hung up the phone and gave himself major points for not throwing it across the room and only dropping it on the couch. How dare his brother and his niece gang up on him about Allie? What was so damn special about her anyway?

CHAPTER 26

Being late for dates was the story of her life, Allie thought as she sprinted up her porch steps and tried to jam the key in the door. Something made her stop, stand up straight, and turn around. She walked back to the steps and used her foot to test the landing. It didn't budge. She grabbed ahold of the banister and tried to ease it back and forth. For all her effort, it didn't move.

Late or not, she had a phone call to make.

Craig barked a greeting into the phone. Allie held the receiver away from her ear before speaking nicely. "Hello, Craig."

"Allie?"

"Yes, it's Allie. Where are you and what in the world is that noise?"

"I'm at the house I'm renovating." She heard the noise recede into the background and recognized the strain in Craig's voice. He sounded exhausted. "They're working on the floors."

"Oh. Listen, I just got home and realized you fixed the step and the banister. I wish I had something better to say, but thank you. That was..." lovely, charming, and downright the sweetest thing anyone had ever done for her, "really great of you."

"It was nothing."

"It wasn't nothing, Craig. When did you do this and why didn't you tell me?"

"I stopped by yesterday. You weren't home, and I had my tools in the truck. It pissed me off that you hadn't fixed it yet, so I just hammered in a few nails. Like I said, no big deal."

"Well, it is to me, so thank you."

"You're welcome."

He didn't seem inclined to say anything more, and she'd missed the sound of his voice. "So, how are you?" she asked.

"I'm good. Busy, but good. You?"

"Good. Busy also, which is always good. I've been fighting something for the past week or so and I finally got some antibiotics, so I'm feeling better."

"Sick to your stomach?" he asked.

"No, just a cold that morphed into a sinus infection. It's almost gone."

"You been on any more dates?" he asked.

At the word date, Allie glanced at her watch. If she didn't hurry up, she'd never make it out of the shower before Jamie arrived. "Yes. As a matter of fact, I've got one tonight."

"First date?"

She let out a breath and said, "Believe it or not, this will be our third."

When he said nothing and the silence stretched out to an unbearable level, she said, "Craig?"

"Yeah, I'm here." She felt...uncomfortable talking to him. For the first time ever, their discussions about her dating seemed forced. "Third date, huh? Wow."

"Yeah, wow."

"Who's the lucky guy?"

"His name's Jamie and I didn't meet him online. Do you remember that girl I introduced you to at Sharon's wedding? Beth Morgan?"

"The one in the red dress a couple sizes too small?"

She had to laugh. Only Craig would remember her that way. "Yes. She and I met up over the weekend and we happened to run into her brother. We got to talking; he invited me to dinner. We really connected. We're going to the movies tonight, and on Saturday, he's taking me to Bones for dinner."

"Get the ribeye," Craig suggested. "You won't be disappointed."

"Ribeye," she said. "Check. What about you? Any dates, past or future, you'd like to share?"

"I've been too busy to do anything but crash when I get home." He ordered some guy to take his shoes off before going inside the house. "Sounds like I'd better get busy or I'm going to need a date to your wedding."

"Stop, please," she begged. She was having a hard enough time not getting ahead of herself with Jamie. "You do need to get out there, Craig. It feels good to be dating a normal person for once. It kind of makes all the bad dates worth the bother."

"I'll have to take your word for it. You make sure he treats you right."

"He does, don't worry."

"I mean it, Allie. Make sure he listens when you talk."

Allie laughed. Oh, Craig, she thought. Sweet, wonderful, misguided man. "He listens, and he doesn't stare at my chest or have any kids or ex-wives."

"He sounds perfect."

"No one's perfect, but he's pretty darn close." She leaned on the banister he'd fixed without her even asking. "I spent all this time looking, and when I'm least expecting it, there he is." She sighed wistfully. "I've got to go, Craig, but thank you so much for fixing my step and the rail."

"It was no trouble. Have fun."

"I will, thanks." She hung up and ran her hand along the wood. He'd done something nice for her. He'd stopped by and she hadn't even asked him why. She didn't have time to call him back or even wonder why he'd come to see her. She tried to tuck it away, through her shower, through her mad rush to pick an outfit, even through the movie where Jamie held her hand and bought her popcorn and Twizzlers. Craig Archer, with his pessimistic attitude and nasty streak of kindness, was never far from her mind.

***

Craig dropped down on the couch and kneaded the sore muscles of his neck. "Too much time on the damn ladder," he muttered as he reached for the remote. He flicked through channels with one hand and cradled his fourth beer of the night with the other. He thought about stopping at three, but figured what the hell. He had nowhere to go and nothing to do but watch TV with his dog. At least he had his dog.

He eyed his watch. Nine-thirty on Saturday night. Bones was probably packed with couples old and young, drinking expensive wine, eating luxuriant food and the best steaks in town. He wondered if Allie would order the ribeye like he'd suggested or be concerned it would send the wrong impression to Jamie.

Who named their boy Jamie anyway? "Guy sounds like a prick," he told Blackjack and lifted his feet to the coffee table. "If she wants to go out with Jamie, be seen around town with Jamie, have great sex with Jamie, what do I care?"

The dog whimpered and rested his head on Craig's leg. "We don't need a woman, do we, BJ?"

Blackjack shifted to give Craig better access for a tummy rub. Craig obliged without thinking and took a long pull from his beer.

He should call her, he thought. Pretend he forgot about her date and see what's up. No, too obvious. He flicked the channel to ESPN and considered what would be a reason to call her. Leah? Nah, he tossed the idea aside. Too complicated.

He tried to get into the game he'd looked forward to watching, but couldn't bring himself to care who won the SEC matchup. It wasn't like him not to care when it came to college football. He finished off the beer and reached for the phone. Obvious or not, he didn't care.

CHAPTER 27

The restaurant was smaller than Allie had expected, but had the ambiance of a country club with its dark wooden walls and white tablecloths. Jamie had ordered the wine, a French Rhone that slid like butter down her throat. She'd worried about the delightful little buzz she felt until she'd been presented with the enormous ribeye she'd ordered on Craig's suggestion. She'd have dinner for a week on what their server had boxed and waiting for her to take home.

Something felt off. Allie had tried all night to shake the nagging feeling that despite the seemingly perfect night, she couldn't focus on her date and what they both assumed would be a big step in their relationship. Jamie looked gorgeous in his blazer and open neck shirt. The way his expertly gelled dark hair shone in the muted light had images of him primping in the mirror zipping through Allie's mind. She couldn't imagine Craig primping.

Their fourth date in one week. They'd known about each other for a long time, since college in fact. But did knowing someone existed in the world for a decade and really knowing them mean the same thing? Did she want to take this great big leap with a man who'd dazzled her, but that she'd really only recently discovered? She felt a little like she was expected to play a part in a role that had been written and performed many times over.

Dinner date, check.

Coffee date, check.

Movie date, check.

Expensive night out, check.

Sex...she wasn't so sure.

The waiter had just delivered the dark chocolate torte Jamie ordered when Allie felt her phone vibrate in the clutch she'd set on her lap after applying gloss to her lips. She stared at the screen and chewed her lip when she saw Craig's name on the display.

"I've got to get this," she said and stood up from the table. "I'm sorry." She rushed off to the bathroom to answer without a backwards glance.

"Hey," Craig said. "You won't believe the date I had tonight."

"Really?" She opened the bathroom door, and when the noise from inside was too loud, she scooted to the end corner of the hallway.

"Oh, yeah," he went on. "You won't believe what this girl said to me."

A loud noise from the adjacent kitchen stopped Craig mid-sentence. "Are you out?"

"Yeah, I'm at Bones. With Jamie."

"I'm sorry, Allie. I totally forgot. I'll call you later."

"No, no," she found herself saying even though talking in the cramped hallway, dodging disapproving stares from the servers, made her feel as if she were going to get her cell phone taken away at any minute. "I'm in the bathroom anyway. Tell me what happened."

"Allie. Go enjoy your date. This can wait. I thought you'd be at home."

"You sure?" she asked. Why was she stalling? Jamie was waiting at the table, he'd given her his undivided attention all night, and Craig insisted his call wasn't important. For some idiotic reason, she didn't want to hang up.

"Of course. Have a good time. One of us should."

"Yeah. Okay. See you."

She tucked the phone in her purse and made her way back to the table where Jamie sat scrolling through his phone. When he saw her coming, he sat back as his half lidded eyes took her in from head to toe.

"Everything okay?" he asked.

"Yes. Sorry about that."

"Hey, no worries. I got the pleasure of watching you walk back to the table." He picked up the bottle of wine and filled her glass while his eyes never left hers. "You are so beautiful, Allie."

Smile, she thought. That was a nice thing to say. But it was hard to smile at someone who looked as though he wanted to eat her alive with one very big bite. Was Craig right? Could a man who called her beautiful, a man who openly admitted he liked to watch her walk, hear her? Really listen to her?

She reached for her water and gulped down a swallow as her devious mind started playing tricks on her. Should she do it? she wondered. Could she possibly lie to a man she'd spent all week with just to test him?

"So, you know how I was telling you about going back to school?" she asked as her heart thundered in her chest. Deny it, she willed him. Tell me I never said that.

"Um hum," he said and lifted a bite of torte to her lips.

"I'm going to do it," she said and pulled the fork from his hand. "I'm going to stop teaching and go back to school."

She took the bite as he watched the fork slide in and out of her mouth.

"That's great, Allie." He motioned for their server to bring the check. "Are you ready to get out of here?" he asked.

Her heart and her spirits plummeted to the floor. How could someone so eager to go out, so willing to twist his plans around to see her, not listen to a word she said? "Yes," she said. "I'm more than ready to get out of here."

***

Craig shouldn't have called. He'd have gotten up and drank the rest of the six pack if he hadn't had a dog sprawled over his lap and a nagging headache from the first four he'd quickly downed. It was stupid to call. What had he accomplished? He'd heard her voice, confirmed she was in fact at Bones with Jamie, and made her think he'd been on a date. What the hell good had any of that done but piss him off?

He turned the volume down on the game and laid his head back against the couch. How had he gotten to this place in his life where a woman, one woman, could wreak havoc on his life? Hadn't he sworn off the species for anything more than an occasional tension reliever? He'd been damn happy the way his life was going before she'd barged—or banged—right into him and changed everything.

He didn't want to care about someone. He didn't want to risk giving any control over to another person. He'd vowed he'd never be that vulnerable again. So how, in the span of a couple of months, had Allie come to mean so damn much? How was it that he couldn't get through a day, or hell, an hour, without thinking of her and wondering where she was or what she was doing? How had he let himself slip so far down the slope that nearly killed him before?

His head bolted up at the banging on the door. Blackjack, now fully awake and ready to battle whoever stood on the opposite side, bolted out of his lap to bark furiously at his late night visitor. Craig hushed him with a simple command and opened the door to find a furiously gorgeous woman on his stoop.

Oh no. "Allie?"

CHAPTER 28

"What are you doing here?" Craig asked. He wore faded blue jeans and an old App State sweatshirt. His feet were bare. How dare he look so casual, so innocent, when he'd ruined everything? "I thought you had a date."

She stepped inside the foyer, not waiting for an invitation. "I did. I'd probably still be out with him if it weren't for you."

"I shouldn't have called." He closed the door and then just stood there, his hands in his front pockets. "I'm sorry."

"You think it was the call? You seriously think it was your phone call that ended the date?" She pushed past him into the den. He had some football game on the television and it annoyed her to hear someone, anyone enjoying themselves when she felt so upset.

He followed her into the room and faced her where she stood in the middle of the den. "Ahhhh, how much did you have to drink tonight?"

"Not nearly enough."

"Okay, I get that you're pissed, but what I don't get is why."

"You ruined everything! You told me all this stuff about how men think and what they want. I never would have noticed that he wasn't listening to me. I never would have been offended because he called me beautiful. I would've gone home with him, I would've been having pretty excellent sex right now if his kissing was any indication of his skill in that department. But no. Nope. Now I'm testing him, asking questions of him, making sure that he's listening to me and not just seeing me. And you know what?" She threw her hands in the air. "He wasn't listening at all. Not one little bit. And it's all your fault."

"I take it your date didn't go so well."

"It was. It should have. He's never been married. He's an investment banker. No kids, no bitter attitude about women. He knows wine and sports and he even took piano when he was a kid. He should have been perfect."

"If you were building a man online, I'd say he was perfect."

"He didn't hear a word I said and it wasn't because of my girls." She pointed to her chest, nicely hidden under her long wool coat and behind her conservative, yet sexy black cocktail dress. "Men don't hear me."

He cocked his head to the side and the look of pity on his face made her want to scratch his eyes out. "Not all men, Allie."

"No, you're right." She started forward, inching toward him as a look of sheer panic crossed over his face. "You hear me, don't you, Craig?"

He nodded and seemed more than a little unnerved at having to admit the truth.

"Why do you hear me?"

He shrugged. "I listen."

"You listen all right." She stopped within a foot of where he stood. She felt powerful, wicked, and just a little bit crazed. "When you called, I was sitting at the table with him. I left him right in the middle of dessert so I could hear your voice. And that doesn't make any sense because I shouldn't even like you. You're rude and you're insensitive, and you're so damn honest that you make me feel exposed and not in a good way. But you're kind and you're loyal and all the goodness in you is all the more sweet because you don't want any part of it."

He stood there, straight as a board, not squirming, not denying, just staring at her as she emptied her soul at his feet. "And you never tell me I'm beautiful. Everyone tells me I'm beautiful, but not you."

"I don't like to state the obvious."

"You think I'm shallow."

"Of course I don't think you're shallow. You shouldn't care what I think. You shouldn't care what anyone thinks."

"I care, okay? Not about everyone, not even about most people, but I care what you think. I can't help it."

"You don't want to know what I think."

"Urrrgh," she groaned. "You see? This is exactly what I'm talking about! Why can't you be rude and insensitive and honest when I ask you a direct question?"

"If I thought you really wanted to know the answer, I'd tell you."

"Oh, never mind," she said and pushed past him. She yanked open the door and was almost through when he grabbed her arm and spun her around and crushed her against his chest.

"You want to know what I think? You want me to be honest?" He was so angry, his teeth were clenched. "I think you're the most beautiful woman I've ever known and I'm not just talking about what I see when I look at you. You're soft, and vulnerable, and funny, and ridiculously kind. And if those jack legs you go out with don't listen to you, it's their problem, not yours."

He let her go as abruptly as he'd pulled her to him and she had to reach out and grab his sweatshirt to keep from falling. Her head was spinning from the words he'd just spoken and the musky scent of his skin. "Oh."

"I think you should go," he said and pushed his hands into his pockets. "You need to go."

Every nerve in her body felt alive and tingling as if a charge ran between them. "Is this you being honest, or is this you running from something that might involve actual feelings?"

"I'm not running from anything. I'm saving you from doing something we'll both regret."

"The only thing I'll regret is if I do go. You're so good at self-protection. You can't get hurt if you never let anybody in, right? But it's too late for that. I'm already in, and I'm not leaving unless you kick me out." She put her hands on her hips and stared straight into those misty blue eyes. "Your choice, Craig. Kick me to the curb or take me to bed."

"Damn you, Allie. You don't know what you're asking."

"You wanna bet?" She lunged. There wasn't any better word for the way she simply threw herself into his arms. Their mouths met in kiss meant to destroy. There would be no tenderness with Craig. No soft words or coaxing from his mouth as it streaked from her lips to scrape greedily along her neck.

"It's your smell," she heard him mutter. "You always smell so damn good."

"Put your hands on me, Craig. God, I need your hands on me."

She didn't have to ask twice. When they streaked over her, under her coat, down her dress and up, she felt the sting of the cold air against her legs. "The door."

He shoved it closed with his foot and pushed her back against the carved wood. He dragged the coat from her shoulders and stood back to look at her. "Good God, Allie. It's a wonder the man could put two words together with you dressed like this."

His words, spoken through ragged breaths, had alarm bells ringing in her head. She pulled his lips back to hers and tried to lose herself in his kiss, but the ringing in her ears wouldn't stop. She pushed him far enough away to catch her breath. "Do you remember me telling you I'm quitting teaching and going back to school?"

His brows drew together and his unfocused eyes narrowed. "You never told me that."

It was all she needed to hear. She smiled, giddy with relief, and flipped around in his arms to spread her hands against the door as if he were going to do a pat down. "Zipper runs right down the middle."

***

He'd lost his mind. As he ordered his hands off and down, they went up, seeking her zipper, and down to expose a column of pale white skin, the contrast made all the more stark against the black of her bra. Before he could push the material off her shoulders, he ran his lips along the base of her neck and nipped at the nape. The dress slithered like a snake over her curves to land in a puddle at her feet. He could only marvel at the beauty of Allie in her underwear and three inch heels.

He unfastened her bra before letting his hands feast on every inch of her milky skin. Everything. She was everything he feared, everything he desired. She leaned against him, a moan of pleasure on her lips. She covered his hands with her own as they cupped her breasts, pinching at her nipples, her bottom snug and swaying against his groin. A man could die from just the feel and taste of her skin.

Who was this woman in his arms, coaxing, urging him to touch, to feel, to take? She turned, and if he'd thought her beautiful before, this Allie, aroused beyond good sense, was magnificent. She tugged urgently at his sweatshirt, yanking it up and over his head. She tossed it aside and made quick work of his jeans as he slipped his fingers inside her panties and found her more than willing, but ready. His jeans fell with a thud on the floor.

"Allie," he croaked as she wrapped her long fingers around him, guiding him toward her. "I'm not going to take you against the door."

"Just take me, Craig. I can't stand it," she panted. "I can't wait. Don't make me wait."

He swallowed her moan as he lifted her leg and rammed inside her. When she cinched around him in a torturous vice, the animal inside of him broke free. Flesh pounded flesh as teeth nipped and fingers plundered. There were no tender words or gentle grazes, only man and woman mating in a fight for the finish. Every breath he took, every thought he had was of her. When she exploded around him, it was her name on his lips as the world narrowed to a pinpoint and he emptied his soul.

***

Allie felt as exposed as a live wire. She had both feet on the ground, but it would be a while before she felt steady on her feet. She gulped air into her lungs and fought the urge to slide bonelessly to the floor. The sound of Craig's breathing echoed in her ear as his hair tickled the raw skin of her neck. They'd battered and battled and somehow remained vertical when the world crashed around them in an explosion of glorious smoke.

He shifted and rested his forehead against hers. "Christ," he said in a whisper. "Are we still alive?"

She chuckled and let her hand drift along his nicely muscled back to rest on his butt. Everything about the last few...minutes, hours—God only knew how long they'd wrestled against the door—was a blur. She knew she'd need more from him even as he pulled back and left her shaking. "If we're dead, I'm doing pretty good in the afterlife."

"Blondie, you're more than good."

Was it possible to blush when she'd just begged for and been ravished to within an inch of her life? "I'm feeling just reckless enough to admit I want more, but since I can't stand up much longer, I'm going to have to insist on a bed."

He did the unthinkable. Just when she expected him to push her toward the couch, he scooped her into his arms and began carrying her up the stairs. Oh, yes, she thought. She was going to need to spend some serious time getting a good look at this body of his. So strong, he carried her as if she weighed nothing. He set his lips on hers in a kiss of devastating tenderness before dropping her like a sack of wheat on the bed. The room was lit only by a small lamp along the wall in the adjoining seating area.

He climbed over her and slung onto his back, his breath coming out in pants. "I'm going to need a minute or two."

"Take your time," she said. Too late to feel shy or awkward around him, she didn't want to waste a second on such worthless emotions. She leaned up and cupped her head in her palm as her other hand stroked along his abdomen. "Yeah," she said. "I'd say you're more than average."

He chuckled and sucked in a breath when her hand reached lower to tease. "Ummm, much better than average."

It took more than a minute, but less than five to have him reversing their positions and working his way over her. Here was the man who'd fixed her porch, the man who read her moods and heard her words, the man who could read her mind if the direction of his mouth were any indication. Both of him, all of him, the Craig who'd taken her with abandon against his front door and the one who suckled tenderly at her breast and beyond were the man who'd won her heart. She gave herself to him in a way she'd never done with another, body, heart, and soul.

CHAPTER 29

He'd forgotten to shut the blinds. That was the first thought Craig had as the sun slanted across his face and his eyes fluttered open. When his arm wouldn't budge, the cloud lifted from his brain and he whipped his head around to find Allie, gloriously naked, sprawled along the edge of the bed, her hair like a riotous halo over his arm and the pillow.

He rubbed his hand over his face even as other, more potent parts of his body sprang to life. What had he done? What in the name of God had possessed him to carry her upstairs to his bed and into his life? When she stirred, he shimmied his hand out from under her head and stared as she turned over and nestled on her back. She fisted the sheet in her hands on her stomach, leaving her breasts exposed and as tempting as a tallboy filled with bourbon at an AA meeting. He sprang up and dashed into the bathroom. It would be a cold shower for him this morning. A very cold shower indeed.

***

Allie stretched as muscles, long unused, heated. Her conscience flared to life. She reached her hand across the bed and found it empty. Blinking against the sunlight that streamed through the up drawn blinds, she sat up and gasped as the bathroom door opened and Craig appeared, still dripping water from his shower, a towel hanging low on his hips.

"Good morning," she said. She couldn't read his expression. It teetered somewhere between annoyance and shock. She wasn't sure, on so little sleep, which she preferred.

"Morning." He averted his eyes and made a beeline for the closet.

Okay, Allie thought. He's uncomfortable. Not exactly the reaction she expected after they'd spent half the night wrapped around one another. But this was Craig she was dealing with, which meant she needed to proceed with caution. "What time is it?" she asked.

"After nine," he called from the closet.

"Nine?" She couldn't remember the last time she'd whiled the morning away in bed.

"You're welcome to stay as long as you'd like, but I've got to get to the house. I'm meeting a contractor in half an hour."

"Oh." It hurt. Unquestionably it hurt for him to rush out of his house with her naked and more than willing in his bed, but he did have a job to do. So did she, when it came right down to it, even though she'd chuck all responsibility out the window to feel his hands on her again. "Okay."

"There's not much in the way of breakfast. Couple boxes of cereal that Leah likes and maybe a box of frozen waffles."

"I'm not worried about breakfast, Craig."

"Good." He emerged wearing a fresh pair of jeans and a worn red flannel shirt. He wouldn't look her in the eye. "I mean, have whatever." He sat on the bench in the sitting area and laced up his work boots.

This wasn't good. He was back to running scared. This wasn't about her, she told herself as the seconds slipped to minutes in absolute silence. She let the sheet fall where she'd held it clutched to cover her chest. It was weak and shallow, but she'd use any trick in the book to break him out of that infuriatingly distant mood.

She should be pleased to see he wasn't immune after all. The swell in his crotch was unmistakable as he moved past the bed on his way to the door. When she pulled the sheet away from her body and slid to the side of the bed to stand up, he practically jumped for the door handle.

"I'll buzz you later," he called over his shoulder.

Naked and more exposed than she'd ever felt in her life, Allie dropped to the side of the bed and cried.

CHAPTER 30

Melissa rushed into the restaurant as fast as she could maneuver the stroller through the throngs of holiday shoppers. She searched over the crowd until she spotted Allie in a corner booth by the window. She left the stroller by the entrance, snagged a booster seat on her way, and wrestled with Henry as he bucked and fought the enclosure. She hadn't gotten more than a glimpse of Allie's face, but she knew something was wrong.

"He's really feisty today, huh?" Allie said.

"Unusually so." She fished a toy out of her bag and he thanked her by throwing it at her head. "Okay, how about nothing, then."

With an exasperated sigh, she eased into the booth. "Oh no. What's going on?"

"What do you mean, oh no?"

"I mean I can tell something's wrong. So spill. I might not have much time."

The waitress showed up and deposited silverware and took their drink order. Allie had that glazed over look like she had in the weeks after Nick had dumped her. "So?" Melissa asked as soon as the waitress turned her back on the table.

"I slept with Craig."

"Okay. Why do you look like you've lost your best friend?"

"I haven't heard from him since."

"When did it happen?"

"Two weeks ago."

Melissa tried, but failed to keep the surprise from her face. "Two weeks. Yikes. Have you called him?"

"Yes."

"And? Come on, Allie. Don't make me pry this out of you detail by detail."

"We made love, repeatedly, and in the morning, he bolted from his own house like his pants were on fire. He said, 'I'll buzz you later,' and I haven't heard from him since."

"How many times have you called?"

"I waited three agonizing days before calling him. I left a message on his cell, which is always with him. No answer, no return call. I waited until the following week, a week ago Tuesday, and left another message on his cell. Nothing. I called him once at home, but didn't leave a message."

"So you have no idea what happened to scare him off? Was the sex bad?"

She let out a mirthless laugh. "No. It was *not* bad, for either of us."

"Okay, tell me what happened in the morning."

"I woke up and he was in the bathroom. He came out, freshly showered, and wouldn't even look at me. He hid in the closet and emerged fully dressed while regaling me with the various breakfast items I could help myself to after he left for a work appointment."

Melissa pulled a container of Goldfish out of her purse and dumped a few on the table when Henry began his Houdini routine. "Let's back up, since it sounds like you didn't have time to say or do something the morning after. How did you end up together?"

"I went out with Jamie. You remember Jamie Morgan? Beth's brother?"

"Yeah, big guy, dark hair?"

"Yes. I told you we went out and had a good time. We went out four times in one week. I was getting stars in my eyes the way I always do when someone I like is interested. On Saturday night, he took me to Bones."

"Very nice."

"Yes, it was. But...I had this feeling that something wasn't right. I mean, we'd been on four dates and I knew he expected to take me home. I was okay with that—I thought I was, but something didn't feel quite right. So I tested him."

"Tested him?"

"Craig said men wouldn't listen to me because of the way I look. He said they'd pretend to listen, but not really listen. So I asked Jamie if he remembered me telling him something, something kind of important, and he said yes. Only I'd never said what I reminded him I'd said, so I knew he wasn't listening."

"Okay..."

The waitress set down their waters and said their food would be out in a jiffy.

"I got mad at Craig. I was furious at him for making me understand men so clearly and causing an abrupt end to a promising new relationship. I know, my rationale was twisted, but I was upset. I went to his house and confronted him, basically yelled at him because he did listen. He did pay attention. He always has."

Her face got all soft and Melissa could tell she was fighting the lump in her throat. Poor Allie, she thought. The girl was sunk. "So what did he do?"

"He tried to get me to leave. He said...what did he say, exactly?" She rubbed her temple and closed her eyes, thinking back to the night she was trying to describe. "He said I needed to go before we both did something we'd regret."

"But you didn't go?"

"I told him to kick me to the curb or take me to bed."

Melissa nearly choked on her water. "You said that?"

"Yes." Allie smirked. "I did."

"So he took you to bed."

She shook her head from side to side. "Right there against the door. It was incredible and it wasn't just me. I've lived with the afterglow of mediocre sex and this didn't come anywhere near that vicinity."

"Wow," Melissa said. She flicked some condensation from her glass onto her face. "Is it hot in here, or is it just me?"

"Then he carried me to bed—carried me up the stairs—and made love to me like I was the most precious, the most desirable woman in the world."

Melissa let out a breath and thought fleetingly of the last time she and Ben had had sex. The quickie in the closet didn't even count as far as she was concerned. "I can see why you're a little confused by his morning after routine."

"It wasn't just that he bolted. He's skittish with his situation and all, I get that. But this non-communication? I don't get this. He's not a coward, and it's not like I've been stalking him. And if he didn't want to see me again, he should at least have the decency to call and tell me. Even Nick, the stupid jerk, confessed to cheating on me to my face."

"I don't know what to tell you, Allie." Their food arrived and they both stared at each other over their plates. "Don't get mad at me for asking this, but are you sure you're not just romanticizing the night?"

"Believe me, Mel, I'm not. He was right there with me the entire time until the morning." She picked up her fork and pushed the lettuce around the bowl.

"What about the brother?"

"What about him?"

"Have you asked him about Craig?"

"No. What am I supposed to say? *Hey, Mark, did Craig happen to mention the night we spent together and that he's avoiding my calls?*"

Melissa gave Henry the breadstick that came with her salad. He dropped it on the floor. "How about asking if Craig is okay since you haven't heard from him in a couple of weeks?"

Allie sighed. "I don't know. That seems too obvious."

"Do you want to know or not?"

"At this point, I'm pretty sure I know. And it pisses me off."

"Good." Melissa reached across the table and grasped Allie's hand. "As long as you don't start blaming yourself for his inadequacies. His immature behavior has nothing to do with you, Allie, and if you start blaming yourself, that's going to piss me off."

***

Craig honked his horn and screamed around the car in front of him as it let off a carload of people in a no stopping zone, but he had to slam on the brakes when he almost barreled into a pedestrian. He loosened his hold on the steering wheel and took a deep breath. Get a grip, he told himself as he counted in his head to ten before exiting the home remodeling center.

His cell phone slid from the passenger seat to the floor. When he reached over and picked it up at the red light, he scanned his calls. No more messages or missed calls from Allie. He wanted to feel relieved, but he didn't feel anything but foolish for avoiding her and for letting her get under his skin.

He knew he couldn't hide from her forever. He'd made a mistake being with her. He knew he couldn't trust himself not to make it again if he talked to her or saw her before he had his emotions in check. She'd be pissed; he knew her well enough to know that he'd hurt her and she wouldn't make it easy. If she were anyone else, he'd have walked away and never looked back, but this was Allie.

Leah had called and left a message. He banged his fist against the wheel after listening to her beg him to come to dinner that night. Tuesday. The night Allie would be there for her lesson. The night she stayed for dinner.

His phone rang as he scowled at the display and he knew he couldn't avoid her forever. "Hey, squirt."

"Are you coming for dinner?" Leah asked.

"I'd like to, but I'm juggling two jobs right now."

"You're too busy for your family?"

He recognized that tone. It didn't bode well for his chances. "I'm too busy, period."

"I haven't seen you in forever, Uncle Craig. Please, I'm begging you. It's lasagna. You know you love Dad's lasagna."

"Leah..."

"Please, Uncle Craig. Please?"

His head was pounding; he had four loads to drop off before heading to the new house for measurements and an assload of paperwork waiting at home. "I can't," he said. "I'll try and stop by another day after work."

"Don't bother," she said. "We're obviously not that important."

"Leah…"

"Whatever. I gotta go."

Craig sighed when the line went dead. It was time to face things head on, one angry woman at a time. Leah would have to get in line.

CHAPTER 31

Allie put on her best happy face and got through the lesson with Leah as best she could. The girl, it seemed, was as down as Allie. "That's good," she told Leah after her second run through of her new recital song. "I can tell you've been practicing."

"Yeah."

"Leah!" Mark called from the kitchen.

Leah rolled her eyes. "Yes, ma'am."

"You okay?" Allie asked and ran her hand along the girl's back. No matter how bad things were with Craig, she wouldn't let him ruin her relationship with Leah.

"I guess."

"Want to talk about it?"

"Not really. Can you stay for dinner tonight?"

Allie sighed and pinched her lips together. Leah was looking at her with puppy dog eyes, but the thought of pretending everything was okay for another hour seemed unbearable.

"Please, Ms. Allie. Uncle Craig already said no, and I really want you to stay."

Allie felt relieved and bemused by Craig's absence. He wasn't usually around for dinner on Tuesday nights, but he rarely told Leah no. "I suppose I can make the time."

The girl sprang up and started to close her music book.

"*If* you run through the song one more time."

"You drive a hard bargain," Leah said.

It wasn't hard to act natural through dinner. Mark and Leah kept up their usual banter, while she and Carolyn did their duty to laugh and make fun when necessary. Allie offered to help Carolyn with the dishes after dinner while Mark challenged Leah to a game of one-on-one in the driveway.

"Is everything okay?" Carolyn asked. "You seem kind of distracted tonight."

"I'm fine," Allie said. She took the freshly rinsed pot Carolyn handed her and dried it with a towel. "Busy. I don't mean to seem aloof."

"You're not. I just wondered if everything was okay. Leah said you've been spending some time with Craig."

Oh no. The last thing she wanted to discuss was Craig. "We're friends," she managed to say without choking. "How are things going with you and Leah?"

"Oh, they're better. We still have our moments, but ever since she ran away to Craig's house and we got a lot off our chests, things have improved. Why?" Carolyn asked. "Do you think she's backsliding?"

"No, not at all. I'm just curious. She seemed a little down tonight."

"She's mad at Craig."

Get in line, Allie thought.

"She wanted him to come to dinner tonight, but he said he was too busy. He's been busy for a couple of weeks now, and she's feeling neglected."

What was Allie supposed to do? Defend the jerk? "I haven't heard from him either, so I suppose he must be busy."

"I don't know…" Carolyn said, shaking her head and scrubbing the cooked on edges of the lasagna pan.

"What do you mean?" Allie asked. She didn't want to seem too interested, but if Carolyn had any information that could shed some light on how she should proceed, she'd listen.

"I'm not sure, but I think something's going on with him. He and Mark talk pretty regularly, and Mark said he's been short with him and acting funny."

"He is kinda moody," Allie offered.

"You know, I feel like I know him a lot better than I actually do. I mean, Mark spent three years talking about him and Leah, so I feel like I know everything about them. I've wanted so many times to give Craig a great big hug for what he's been through and the way he put everything on hold to help Mark and Leah after Becca died. I mean, the accident cost him his wife and the baby…"

"The baby?"

"Julie was pregnant when she died." Carolyn rinsed the lasagna pan and set it on the drying rack when Allie couldn't reach for it in her state of shock. "Craig didn't know," Carolyn continued. "Mark said Craig was so strong until he found out about the baby and then he just lost it. Apparently he was a mess until about three months after and he just kind of snapped out of it. Mark said it was like someone had flicked a switch and the old Craig was back."

Allie had to turn away while Carolyn prattled on about Craig and Mark and Leah and how they all suffered and got through the first year together, about how one year bled into another and they basically raised Leah together. Allie braced her hands on the counter and struggled for breath.

"Hey, hey," Carolyn put an arm around Allie's waist. "Are you okay? You look kind of pale?"

"I'm feeling a little lightheaded all the sudden."

Carolyn led her to the table and helped her into a chair. She got Allie a glass of water and ordered her to drink.

"I'm sorry," Allie said. "I'm not sure what happened."

Carolyn stared into Allie's eyes. "Your color's coming back. Whew," she drew her wrist across her forehead. "You scared me. For a second there I thought you were going to pass out."

"I'm fine now. I'm not sure what that was."

Carolyn stood up. "I'm going to get Mark, get him to drive you home."

"No," Allie said. "No, that's sweet, Carolyn, but I'm fine. Whatever that was, it's passed and I feel fine."

Carolyn stared at her from across the kitchen. After a slow, appraising glance, she said, "Are you sure? What if you get lightheaded on your way home?"

"I'm not far and if I feel dizzy, I'll pull over. I'm fine, Carolyn, really. There's no need for Mark to drive me home."

"It's no trouble, Allie."

Allie felt panicked at the thought of being around Mark or any of them now. She desperately needed to get out of there and think. She just needed time to think and process everything Carolyn had just told her. "I'd feel silly and embarrassed. I'm embarrassed enough. Please, I'm fine."

Carolyn sighed. "All right, but do me a favor and give me a call when you get home so I don't worry."

"Absolutely."

Allie gave Carolyn her brightest smile, gathered her things, and waved to Mark and Leah as she got in her car. She pulled out of the driveway, onto the street, and around the corner before pulling over to the curb because her hands were shaking so badly she could hardly grip the steering wheel.

Oh, Craig, she thought. You poor, poor man. What in the world did that woman do to you and how in in God's name have you lived alone with this for so many years?

***

Craig was just about to leave when he saw the headlights coming down Allie's quiet residential street. He stood up from the porch step and stared as her car pulled into the drive. She knew he was here; she'd have known since she pulled in the driveway and saw his truck in front of her house. He felt a twinge of guilt for ambushing her when he hadn't called her back, but there wasn't any way to explain what he needed to say other than face to face.

She took her time getting out of the car. He shoved his hands in his jeans and watched her. She wore wool pants, heeled boots, and chunky sweater to go with the unreadable look on her face. He'd expected her to be fuming when she saw him and this...pale and sullen Allie had his stomach knotted in worry.

"Hey," he said as she stopped on the walk in front of him. He towered over her from his perch on her porch.

"Hi." She just stood there, her bag in her hand, her purse slung over her shoulder, that damn puzzling look on her face.

"How was the lasagna?" he asked.

She cocked a brow. "Am I why you stayed away?"

"No. I can have Mark's lasagna whenever I want. Kinda takes the appeal away."

She didn't even crack a smile.

"Listen," he began. "I need to talk to you. I'd like to explain."

She just stared at him without moving. He climbed down the stairs when it became obvious she'd rather freeze to death than invite him in. "So explain."

"Allie, I can't do this. I wish I could and believe me, if I could, you'd be the one, but I just can't."

"I know you can't. It hurts like hell, but I know you can't and I even understand why."

What the hell? "You're not mad? Why does this feel like a trap?"

"Mostly because you're the one who spews the cold, hard truth and you're not used to having it spewed back at you. I can honestly say, of all the things that have come out of this relationship we're in—and don't turn white on me, Craig, we are in a relationship—it's that you've taught me to be honest. With others and most especially with myself." She sat down on the porch step and put her case between her legs. "Carolyn told me about the baby. Julie's baby."

Sucker punched. She'd sucker punched him when he least expected it. "That doesn't have anything to do with this."

"Now who's not being honest?"

"I don't do relationships, Allie. That's all this is about."

"You don't do relationships, Craig, because you're not done having one with your wife."

"That's bullshit!"

"Not from where I'm sitting. You stopped grieving." She snapped her fingers. "Just flat stopped the minute you discovered those emails. And I don't have to be a psychologist to know you can't adequately grieve for your dead wife in three months."

Anger, fierce and hot, rose up in his gut. "Oh, so you're a therapist now?"

"No, I'm someone who cares about you. Probably more than you're ready to hear, but we'll save that for later. You never told your brother about the emails. You never told anyone but me, and I'm pretty sure you never would have told me if I hadn't been so weak and sniffly at the time."

"I shouldn't have said anything."

"Most people would think you kept everything close to the vest so you wouldn't be pitied, but I know you better than that. You didn't know how to be angry and sad at the same time, and it pisses you off when you can't figure something out. You lost your wife, your child—"

"It might not have been mine." The words, so long trapped in his head, in his heart, came out in an angry whisper. He sank down on the step next to her, his head in his hands.

"It could have been," she said. "And it's gotta be pure hell not to know one way or the other. So because you didn't know how to grieve, you just decided not to, and you're just stubborn enough to follow through."

"I don't want you analyzing me, Allie. You don't know what you're talking about. You didn't know me then. I wasn't the same person I am now."

"You should probably grieve for him, too."

"I was a coldhearted bastard. I worked all the damn time. I told myself it was for Julie, for all the things she wanted and the lifestyle I wanted to give her, but we both knew it was my own greed and pride that kept me away from home." He ran his hands through his hair and tried to calm his racing heart. "I don't blame her for taking up with some other guy."

"Now you're just flat lying. There are lots of reasons to cheat, Craig, and I'm sure when you're tempted, you can come up with some pretty good ones, but that doesn't ever make it okay."

"That's your own divorced parents/old boyfriend baggage talking now."

"Probably. I can't forgive or be with a cheater and neither could you. Now or then. If she'd have lived, you'd have left her when you found out about the cheating."

It was the question that haunted him. What would he have done, if given the chance? "Yeah," he admitted after staring off in the distance. "I would have."

"But the baby might have changed things. She didn't tell you about the baby, so you don't think it was yours. There are so many ways it all could have played out if it weren't for the accident. Too many ways. It makes my head spin just thinking about all the things that could have happened, and I just found out. I could play 'what if' for hours, but the only thing I can't see is you forgiving her and moving on. I don't think you're built like that."

He just stared at her. She looked like a ghost in the soft light of the porch lamp, but there was steel underneath her polished exterior.

"You couldn't forgive her, alive or dead, and you've never been able to forgive yourself. And that brings us back to now."

She'd cut him to the quick and he intended to return the favor. "You think you know everything now that we've slept together once and my new sister-in-law told you some juicy gossip?"

"It wasn't just once, Craig, and we both know it wasn't just sex."

She was twisting everything around and tying his insides into knots. He wanted so badly to rail at her, to be pissed, but everything she said felt like a slap to his face. So instead of being mad, or appreciating her honesty, he fought back the only way he knew how. "I can't do this with you, Allie, because I don't want to. You're a little too much for me and we both know it."

The shaky breath she let out made him feel worse than all the things she'd said. "I can't control your feelings any more than I can control mine, so I may as well be honest. I'm in love with you, Craig, but I'm not going to let you hurt me or lie to me. We can't be together now because you're in no position to be with anyone. I love you enough to understand. I also love myself enough not to wait for you. I can't fix you and I can't make you love me back, but I may as well lay it all out for you and, if anything, give you an easy out."

"What the hell do expect me to say to that, Allie? Just what the hell do you want?"

"I want you to be happy, Craig. I want me to be happy, too. If we can figure out how to be happy together—after you've dealt with your grief—then I think we'd make one hell of a couple. But if we can't, I still want us both to end up happy."

"You don't love me," he said.

When she smiled at him, if he weren't already sitting, it would have brought him to his knees. "You can't tell me how I feel."

"What do you expect me to do with this?"

"That's for you to decide."

"But you're not going to wait? You think you love me, but you're what? Going to go back to online dating?"

"I'm going to get through this one day at a time. You're just stubborn enough not to do anything and to let me and what we could have together slip away. I deserve better than that."

"What if...what if I get my shit together—I'm not admitting I need to—but what if I do and you've met someone else?"

"I guess that's the chance we both have to take." She leaned over and planted a kiss on his lips, lingering long enough for him to consider, just for a second, grabbing hold and never letting go. She walked inside without a backwards glance.

CHAPTER 32

Melissa hitched Henry on her hip and pounded on Allie's door. She'd seen her car in the garage and wasn't leaving until her friend showed her face. Melissa wasn't sure what she'd said or done to hurt Allie's feelings, but it was just plain rude not to answer her phone calls and let her wonder.

Melissa was ready to pounce when she heard the door lock slide open and the door inched back, but it was a gasp that came out of her mouth when she caught sight of her friend. "What the hell happened to you?"

"Excuse me?" Allie asked. She shuffled back to the couch where, from the look of the throws and pillows stacked at one end, she'd dragged herself from to answer the door.

"It's the middle of the day," Melissa said after closing the door. "You haven't answered your phone or returned my calls. You're lying around on the couch in your pajamas—which you never do—and you look like hell. What gives?"

"I'm sick."

"You're sick. Are your fingers broken, too?"

"What?"

She pointed to the phone where it rested on the cradle. Even from the opposite side of the room, Melissa could see the message light flashing. "Your phone."

"I don't feel good, Mel."

"Have you been to the doctor?"

"No." Allie sat down and bundled under the covers. "I'm just tired."

"Too tired to answer the phone?"

"I didn't feel like talking to anyone."

"Did you ever think some of us might be worried when you didn't answer your phone?"

"No. I should have. That's really rude of me. I'm sorry."

Melissa sat down on the coffee table in front of Allie and studied her friend. "What happened? Are you moping around because of Craig? Because really, after all this time, you've got to get over him."

"I'm not moping around. I told you I don't feel good."

"What are your symptoms?" Melissa asked. Henry, God bless him, sat quietly in her lap playing with her necklace.

"I'm tired, I don't have any energy, and my stomach isn't always steady."

"Oh my God, Allie. Tell me you're still on the pill."

"What? Don't be silly. Of course I'm on the pill. I'm not pregnant."

"When are you supposed to get your period?" Melissa asked.

"I don't know." Allie rubbed her temple with her fingers. "Couple of days."

Melissa shot to her feet. "I'm going to the store right now and getting you a pregnancy test."

"Don't you think you're jumping the gun? I'm not even late. I could just have a bug or something. Or, let's think this through. A few weeks ago, I told the man I slept with I love him and haven't heard a thing from him since. So maybe, just maybe, I might be a tiny bit depressed."

"Yes, you could be all of the above, including pregnant. Let's start by ruling out the big one and work our way back from there."

"I'm not pregnant."

Melissa turned at the door. "How can you be sure?"

"Because God wouldn't be that cruel." She covered her head with the blanket and Melissa bolted out the door. Pregnant or not, God had little to do with it.

***

The sinus infection. A ten-day course of antibiotics had changed her life forever. Allie swore never to take antibiotics again.

She stepped off the elevator and stumbled in a daze to the glass doors, pushing one open and stopping under the overhang where she could take a deep breath of cold air and think. Okay, she was pregnant. The pee test and the doctor's confirmation hadn't made reality sink in, but listening to the heartbeat, watching the little bean shaped being inside her on the black and white screen had felt like a sledge hammer of truth. She was having a baby. Craig's baby.

She pulled the keys from her purse and walked numbly to her car. It wasn't until she saw the reflection in the driver's window that she realized she was touching her uterus.

She unlocked the car and got in. She had to tell him. Just the thought of telling him made her want to driver her car off a cliff. She contemplated everything she'd said; all her brave talk about not trying to fix him and not waiting for him sounded so hollow considering she'd just tied herself to him forever. He was going to be mad, he was going to feel manipulated, but come hell or high water, he was going to know.

Now all she had to do was find him.

**

Craig picked up the towel and used it to wipe his brow. He welcomed the sweat and the ache in his muscles from swinging the ax. His mom needed firewood for the season and he needed to work out some things in his head. Sometimes, there was no better way to get your head right than to exhaust your body.

And Craig was damn exhausted.

He'd worked like a dog getting Davis and Stacy Hollingsworth's house complete. They'd been as thrilled with the accelerated schedule as his contractors had been pissed. It all worked out in the end and everyone was happy—everyone but Davis' buddy whose job Craig had quoted and then pulled his name from consideration. Allie had thrown him a curve ball and it was time to adjust his swing. If only he could get a grip on the bat.

His mom interrupted his musings with a glass of lemonade and sandwich with thick slices of ham. God love Patsy Archer, all five feet of her dressed in old jeans and a flannel-lined coat.

"You've worked up quite a sweat in this chilly air," she said. She set the sandwich and drinks on the table his dad had made from an old oak stump. Patsy sat down in one of the two porch rockers that Craig had noticed could use a fresh coat of stain. "Figured I'd better keep you hydrated and energized if you're going to make it through the rest of the day."

"You figured right." He leaned over and kissed her cheek before easing into the other rocker. He let out an "ahhh" for both the taste of the sandwich and the relief of his back.

"I know you didn't drop everything at home and come here just to chop my wood and eat my excellent sandwiches."

Craig scowled into the distance. He loved the view from the front porch; he always had. A man could do some serious soul searching staring into the endless twists of the forest and listening to the call of the birds. At night, if he listened hard enough, he could hear the owls. He'd always loved the owls. "I had some stuff on my mind. I can go whenever you want if I'm cramping your style."

"You're not cramping my style. I just thought a week was long enough for you to stew before I ask you straight out what's wrong."

"Got some things on my mind."

"You can't think at home?"

Craig smiled at his mother's sarcasm. "Not like here."

"Nothing better than clean mountain air to clear the brain." She stopped her rocker with the toe of her work boot. "Unless it's not your brain that needs the clearing?"

"What else is there?" he asked.

"You've got a pretty dusty heart inside your chest. I figured— all right, hoped—you'd maybe met someone who's good with a dust rag."

"Leave it be, Ma."

"Your brother's happy. I want to see you happy, too."

"Who says I'm not happy?"

"Craig," she stood up and swiped a hand across his shoulder. "I've seen you happy, boy, and this," she waved her hand in front of his face, "isn't it. Do whatever you need to do, take whatever time you need to take, and get happy. Life's too short to waste a second on anything else."

Why did every damn body want him to be happy? Not everybody, he admitted, only the ones who cared.

CHAPTER 33

Allie's stomach curled with each turn on the winding road. Every corner seemed to have the blacktop folding back on itself in an endless climb through the naked woodlands. A month earlier and the leaves would have been spectacular, but now the view seemed as cold and desolate as the task that lay before her. *If* she made it up the mountain roads without losing her lunch.

After everything she went through to get here, the least of her worries had been the treacherous drive. She'd looked forward to having the time to put her thoughts in order and formulate a plan. So much for a plan. At this point, the only plan was to keep her eyes on the road and not throw up when she arrived. If she ever arrived.

Mark should have warned her about the hairpin turns, but then he'd jotted down the address and some basic directions before he changed his mind and honored his brother's request not to tell anyone where he'd gone. Allie had Carolyn to thank for her quiet, but powerful influence in helping to sway his decision. She hadn't told them why she'd needed to see Craig, but Carolyn understood, in the way only a woman would, that it was vitally important.

Melissa warned her not to come, said he didn't deserve to know, that he'd forfeited his right to a say when he'd walked out on her. But she wouldn't be the second woman in his life to take the knowledge and choice out of his hands. This time, Craig would know from the very beginning.

When the road leveled out and Allie spotted signs of life along the road, a country store here, a gas station there, she felt the queasiness in her stomach turn to nerves. She spotted the fly fishing shop Mark had said to use as a landmark and turned right at the cross street. After two more turns, she spied the mailbox, a fish mounted on a wooden post with the name Archer illuminated in reflective letters. Allie pulled to the side of the road, took a deep breath, said a small, but potent prayer, and turned up the gravel drive that led through the woods.

She wasn't expecting to find Craig sitting on the porch smiling at a short woman with a capful of white hair. Craig's face fell when he spotted her car and she knew he wasn't expecting her. At least Mark had kept his word and not alerted Craig to her impending arrival. Without any chance to change her mind and escape, she put the car in park, reached for her coat, and got out of the car.

Craig and his mother met her at the top of the porch. The scene reminded her of when a judge and bailiff meet the accused. "What are you doing here?" Craig demanded.

His mother elbowed him in the side. "I'm Patsy Archer," she said with a warm smile.

Allie extended her hand in greeting, but stayed below on the walkway. Craig's posture—his hands on his hips, the muscle twitching in his jaw, and the waves of disapproval that emanated from him—didn't invite her to approach. "I'm Allie Graves. It's nice to meet you, Mrs. Archer."

"Call me Patsy. Would you like some lemonade, Allie? I've just made a fresh batch. It's Craig's favorite."

"No, ma'am. I'm fine, but thank you."

The silence only magnified the tension between Allie and Craig.

"Well, I'll leave you two to your business." She ducked inside the large wooden home.

"I'm sorry to bother you, Craig."

"Why are you here?" He scowled down at her. "How did you know where I was?"

She felt ridiculous standing below him, yet didn't feel steady enough to join him on the porch. She desperately wanted to ease into her reasons for coming, and yet the way he stood staring at her as if she had three heads, demanding an answer, left her no choice but to summon her courage and spit it out. "I need to talk to you."

"So talk."

She raised her arm and motioned around her. "Can we take a walk or something?"

"I'm pretty sure you didn't drive all the way up here to have a walk in the woods. Tell me. Is something wrong with Mark? Is it Leah?"

"No, no not at all. I'm sorry if I scared you."

"Okay." He blew out a breath. "Now I'm just curious, since the last time we talked you told me to get out of your life."

She hadn't told him to get out of her life. *Dear God, grant me patience with this man.* "I have to tell you something."

"I think you said enough the first time."

"There's more you need to know. Something I didn't know before."

He ran his hands through his hair and let out a shaky breath. Good, she thought. She wasn't the only one unnerved by being together again.

"Spit it out, already," he demanded.

Allie gathered her strength, touched a hand just below her stomach, and walked up the three stairs to look the man she loved in the eye. She wouldn't allow him to look down on her when she told him the news. "I'm pregnant."

His body swayed, jolted to a stop, and his face drained of color. "What?"

"I said I'm pregnant."

"How?" he asked.

"Well..."

"You were on the pill. You told me you were on the pill."

"I am; I mean, I was—"

His eyes narrowed into a dangerous stare. "Are you sure it's mine?"

She didn't realize what she'd done until she saw his face lash sideways and felt the sting of her hand. Her reaction left them both stunned and speechless.

When Craig finally spoke, she would have known his anger from the quiet fury of his voice even without the murderous look in his eye. "When did you get off the pill? When you found out I was loaded?"

He couldn't have hurt her more if he'd taken the ax against the banister to her heart. "Go to hell."

She turned, took each step with care, and walked to the car while pieces of her shattered heart fell like broken glass at her feet. She was amazed, when she put the car in reverse, that she didn't see a trail of blood marking her steps.

***

Craig stared at the leaves as they danced to the ground in the wake of Allie's departure. He was frozen to the spot; his feet refused to move. He gripped the porch's log post and leaned his head against the soft grain. Allie pregnant? He couldn't get a hold of his emotions or even understand what he felt. Surprised? Hell yes. Afraid? More than he could express. Happy? He wasn't quite sure. The only thing he knew for sure was that he'd hurt the most precious thing in his life and let her drive off upset. He turned to retrieve his keys from the house and met his mom in the doorway.

"I'll be back," he said as he opened the screen and tried to move past her. She stood firm and didn't budge. "Ma, please. I've got to catch her."

"She's not going anywhere. I put a call in to the sheriff. He's going to head her off before she hits the highway. He won't let her leave."

"What?" Recognition dawned as his mother stared at him, disapproval written all over her face. "You heard."

"Hard not to."

"I have to talk to her."

"After the way you treated her, Craig, it had better be from your knees."

217

"I know, Ma. I'm sorry." He shut his eyes, but opened them again when the image of Allie's face, fraught with pain, appeared in his mind. "I panicked."

"I can see that. You're in love with her. She's the reason you've been hiding out up here for over a week."

"Yes."

"Love's a gift, son, one you're damn lucky to have been given twice in a lifetime. I can't imagine why you wouldn't do everything in your power to grab hold and never let go. And now a baby..."

"It's not that simple. I can't...I'm not..."

"You're scared is what you are, scared to the bone." She stepped outside and let the door slap closed behind her. She reached up and cupped his cheek. "Just because Julie died doesn't mean every relationship is going to end in heartbreak."

"It's more than her dying, Ma. I wish it were that simple."

"She hurt you, Craig."

He stared at his mother, at the way she was looking at him as if she knew what he'd never told anyone but Allie. "What do you mean?"

"Ms. Keller was hurting real bad after the accident. Julie was her only daughter and she was looking for someone to blame. She said if you'd been a better husband, her daughter wouldn't have had to look outside the marriage for comfort."

"Jesus, Ma. You knew all this time?"

"She apologized, begged me not to say anything to you or anyone else. I didn't want to be the one who told you. You were upset enough as it was. And when you stopped being upset and you turned so bitter and cynical, I figured you'd found out."

"Why didn't you ever say anything?"

"It wasn't my place. But now that we're talking about it, I'm going to say what I should have said a long time ago. I knew Julie Keller since the day she was born. You two were kids when you fell in love, and in many ways, she was still a kid when she died. You and Julie never had to work very hard at being in love, you both just stumbled headfirst, and when times got tough, neither one of you knew how to work at it. When your work took off and she had to compete for your attention, she didn't know what to do. I've seen it played out too many times over the years not to know what happened."

"I should have paid more attention. I should have set work aside and been home more."

"There's two sides to every story, and you can shoulda, woulda, coulda all day long. Doesn't change a thing. She loved you, Craig. She didn't know how to breathe without loving you."

He turned his back when he felt his throat close up. "I wouldn't have cheated on her. I couldn't have."

"She wasn't as strong as you. You have to forgive her. All this bitterness is making your heart so hard. I haven't heard you laugh in so long. I haven't seen so much as a blip on your emotional radar until that beautiful girl came driving up to the house."

"She thinks I can't have a relationship because I'm not over Julie. I'm so over Julie I could spit."

"You've never forgiven Julie. As long as you cling to the bitterness and anger you feel towards her, Allie's right, you're not going to be able to move on."

"I don't know how to forgive her, Ma."

"It's three little words, Craig. Three little words that will set you free. Say them, mean them, and get on with your life. Allie doesn't seem like the kind of woman who'll run away when things get ugly."

"I guess I'm about to find out." Craig felt the fist on is throat loosen. "She's irritating."

"So was your dad. It was one of the things I loved most about him."

"I'm mean to her, not quite as mean as I just was, but honest. I tried everything I could to keep her away, but she wouldn't listen. She loves me, or at least she did."

"She's got good taste."

"She smells really good all the time and she's so smart. She doesn't have any idea how strong she is. She doesn't play games."

"Then I'd say you'd better grovel."

Craig nodded. "I'm going to marry her, Ma, and not just because of the baby. I love her."

"Don't tell me, son. Tell Allie."

CHAPTER 34

"I don't understand, Officer. Why am I being detained?"

Allie watched the sheriff of Fidley, North Carolina fidget from foot to foot. He'd taken her license and registration and held them hostage in his car for over twenty minutes. At first she thought she'd been weaving on the road. She could barely see through the angry tears. After a good cry while she waited on the sheriff, however, she started to get worried. She'd moved beyond worried when he meandered back to her window announcing she'd have to stay put while he checked some details that pulled up when her ran her license.

"It's probably nothing, Ms. Graves, but it's standard procedure to check these things out."

"What things?"

He glanced behind her car along the deserted road. "I'm afraid I can't say."

"Why not?" she asked. "Is it because I was upset? Was I speeding or weaving on the road?"

"Now, Ms. Graves, don't go getting yourself all worked up again. I'm sure this will get settled in just a minute or two more."

"Well, what are you waiting on?"

The look of relief on his face had her turning just as she heard the roar of an engine. A diesel engine. Craig's black truck barreled to a stop in front of her car, barring her escape. "What the…"

He hopped out and shook hands with the sheriff after he handed Allie her license and registration. "You have a nice day now." He skipped to his cruiser and maneuvered a hairpin U-turn before speeding away.

Allie fumed. Of all the backwoods, low down, manipulative crap he could have pulled, this was beyond compare. She turned the ignition.

Craig threw his hands in the air. "Allie, I'm sorry."

She ripped the car in reverse and hit the gas. She was forced to brake when he jumped on her back bumper. "Allie, please. Let me explain."

"Why should I?" she shouted.

"Because I'm the father of your baby."

"Oh, now you believe me." She put the car in drive and revved the engine.

"You wouldn't hit my truck," he warned.

"I've done it before."

"Allie…"

She shifted into park and set her head on the steering wheel, defeated. Nothing about this was going even remotely well. "Go away, Craig. I don't have any more skin for you to peel off."

He opened her door and kneeled down so they were eye to eye. "I didn't mean what I said. I know you don't sleep around. I know you didn't plan this. I don't know what to say other than I'm more ashamed than I've ever been in my life."

Allie knew they'd hit rock bottom and there wasn't anywhere to go but up. The question remained whether they came up together or alone. "You hurt me, Craig."

"I don't have any defense except to say that you scared me, Allie. Loving you means you have all the power, and I promised myself I'd never be that vulnerable again."

She raised her head and stared him in the eye. It seemed she had some fight left in her yet. "That's crap. You hold just as much power and—as demonstrated—you know how to aim where it hurts."

"Allie…" He reached inside and released her seatbelt. "You'll never know how sorry I am for what I said to you. You scared me and I panicked. I get mean when I'm scared. I love you and I don't want to lose you."

"Don't," she said. She knew her eyes were still swollen and puffy. She felt as fragile as a thin piece of glass. "Don't tell me what you know I want to hear when you think so little of me. I had to tell you about the baby, but I'm done."

"It's the truth."

"No, Craig, it's not. You don't love me. You think I'm after your money? Please, there isn't enough money on the planet for me to put up with you. You think I did this on purpose? Who would do this to themselves? Who would bring a baby into the middle of this mess? Not me, Craig. I may have been stupid enough to fall in love with you, but I'm not stupid enough to want a baby on top of it all."

He rocked back on his heels. "You don't want the baby?"

***

"Quit twisting my words around," Allie said as tears began leaking out of her eyes. "Of course I want the baby."

Craig dropped to his knees and pulled her out of the seat and into his arms. He'd earned her distrust with his careless words. He'd use better words, spoken from the heart to make her believe. "You want to know what I think of you? I think you're the strongest woman I've ever known. I've been falling for you since the moment you crashed into my life. I'm not going to lie, at first it was your looks. You're the most stunningly beautiful woman I've ever seen, but if that's all that you were—a pretty face—I'd have walked away months ago. You're so much more. You've got this insane kindness, a tender and generous heart, and the most optimistic outlook on life I've ever seen. I can't make this love I feel for you disappear; I can't stifle it or wish it away. As these last few weeks have proven, I could fly to the moon and still be in love with you. So if you walk away, Allie, it had better be because you don't love me, because there isn't another man alive who could ever love you more."

It felt so easy to tell her the truth, to open his heart to her. She'd been everything he needed all along and he'd pushed her away from the start. "I need you, Allie. Please forgive me."

She pulled out of his embrace and grabbed his arms. When their eyes met, he knew he hadn't lost her quite yet. He felt the web around them growing stronger. This time, he welcomed the tug.

"What about your wife?" she asked.

He wiped the tears from her cheeks. "We were kids when we fell in love. What we had wasn't a grown up kind of love. It wasn't meant to last forever. Ma helped me forgive her. It was as simple as saying it and meaning it. I'm finally free."

"Tied to me and the baby is more like it."

"If I could, I'd tie the knot so tight it'd never break."

She gave him a hard push, but he held firm. "How can I trust what you're telling me? Thirty minutes ago you doubted the baby was yours, and now you say you love me? Don't lie to me, Craig. Like it or not, we're connected through the child we made. That connection won't break no matter how we feel about each other, but I won't let you lie to me or to yourself because of the baby."

"I've never fought so hard against something in my entire life and if I have to, I'll fight even harder to make you believe in me. In us."

"Why does everything with us have to be so hard?"

"Everything?" He slid his hand up her back and cupped the back of her neck, inching her face to his. He kissed the tears on her cheeks, her eyelids, and her chin before tugging her hair so she'd open her eyes and see the love reflected back in his.

"You left me naked in your bed."

"I was trying to save you."

"You were scared."

"Yes. A lesser man couldn't have walked away."

"You mean smarter?"

"It took Herculean strength. And just so you know, you don't need to lose weight."

Allie snorted and dropped her forehead to his. "That's good to know because I'm going get fat in the next few months."

"I'll still love you when you're fat." He kissed her temple. "And when you're old and gray. Do you forgive me?"

"I don't have the energy to fight you, Craig. I'll say it and mean it once and for all. I forgive you for being an ass."

He'd never heard sweeter words. "It probably won't be the last time."

"I know it won't." She pushed him back when he went in for her lips. "You need to hear this. And you need to listen."

"Don't I always?"

She took a deep breath and stared into his eyes. "I've got a boatload of flaws, Craig, but they aren't the same as Julie's. If I'm feeling ignored or taken for granted, I'll tell you. If I'm feeling unloved, the only one I'll come to is you. And if I ever feel tempted to stray—which I wouldn't because you only stray when you're looking—you'd be the first to know. I respect us both too much to do anything else."

What the hell had he been so afraid of in the first place? But he still needed to hear the words. "Does that mean you still love me?" he asked.

"I don't want to. I really want to drive away and not give a damn what happens to you, but I can't. You're it for me, and now there's a baby to seal the deal."

"Would you love me if it weren't for the baby?"

"I loved you before the baby. The question is, would you love me if it weren't for the baby?"

"Yes," he said without hesitation. "I've loved you all along."

"Well, what in the world were you waiting for?"

Good question. "A sign from God, I guess." He slid his hand inside her coat and rested it above her jeans on top of her sweater. "It's in here. Our sign. Marry me?" he said. "I don't want to waste another second."

"I didn't come find you so you'd propose marriage. It didn't feel honest keeping the baby from you."

"I'm not proposing because of the baby. I love you, Allie, with everything I've got. I'm so damn tired of fighting what I wanted all along. I want you. All I want is you. You're all I've ever wanted."

"Oh, Craig. You make it hard to say no."

"Then don't say no."

"I'm not saying no. I'm saying yes."

He snaked his hands inside her coat, around her back, and pulled her close just as a car zoomed past honking the horn in greeting. He found her lips and everything inside of him settled and heated in the most powerful combination. "I love you, Allie. You're going to get sick of hearing me say it."

She burrowed into his chest. "I'll let you know when I am."

"I've got to get a ring."

"Craig." She gripped his jacket and pulled his lips to hers. "I don't need a ring. All I need is you."

"Oh, wait." He hopped to his feet. "Wait right here." He ran to his truck, opened the driver door, and pulled the tiny blue bud vase Allie had admired at Sharon's wedding into his palm. He dropped to his knees in front of her and opened his hand. "It's not a ring, it's nothing really, but I wanted you to have it."

She picked it up and he had the pleasure of watching her shed tears of joy instead of sorrow. "When did you get this?"

"Before I left town. You loved it, Allie. Your whole face lit up when you saw this. Don't cry."

"I can't help it."

"You're still getting a ring. A big one. Guys will see it for miles. It might even flash or glow in the dark."

"A glow in the dark ring with flashing lights. Could it play music?"

"I'm sure I could make that happen."

"Okay. I'm sold, but this is it for me, Craig. For better or worse, you're going to be stuck with me."

"That works both ways. We're stuck with each other."

"And the baby."

His eyes misted with tears. Oh, yeah. This was it all right. "And the baby," he whispered. "We should have known. Look at what happened when we crashed. We fell in love. What the heck did we think was going to happen when we made love?"

"We made a life," she said.

"The first of many, I hope." He helped her to her feet and then promptly whisked her off her feet. "You know what they say about sex?"

She nuzzled her face in his neck. "I'm afraid to ask."

"Practice makes perfect."

"In your mother's house?"

He nipped her ear. "I was thinking about the cab of my truck."

"In the middle of the day? We'll get arrested."

"I've got an in with the sheriff."

"Well," she said, "at this point, I guess we've got nothing to lose."

EPILOGUE

Allie felt nervous as Leah wobbled onto the stage wearing the two-inch heels Carolyn had tried in vain to discourage her from wearing. When Leah scooted behind the bench and took a seat, Allie let out the breath she'd been holding and gave the girl a nod. The song began at just the right tempo. Practice, Allie knew, made all the difference.

Allie bobbed her head in tune with the song and stifled a smile at Leah's fierce expression as the melody carried nicely through the small auditorium. She glanced at Mark and smiled. He gripped Carolyn's hand, his foot tapping to the beat, and stared with wonder at his daughter. She couldn't decide who looked more proud—Mark or Carolyn.

Craig didn't look anxious at all, not with his ankle crossed over one knee and his arm stretched along the back of Mark's chair. He looked so handsome in the blazer she'd found in his closet and insisted he wear. The man had a lot of nice clothes. He caught her staring and gave her a wink that had the tips of her ears burning and gave a nice little flutter to her stomach. Allie turned her attention back to Leah as the passionate crescendo of the piece brought memories of the night before floating through her brain.

She'd played for him, naked as requested, and they'd done some very interesting post performance antics. She couldn't believe how things had changed, how open and giving and playful Craig had become. Every day they spent together, every night they shared, felt like a gift.

Leah's piece ended with thunderous applause and she exited the stage, followed by Allie's last performer, six-year-old Madelyn, who brought the house down with her rendition of "Santa Clause Is Coming To Town."

After her backstage congratulations and hugs, Allie and Leah came down the auditorium stairs arm in arm. "You did great, Leah. I'm so proud of you for mastering both songs."

"Dad made me practice. A lot," Leah admitted. "I'm glad he did."

"There's my girl." Mark extended his arms and Leah skipped to greet her father. "You played wonderfully, baby. I'm so proud of you."

"Thanks, Dad."

Carolyn gripped Leah's hands. "I can't believe how grown up you looked on stage. You were lovely, Leah."

Leah's cheeks turned a nice shade of pink before she averted her eyes and smiled. "Thanks. It was fun."

Craig came through the side door from the parking lot with a bunch of roses in his arms. He bowed in front of Leah and presented her with the dazzling bouquet. "For the artist. You were magnificent."

Leah buried her face in the deep red blooms. "Oh, Uncle Craig. I love them."

"You earned them." He returned her hug and casually placed his hands in his pants pockets and rocked back on his heels. His gaze, dark and direct, landed on Allie. "And you," he said, pivoting to face her. "You earned this."

He pulled a small velvet box from his pocket and plopped it in her hand. "What is this?"

"Open it up and find out."

Allie pried the lid open and gasped. "Craig. You didn't."

"Of course I did. Do you like it?"

"Like it?" She looked up into his eyes. "It's beautiful...so perfect."

"Just like you." He plucked the ring from the box and slid the emerald cut diamond on her finger. It sparkled even in the muted light. "Perfect fit."

"You shouldn't have, Craig. I said I didn't need a ring. We're getting married in three days."

"We may be doing this fast, Allie, but we're doing it right. I'm not going to scrimp on the details. We're engaged and now it's official."

"I was officially yours when you said you loved me."

"So," he said. "Call this an encore."

"That's some kind of encore, Allie." Carolyn grabbed her hand and admired the ring.

Allie wrapped her arms around Craig's neck. "Why don't we call it a prelude?" she suggested. "To a life full of love and happiness."

"And babies," he whispered as her lips hovered near his. "Lots and lots of babies."

ABOUT THE AUTHOR

Christy Hayes writes romance and romantic women's fiction. She lives outside Atlanta, Georgia, with her husband, two children, and two dogs.

Please visit her website at www.christyhayes.com for more information.

Made in the USA
Lexington, KY
13 September 2016